EASY MONEY

In the showers after the audition, Mitch was anything but shy. He stripped bollock naked before Cary even had a chance to unzip his sports bag. Cary studied Mitch discreetly. Buttocks as round and firm as bowling balls; pale skin framed by a delicious tan line; a nipped-in waist leading up to a broad back, with shoulders to match and footballer's legs covered in coarse black hair. Cary focused on the crack between Mitch's arse-cheeks. Was, in fact, so distracted by the thought of tracing the line with his tongue that he didn't notice that Mitch was now looking over his shoulder directly at him.

'What's the matter? Never seen a naked man before?' Mitch asked, with a laddish grin. 'Or are you just sizing up the competition?'

EASY MONEY

Bob Condron

First published in Great Britain in 1999 by
Idol
an imprint of Virgin Publishing Ltd
Thames Wharf Studios,
Rainville Road, London W6 9HT

Copyright © Bob Condron 1999

The right of Bob Condron to be identified as the Author of this Work has been asserted by him in accordance with the Copyright, Designs and Patents Act 1988.

ISBN 0 352 33442 8

Cover photograph by Colin Clarke Photography

Typeset by SetSystems Ltd, Saffron Walden, Essex
Printed and bound in Great Britain by
Mackays of Chatham PLC

This book is sold subject to the condition that it shall not, by way of trade or otherwise, be lent, resold, hired out or otherwise circulated without the publisher's prior written consent in any form of binding or cover other than that in which it is published and without a similar condition, including this condition, being imposed on the subsequent purchaser.

SAFER SEX GUIDELINES

We include safer sex guidelines in every Idol book. However, while our policy is always to show safer sex in contemporary stories, we don't insist on safer sex practices in stories with historical settings – as this would be anachronistic. These books are sexual fantasies – in real life, everyone needs to think about safe sex.

While there have been major advances in the drug treatments for people with HIV and AIDS, there is still no cure for AIDS or a vaccine against HIV. Safe sex is still the only way of being sure of avoiding HIV sexually.

HIV can only be transmitted through blood, come and vaginal fluids (but no other body fluids) passing from one person (with HIV) into another person's bloodstream. It cannot get through healthy, undamaged skin. The only real risk of HIV is through anal sex without a condom – this accounts for almost all HIV transmissions between men.

Being safe
Even if you don't come inside someone, there is still a risk to both partners from blood (tiny cuts in the arse) and pre-come. Using strong condoms and water-based lubricant greatly reduces the risk of HIV. However, condoms can break or slip off, so:
* Make sure that condoms are stored away from hot or damp places.
* Check the expiry date – condoms have a limited life.
* Gently squeeze the air out of the tip.
* Check the condom is put on the right way up and unroll it down the erect cock.
* Use plenty of water-based lubricant (lube), up the arse and on the condom.
* While fucking, check occasionally to see the condom is still in one piece (you could also add more lube).

* When you withdraw, hold the condom tight to your cock as you pull out.
* Never re-use a condom or use the same condom with more than one person.
* If you're not used to condoms you might practise putting them on.
* Sex toys like dildos and plugs are safe. But if you're sharing them use a new condom each time or wash the toys well.

For the safest sex, make sure you use the strongest condoms, such as Durex Ultra Strong, Mates Super Strong, HT Specials and Rubberstuffers packs. Condoms are free in many STD (Sexually Transmitted Disease) clinics (sometimes called GUM clinics) and from many gay bars. It's also essential to use lots of water-based lube such as KY, Wet Stuff, Slik or Liquid Silk. Never use come as a lubricant.

Oral sex
Compared with fucking, sucking someone's cock is far safer. Swallowing come does not necessarily mean that HIV gets absorbed into the bloodstream. While a tiny fraction of cases of HIV infection have been linked to sucking, we know the risk is minimal. But certain factors increase the risk:
* Letting someone come in your mouth
* Throat infections such as gonorrhoea
* If you have cuts, sores or infections in your mouth and throat

So what is safe?
There are so many things you can do which are absolutely safe: wanking each other; rubbing your cocks against one another; kissing, sucking and licking all over the body; rimming – to name but a few.

If you're finding safe sex difficult, call a helpline or speak to someone you feel you can trust for support. The Terrence Higgins Trust Helpline, which is open from noon to 10pm every day, can be reached on 0171 242 1010.

Or, if you're in the United States, you can ring the Center for Disease Control toll free on 1 800 458 5231.

One

Framed in the picture window, the soft afternoon light accentuating his taut muscularity, Mitch looked like a work of art. Saint and sinner. An angel-faced piece of rough redeemed by Michelangelo. But no still-life. In the moment, he screwed up his face, threw back his head and from deep within his throat came a primeval moan, one fist clamped manfully around his thick, long length; the other hand tugging on his ripe bollocks. Effort strained the cords in his neck. A sheen of sweat glistened on his skin.

Frowning with concentration, Mitch dropped his chin to his chest and caught sight of himself in the glare of a full-length mirror. He had to smirk. He knew he was some performer – that he had it all. His hair cropped to a dark shadow, muscles and tattoos, and the face of a fallen angel. Devilishly handsome, his square jaw embellished by a trim, black goatee. All he would have needed to complete the image was a pair of baby horns. Every inch the working-class lad, and a born crowd-pleaser to boot.

With a final whoop, a deluge of come jettisoned from the tip of his crimson arrowhead and flew high in the air, shimmering as it was caught momentarily suspended in the dust-speckled shaft of sunlight. Then free falling to crash-land with a resounding splat on the polished oak floorboards. And again and again.

Guttural cries accompanied each copious spurt and threatened to bring the roof down around his ears.

An audience of one struggled in vain against the ropes that bound him to the seat of his hard-backed chair and he smiled blissfully as he too shot his load, squirting into white cotton boxer shorts, his cock restrained beneath his buttoned fly.

Moments passed in stillness, save for Mitch's heaving chest. He gasped for breath like an athlete who'd just completed a marathon. Finally, with binds untied, Mitch's satisfied customer dug deep into the pocket of his pinstriped trousers, producing a damp wad of notes.

Easy money, thought Mitch. Easy money.

Cary could not relax. He shuffled in his seat, checked his watch endlessly, willed the mountains to move, but to no avail. The regional train to Lewisham ambled along at its own pace, along its own lines and in its own time.

Inexplicably delayed, somewhere between Peckham and his final destination, Cary plucked the carefully folded scrap of newspaper from the back pocket of his jeans in an effort to distract himself. And for the umpteenth time that day he read: *18–20? Handsome? Can sing? Can dance? A positive attitude and the will to succeed? We want to hear from you! A new boyband is being created to storm the new millennium! Got what it takes? Contact us now! Photo essential. Box . . .*

He had travelled down from Newcastle the day before and spent the night at his uncle's place in Wimbledon. He needed to be rested for today's upcoming event but already he was feeling tired and worn. The letter was burning a hole in his pocket; the letter inviting him to try his luck.

Cary's heart sank as he entered the audition hall. The group audition turned out to be more like a three-ring circus. It seemed as if a hundred hopefuls cluttered the space. The majority were engaged in a warm-up of some sort, either vocal or physical. The corresponding surge of noise and activity was such that he failed to notice the smartly dressed young woman who had been trying to attract his attention until she tapped him lightly on the shoulder.

The woman smiled perfunctorily as he turned towards her, then looked directly at her clipboard.

'Name, please?'

'Cary Clarke.'

'OK, Gary. You're in Group C. Could you join the boys over in that far corner? You'll need this.' She handed him a sheaf of papers. 'Fill in the questionnaire. Choose a song from the selection. Check the lyric sheet if you need to. I'll be with you in about –' she checked her watch '– twenty minutes. By the way my name's Gayle.'

Gayle turned and marched away before he had had a chance to correct her error; an error that people invariably made. *Cary* not Gary. He comforted himself with the assurance that one day everyone would know his name.

Everyone.

As he filled in the questionnaire, he was surreptitiously checking out the competition. Not so steep, he concluded, except maybe the cute skinhead. Even as he thought it, the skinhead's eyes met his and fixed on him, then smiled warmly. Cary felt a surge of colour in his cheeks and looked away. When he had eventually worked up the nerve to look back the skinhead was grinning from ear to ear.

At that precise moment, Gayle appeared at his side. 'Ready, fellahs? Follow me.'

The group of ten followed dutifully behind her. Trooping up one flight of stairs, along a maze of corridors, they finally entered a darkened studio space. Dark except for a spotlight aimed directly at a lone microphone stand, a performance space fringed with chairs that were barely illuminated.

'You first, I'm afraid,' Gayle whispered, as she nudged Cary in the direction of the spotlight. 'And,' she instructed the others, 'could the rest of you guys take a seat in front.'

Cary stood before the captive, if not hostile, audience. Effectively blinded by the light shining in his face, he was unprepared for the rich, masculine voice that came out of the darkness.

'Name, please?'

'Cary Clarke.'

'OK, Gary. And which song have you chosen?'

'Sorry, it's *Cary* not Gary.'

'Come again?'

'My name's Cary. As in Grant. Cary Grant.' He tried his best to smile boyishly – working on the principle that you catch more flies with honey than with vinegar.

'OK, Cary. And the song?'

'"The Sun Ain't Gonna Shine Anymore".' For no other reason than it was one of his mum's favourites.

'Take it away.'

And with that command, the backing tape kicked into action. For a few brief seconds Cary thought he was going to dry, was going to blow his big chance. But then he opened his mouth and something wonderful happened – he found his voice.

At the back, hidden from view in the dark recesses of the studio, Rab Mackay looked on. First at Cary and then to Gayle. Her smile of approval mirrored his own and confirmed his opinion: they had found a serious contender. This guy could sing! More than this, he was devastatingly handsome – beautiful, even: a fringe of ash-blond hair flopped over big green eyes, the most kissable of mouths was accentuated by pale, perfect skin. He was tall, athletic and completely self-possessed. Gayle stood in awe of the transformation. In the cold light of day this guy would turn heads but under the spotlight he could break hearts.

It seemed to Cary that it was all over in the twinkling of an eye. An anticlimax. His performance appeared to have vanished into a vacuum. There was no applause, just a bout of nervous coughing from the ring of seats before him and a polite thank-you from the invisible man at the back. And whilst the skinhead took his place, Cary took his seat.

'Name, please?' the disembodied voice said.

'Mitch. Mitch Mitchell. As in Grant.' He grinned playfully into the spotlight.

'And the song?'

'Well. You didn't have "Nessun Dorma". So how's about "Unchained Melody"?'

'Take it away.'

Sixty seconds in and Rab couldn't believe his luck. He had spent the whole morning suffering through a string of no-hopers with only a mere handful of possibilities and now here were two winners in a row. True, Mitch did have a touch of the football hooligan about him and, also true, Rab had expected a voice from the terraces but there was none of it. Mitch sang with real sensitivity and tenderness. And the contrast of tough shell and soft centre was what made him truly fascinating to watch.

Rab rubbed his chin thoughtfully. Now if this pair could only dance as well as they could sing . . .

The other eight contenders ranged from passable through dire to pitiful. And it was with a sigh of relief that Rab finally watched them exit through to the main hall. Only Cary and Mitch would remain once Gayle had offered her commiserations.

'Right, fellahs.' Gayle turned towards the delighted pair. 'Hope you brought your dance togs 'cause that's what's coming next.'

'Sure. Where can we change?' Cary asked.

'Don't tell me you're shy?' Mitch teased.

Cary shot him a warning glance, but Gayle swiftly interceded.

'Changing room over on the left. But be quick about it. Ten minutes and we start.'

'We?' Mitch asked.

'Yeah.' Gayle raised an eyebrow. 'I'm your choreographer.'

One thing was patently obvious to Cary – Mitch was anything but shy. He stripped bollock naked before Cary himself had even unzipped his sports bag. Cary studied Mitch discreetly. Buttocks as round and firm as bowling balls; pale skin framed by a delicious tan line; a nipped-in waist leading up to a broad back with shoulders to match and footballer's legs covered in coarse black hair. Cary focused in on the crack between Mitch's arse-cheeks. Was, in fact, so distracted by the thought of tracing the line with his tongue that he didn't notice that Mitch was now looking over his shoulder directly at him.

'What's the matter? Never seen a naked man before?' Mitch asked, with a laddish grin. 'Or are you just sizing up the competition?'

'What competition?' Cary retorted. 'Did I miss somebody come through the door?'

Knuckles rapped on the outside of the changing room. Once again, Gayle's timing was perfect. 'Ready, you guys? Time's up.'

She certainly knew her stuff. After a thorough warm-up Gayle put them through their paces in an elaborate dance routine intended to test their ability to the max. Of the five guys taking part in this phase of the audition process only Mitch and Cary truly excelled, their excellence now fuelled by a competitive spirit. Cary was quick on the uptake and stylish, while Mitch brought his laddish physicality to the movement motifs. Each kept the other in their sights, determined not to be outshone.

Behind the one-way mirror, Rab looked on approvingly. Cary and Mitch had a certain chemistry between them. This was obvious. Kindred spirits? A personality conflict? Sexual tension? He wasn't sure. But whatever it was, it worked. The combination worked.

Half an hour later, packed up and ready to leave, Cary felt a hand grip his shoulder.

'You did good.' It was Mitch's voice. 'Got time for a quick pint?'

'Sorry. Have to rush. Got to get a train back to Newcastle.'

'Newcastle? But you've got no accent.'

'Dad was in the army. Senior officer. Moved about a lot. I spent most of my education at public school.'

'I'm from Manchester.'

'Yeah. I guessed as much.'

'So . . . What's your hurry?'

'Exams.'

'You're never still at school?'

'University.'

'Oh!' Mitch snickered. 'I'm in the presence of an intellectual!'

'Hardly.' Cary felt suddenly defensive. 'I'm studying performance art. It's a practical exam.'

Mitch punched him playfully on the upper arm. 'Break a leg!' He threw his sports bag over his shoulder as he made his exit. 'No doubt I'll be seeing you.'

'No doubt,' Cary replied as the door swung shut. He slipped on his jacket. 'If only I had his confidence,' he muttered to himself alone.

Rab had made the most of the ride back into Central London. Within the comfort of his chauffeur-driven limousine he had discussed matters with Gayle and drawn up his final selection before dropping her off en route. Even as he entered his Earl's Court apartment, he imagined Gayle would be typing up the final set of invitations. She was nothing if not efficient; a trusted employee. The day-to-day running of the project would be in her hands; safe hands, he was confident of this.

At long last, he felt he could let himself relax. Murat's meaty fingers ground into his flesh. Murat was Rab's own personal bodyworker. Rab would be getting just what he needed: a nice, relaxing massage polished off with a well-oiled fuck. He loved the luxury of sprawling on his belly, of being pampered, of releasing all the tensions of the day, of giving over control to his Man Friday. Murat didn't disappoint, not ever.

It was more than a business relationship, one of employer and employee. What had begun as a mutually beneficial arrangement had developed into something much more complex and rewarding. The original arrangement had meant that Murat got to leave Turkey first-class, a resident's permit (thanks to Rab's machinations) and the opportunity to live in relative luxury; while, for his part, Rab got his every need catered for by possibly the most handsome man he had ever known. Trust and loving friendship had been an unexpected bonus; one that both men valued above all.

Of course, Rab was technically the boss. He was the one who

paid Murat his generous salary each month. It was part of the deal. There was no shame involved. Murat more than earned his wages and Rab was fully satisfied. He was a firm believer in the old adage that you get what you pay for and Rab never paid for anything but the best.

To those who might say money can't buy you happiness, Rab could simply and honestly reply, 'Bollocks! Only misery is cheap.' Money had often bought him happiness. It had changed his life. For a boy who grew up in abject poverty – feeling like he had no control over his circumstances whatsoever – money had been like an answer to a prayer.

So now what? Now he was in a position to change the lives of others. He could improve their chances of success; could even make dreams come true. He liked the idea of being a Fairy Godfather. He liked it a lot.

And as he found himself drifting back to the massage table, and the three oiled fingers massaging him in that most intimate of places, he could do nothing but believe in a policy of money well spent.

Murat towered above Rab, his liquid brown eyes fixed on the contrast between his own strong, tanned, Mediterranean hands and Rab's pale, chunky, Celtic backside. It made an attractive combination, light and dark. And as his fingers disappeared into the receptive depth between his boss's arse-cheeks he couldn't help but smile. He loved giving pleasure and Rab, moaning softly beneath his expert ministrations and manipulations, reassured him of his ability to do just that. Murat was a man who was truly happy in his work.

The stroll from the rehearsal room to the bus station turned out to be fruitful for Mitch. His rumbling belly persuaded him to pop into a greasy spoon along the way. It proved to be a lucky decision. Along with the all-day breakfast menu he would get himself a place to sleep for the night. Bed and breakfast in one fell swoop.

Having ordered, he spotted a familiar face at a corner table and made his way over.

'Mind if I sit here?' he asked as he placed his tray on the red and white checked table cloth.

'Please,' came the friendly reply.

'The name's Mitch.' He offered his hand in greeting. 'Didn't I just see you back at the audition?'

The other guy took his hand and nodded in the affirmative. 'Yes. My name is Fredo. Pleased to meet you.'

It wasn't just the name but the way he pronounced it – Fraydo – that tipped Mitch off; the subtle yet unmistakable hint of an accent. 'You French?'

'That's right. My parents were originally from Sicily but I was born and grew up in Paris.'

Mitch grinned in response and took his time looking over the handsome stranger sitting opposite from him. Fredo was perhaps twenty years old, dressed in jeans, a white T-shirt, and a silk bomber jacket, just the same as Mitch. In fact, he actually bore a distinct resemblance to Mitch himself, but shorter, stockier. He looked like a real hard bastard but was surprisingly softly spoken. And much to his delight, Mitch spotted the enamel rainbow flag pinned to the flap of Fredo's jacket pocket.

'I don't speak French myself. Studied it at school of course; twice a week for five years. Can't remember a thing!'

'Nothing?'

'*Je m'appelle* Mitch. That's about it. Don't think languages are my strong point. But your English is great.'

'Thanks.' Fredo smiled and took a sip from his coffee cup. 'So what *are* you good at?'

Mitch was caught short, half a sausage primed with a fork before his open mouth. Fredo was flirting with him.

Taking his time, Mitch replied, 'That is for me to know and for you to find out.'

Fredo smiled enigmatically. 'I just have to ask the right questions?'

'Something like that.' Mitch changed tack. 'How did it go back there? How did you do?'

'I didn't get a call back.' Fredo looked a little embarrassed. His long, dark eyelashes momentarily fluttered shut. 'And you?'

'I got through to the second round.'
'Congratulations.'
'Sorry you didn't have more luck.'
'It's not so bad for me, I didn't have far to come. But some of the other guys in my group . . . One came all the way from the Isle of Man! The poor guy, he was really pissed off. Can't say I blame him.'

'No, me neither. I wouldn't have fancied that journey.' Mitch dunked his toast into the soft centre of a fried egg. 'I'm from Manchester. And you, I presume you live here in England?'

'I live in Blackfen, to be precise. It is only along the road.'

'Lucky sod.'

Beneath the table, Mitch felt the pressure of Fredo's leg pressing against his knee.

'You want to see it?'

'See what?'

'My place.'

'Sure. Let me just finish up here and I'll be with you.'

Outside the café the air was fresh, rejuvenating. Mitch zipped up his jacket and then, suddenly, laughed out loud.

'What? What is it?' Fredo asked.

'I was just thinking, isn't life wonderful. One moment I'm meeting you in a café and the next – well, in ten to fifteen minutes I'd guess –' He paused for effect. 'I'm going to rip all of your clothes off. I'm going to be naked with you, Fredo. My flesh will be pressed against your flesh. Your arse is going to be mine. All mine. And you, you're going to love every single fucking minute of it. Every single one. Just wait and see.'

Fredo trembled slightly, letting out a short sigh at the same time. Mitch reached out to stroke the short hairs on the back of Fredo's neck, gently pinching the flesh between palm and fingers. Not another word was exchanged until they had reached their destination.

Fredo's bedsit was unusually large and well laid out. A huge aquarium separated the bed space from the living area. Over by the bay window was a desk and on it an elaborate computer system. Alongside stood the TV, video and hi-fi facing a comfortable-looking sofa. Shelves were stacked with books, videos and CDs. Nowhere were there any hints of Fredo's French origins. He appeared to be an Anglophile, through and through.

Mitch stood in the centre of the room, slipped off his jacket and let it fall slowly to the floor. Meanwhile Fredo crossed to the window to draw the blinds, shutting out much of the late afternoon light.

'Come over here, Fredo. And be quick about it!' Mitch's voice took on a new air of authority.

Fredo did as he was told. Mitch reached out to grab hold of Fredo's straining crotch and squeezed it, gently increasing the pressure until Fredo tried to move away.

'Oi! You don't move until I tell you to, Fredo. And you don't touch me until I give you permission. I'm in complete control. Got that?'

Mitch leant forward and down so that his mouth was only a couple of inches away from Fredo's nose and then he breathed directly into Fredo's nostrils. It was a long, slow, warm breath that made Fredo quiver with anticipation, his head swimming with Mitch's perfumed breath.

'Now, take off my T-shirt and lick my armpits clean.'

Fredo proved he could follow instructions to the letter. Having yanked the T-shirt over Mitch's head, his mouth fell on Mitch's pit and attempted to consume it.

'That's good, baby,' Mitch complimented him. 'You were so thirsty, weren't you? Don't worry, Mitch is going to satisfy all your cravings.'

Fredo switched to the other pit, lapping and sucking on the forest of curls.

'Stop! That's enough!'

Fredo stood to attention.

'Good lad. Now strip. But do it slowly. I want to be able to enjoy it.'

Mitch stood back to get the full view as Fredo yanked his own T-shirt over his head to reveal a heaving, hairy ribcage.

Any preconceptions that the guy was a little on the heavy side quickly diminished for here was one sturdy little muscle packet, his gym-trained body as hairy as an ape. Mitch walked a circle around him, admiring the broad back that was almost as furry as the front.

'Trousers off!'

The glorious sight of Fredo's firm, beefy buttocks had the lump in Mitch's jeans soaring to new heights.

'Turn around.'

As Fredo stepped sideways, Mitch marvelled at the semi-erect pole that came into view. It stood at some forty-five degrees; long and thick and uncut, a dewy drop of precome glistening on the very tip.

Mitch reached out to stroke it, feeling it respond to his touch. A whimper escaped Fredo's lips. Mitch smiled and continued stroking Fredo's member, while at the same time he gripped Fredo's mouth in his other hand, pinching his lips roughly together and forcing his head back. Pain and pleasure, inextricably linked.

Letting go of the throbbing cock, Mitch inserted his thumb into Fredo's mouth and, using this added leverage, he led him roughly over to the bed. He pushed him down on to his haunches and then, with the pressure from a well-placed boot, pushed him over on to his back. Straddling him, Mitch unbuckled his own belt, slipping it through the hoops, taking his time, teasing his victim.

'Won't be long now, baby.'

His fingers found his fly and unbuttoned them, one by one by one. Finally, his cock burst free and twitched in confident expectation.

Mitch dropped to his knees between Fredo's open thighs. He held his cock up for close examination. 'You like what you see, don't you?'

Fredo nodded violently.

'Want to suck me, baby?'

Fredo's voice cracked with longing. 'Yes.'

'Then you'll have to beg.'

'No, please . . .'

'Yes! Beg!' Mitch's tone suddenly softened. 'After me: "Mitch . . ."'

Fredo clamped his lips together and shook his head. Mitch collapsed on top of him, his eyes staring Fredo down, their lips almost touching.

'I *said*, after me: Mitch . . .'

'Mitch . . .'

'I'm begging you . . .'

'I'm begging you . . .'

'Let me suck you dick.'

'Let me suck your dick!'

'No! Not until I'm ready!'

And with that Mitch shut him up, crushing his mouth against Fredo's with such ferocity that, for a moment, his quarry thought he would be smothered. Their tongues battled it out briefly, a fight for supremacy that Mitch was bound to win. Within seconds Fredo willingly submitted. He clutched Mitch's tongue between his lips and sucked for dear life.

As Mitch broke free, he clutched Fredo's wrists together and pinned them above his head. 'You know what, Fredo? I'm bigger than you are. Much bigger. In fact, I'm bigger and stronger and tougher.'

Fredo listened carefully before responding. 'And I love it, Mitch. You can do anything you want to me.'

'I can. I could hurt you, Fredo. I don't want to but I could, you know that, don't you? So you have to pay me respect. You have to beg me.'

'Mitch, I beg you, kiss me again.'

And again Mitch lurched forward and clamped his mouth on Fredo's.

'You love it when I kiss you, don't you? And you know why? It's 'cause I'm a great kisser.'

'Yes, you're wonderful.'

'That's right, I am!' Mitch released Fredo's wrists, then raised himself, letting his hands trail over Fredo's chest. Fingers found erect nipples, straining to be tortured. Mitch began to tug, Fredo began to moan. Mitch tugged harder and began to twist first one nipple and then the other. Fredo began to wail. He pulled the pillow from behind his head and pressed it to his face to smother his groans.

Mitch's palm closed around Fredo's balls and began to tug them in the direction of his toes. Fredo whimpered in a vain effort to elicit mercy but Mitch wasn't about to give an inch.

'Like that, do you?'

Fredo nodded frantically. 'Oh, yes. But please, no more.'

Mitch tugged even harder. 'Yes, more.' Mitch let go of Fredo's nipple and let his free hand grasp Fredo's stiff phallus. He brought his mouth close and spat a big dose directly on to the head of Fredo's quivering manhood. Within moments Mitch had lathered the shaft, gliding his fist from top to base and all the time stretching Fredo's swollen nuts with his other hand.

Fredo was writhing around on the bed, thumping the mattress, thrashing about, hollering. 'Please, Mitch, I beg you, don't make me come. This is great. So great. Don't make me come. I'm begging you.'

Mitch released his grip. 'See. When you beg me, Fredo, I show leniency.' Mitch clambered up the bed so that he knelt beside Fredo's face. Cupping his palm around the back of Fredo's neck, he raised Fredo's head until it was almost touching his drooling prick. Mitch tightened his buttock muscles and made his prong twitch up and down.

'Now I'm ready. Now you can suck my dick.'

And with one deft move, Mitch positioned his cock and plunged it down Fredo's open throat. Bollocks slapped against chin as Mitch fucked face. Fredo was gagging, struggling to accommodate the width and length of Mitch.

Mitch reached out a hand and began to tap Fredo's straining cock. The glans were swollen fit to burst. Then Mitch began to slap it, this way and that. Fredo was squirming, grinding his hips, fighting to free his throat and to hold back his orgasm but he was losing the battle.

All at once, Fredo's prick was spurting. Come was flying in every direction as Mitch looked on, deeply impressed. As Fredo attempted to squeal, Mitch felt the vibrations against his cock heralding his own inevitable ejaculation. He pulled out. Fredo gasped for air. Mitch shot his load over Fredo's chin and neck. Milk-white sperm, thick and jellified, clung to Fredo's skin. Slowly, it eased a path into the hollow beneath his Adam's apple and formed a creamy pool.

'Good boy. That's a good baby.' Mitch sighed.

This energetic pair slept and ate and fucked, and slept and ate and fucked until mid-morning the next day; until the time came for Mitch to leave.

Mitch had showered and dressed. Fredo was showered but wore only his bath towel. They stood in the centre of Fredo's room and kissed. Mitch thought Fredo would never let go. Eventually he did.

'You want my address and phone number?'

'Sure. That would be nice,' Mitch replied with as much enthusiasm as he could muster.

Fredo scribbled the details down on the back of an old envelope and handed the scrap of paper to Mitch. He stuffed it in the back pocket of his jeans as Fredo walked him to the door.

'I'd come down with you but –' Fredo indicated the towel '– the neighbours.'

'It's OK.'

Fredo stared intently into Mitch's eyes and then leant towards his ear. 'It would be so easy to fall in love with you,' Fredo whispered.

'Sweetheart!' Mitch replied, stroking Fredo's cheek. 'I'll give you a call. Yeah?'

It was only once outside, as he made his way on foot towards the bus stop, that Mitch allowed himself time to reflect. 'Easy to love me? He doesn't know me. All he knows is what I let him see. It's all he's interested in.' He took the scrap of paper from his back pocket and screwed it up. 'He doesn't know me. Nobody knows me.' And with that he booted the ball of paper high in the air and continued walking without a second thought.

Two

As the long, black limousine swung through the wrought-iron gates and eased up the gravel path, four mouths fell open. Four faces gawking out through the tinted windows in the back with Murat seated up front. Steering the car home, Murat smiled to himself as he checked the boys out in the rear-view mirror.

Mitch had thought he'd seen it all but who was he kidding? This wasn't just another world, it was another universe.

The car swept through an elaborate ornamental garden before reaching the mansion house. A bronze fountain was the centrepiece of the forecourt. A double set of stone steps, one on either side, swept up to a baroque terrace, strewn with pots of flowers. Heavy oak double doors stood ajar where Rab was waiting to welcome them personally. He leant casually against the door frame, smiling.

'Meet the boss,' Murat said by way of introduction.

It was the first glimpse any of them had had of their mentor, the man who was about to change their lives for ever.

He was a big man in his mid-to-late thirties. Stocky but solid. His hair was copper-coloured and clipped short to match his full, neat beard. He was dressed in Levis, hiking boots and a workshirt, with sleeves rolled up over the spun gold of his hairy forearms. He looked more like the gamekeeper than Lord of the Manor.

The first group meeting was being held two weeks after the auditions had finally finished. Murat had been given the task of collecting the boys from the village station and was about to deliver them safely to Rab's country retreat in darkest Derbyshire.

Rab greeted each of them in turn with a warm smile and a firm handshake, then instructed Murat to show them to their rooms. They would all meet together again in twenty minutes. More than enough time to freshen up. Cary still couldn't take it all in. Not the offer to join the band; not the journey from the station; nor this room with its four-poster bed and views over woodland and the hills beyond. The en suite bathroom was marble, genuine marble with gold fittings. He sat down on the elegant bed beside his unopened rucksack and tried to let it all sink in.

Interrupting his quiet contemplation, the door handle rattled and the door opened to reveal Mitch. Behind him, his adjoining room. Mitch swung through the open connecting doorway.

'Can you believe this!' Mitch exclaimed.

'No.'

'Me neither.' He crossed to the window. 'I tell you, this is the life.'

'Where does he get his money from?'

'You mean you don't know?'

'No. Should I?' Cary asked, more than a little annoyed.

'Our new boss is Rab Mackay.'

'Yeah, I know that much, but what else . . .'

'Where have you been living these past ten years? Rab Mackay the entrepreneur. He was a millionaire by the age of twenty-three; a billionaire by the time he was thirty-three. He's your proverbial working-class lad made good; started off in property speculation and diversified into just about everything; sold off his business empire about two years back. Since then – not a murmur.'

'How come you know so much?'

'I take an interest where money is concerned.' Mitch paused, sniffed, then as an afterthought added, 'Plus I saw a documentary on Channel Four.' After another brief pause, he grinned, then shook his head. 'We've landed on our feet this time. No doubt about it.' And with that he disappeared through the doorway.

Cary couldn't help thinking that for someone who made such a big show of not having two brain cells to rub together Mitch seemed pretty clued up. Surprisingly so.

Suddenly, Mitch's head reappeared. 'Good to have this access. We'll be able to have midnight feasts. I always fancied myself at one of those posh boarding schools. Though I guess you'd know more about what they get up to after lights out than me!' Without waiting for a reply his head just as quickly disappeared.

Cary stood, crossed to the door, closed it and turned the key in the lock.

'Spoilsport!' came Mitch's muffled response.

The first official group meeting took place in a grand hall around an oval, antique dining table. A crystal chandelier was suspended overhead. Rab formally welcomed the boys and then introduced himself as Murat served the drinks.

'Sorry that everything has been kept so cloak-and-dagger but as some of you will know the things I do tend to be viewed as grist to the tabloid mill, my name being Robert Mackay. But please do call me Rab.'

Cary was the first band member to be invited to introduce himself. He smiled, took a deep breath and began.

'My name is Cary. That's *Cary* – with a C.' He laughed. 'I seem to have spent the best part of the past twenty-one years pointing that out. I was born in Berlin, Germany. My dad was stationed there with the old peace-keeping force. Subsequently, I've lived all over the place.' He thought for a moment. 'And I act, I sing, I dance, I write songs. I'm really glad to be here today. Enough?'

Rab nodded. 'Thanks, Cary. Mitch?'

'Yeah. I'm Mitch. I'm also twenty-one. I'm five foot eight in my stocking feet. Take an eight in a shoe. Manchester born and raised, since when I've done a bit of this and a lot of that. Reckon I'm up for most things. I can do all the things Cary can do. And my name's easier to remember!'

'Thanks, *Rich*.' Rab added dryly, 'I'll be sure to remember.'

Then it was the turn of the newcomers. Damon Trent was cute and baby-faced. Huge brown eyes seemed to dominate his face. Strawberry-blond hair, cut in a mop-top, fringed his long eyelashes. He was short and slightly built. And when he spoke his voice was soft and measured.

'The name's Damon. Believe it or not, I've just turned twenty – though everyone seems to think I look like I should still be at school. As you've probably guessed from my accent, I come from the East End of London. Any special talents? The only remarkable one I have is an encyclopedic memory for pop music. This means I can give you the full rundown on the history of any pop song – highest chart position and date, band personnel, etc. Which is why I work in a record store.'

'*Worked* in a record store,' said Kenny, the last of the recruits.

'Oh, yeah.' Damon grinned, revealing a dimple in his cheek. 'Worked.'

In the silence that followed all eyes turned on Kenny Tauber. At six foot plus he was the tallest member of the band. His eyes were blue. His hair, chestnut brown. High cheekbones and slightly slanted eyes betrayed his Slavic ancestry. His body was athletic and trim.

'Yeah, I'm Kenny. Also twenty. A mechanic by trade. My family was originally from Poland but like my parents I was born and bred in Sheffield and –' He hesitated slightly. 'I can't believe this is happening to me. I can't believe my luck!'

All four lads shared a smile of agreement.

'Luck has precious little to do with it,' Rab said matter of factly. 'You were chosen on the strength of your talent and abilities.' He looked around the conference table at each handsome, smiling face in turn. 'And your looks, of course! The four of you together make a killer combination.'

The situation was explained: the lads would receive a wage until such time as sufficient royalties were generated. For their part, they each had to commit to spending the next three months as residents of the mansion. Each day would be filled with a busy schedule of vocal classes, dance coaching, fitness training, and so on. Seminars would also be held to teach special skills, like how to be media savvy. Nothing was going to be left to chance.

Rab rang the buzzer on his side of the table and moments later the door opened and a familiar figure entered the grand hall closely followed by a fresh face. Gayle smiled and waved in recognition as she approached the conference table. The stranger swaggered confidently behind her. Short, dark, curly hair topped a square head on a bull neck. A cleft chin and hazel eyes. A white and green hooped rugby shirt stretched over his powerful chest but hung loose over the waist of his jogging pants. The ensemble was completed by high-cut trainers and sport socks. In his late twenties, he looked every inch the rugger-bugger. And just as intimidating.

'I believe you've all met Gayle before?' Rab said as she took her seat to the left of him. 'She's project coordinator. She'll be supervising your progress day by day. Any work-related questions or requests are to be directed to her in the first instance. She's also your dance teacher and vocal coach.' Rab turned his attention to the new face. 'Gareth Preston will be putting you through your paces in the gym and he's also your nutritionist – so you'd better be nice to him or you could end up on bread and water.'

'Hi, guys.' Gareth winked as he leant back in his chair, his bass voice rumbling, thick with testosterone. 'Glad to meet you.'

Being nice to this guy wasn't likely to present too many problems, thought Cary. Anybody built like he was deserved respect.

'Gareth is founder and co-owner of a string of fitness centres throughout the North of England. I've recruited him, at considerable expense, to work with you for the next three months. I expect you to make the most of his expertise. And then there's Murat . . .'

Murat was seated on Rab's right hand-side. He gave a broad

grin at the mention of his name, a perfect set of white teeth appearing below his thick, black moustache.

'Murat has the unenviable job of keeping you guys in check. He's the one who'll get you up in the morning and put you to bed at night. Think of him as a second daddy. His role is to take care of you.'

'And what about you, Rab?' Kenny asked.

'I was just getting around to that, Kenny. For the time being, I'll be taking care of business at our London headquarters but I will be here each weekend.' Rab added, 'Any other questions?'

'Only about a million.' Mitch chuckled.

'For instance?'

'These contracts you want us to sign? How do we know they're fair?'

Cary, Damon and Kenny squirmed in discomfort but Rab simply smiled and nodded towards Gayle.

'You don't,' she replied. 'However, should you wish to have them checked out by a specialist in entertainment law, you're welcome to do so. We'll see to it that whatever fees you incur are paid.'

'And in the meantime you don't have to sign anything,' Rab added. 'I only need your word to start the ball rolling.'

Cary blurted out, 'I'm sure Mitch didn't mean to suggest . . .' but Rab merely held up his hand.

'It's a fair question. An intelligent question. I wouldn't expect any less.'

Mitch grinned.

'I think you'll find the contracts are exceedingly fair.'

'One more question, Rab.'

'Yes, Mitch?'

'If what I read is accurate, you're not short of a bob or two.'

'Is that the question?'

'Not exactly. I was just wondering . . . What are you doing all this for? I mean you're laying out all this dosh with no guarantee of a return. So I guess the question is: why?'

'Would you believe me if I told you I'm a frustrated pop star?'

'Geddaway!'

'Sad but true, lads. A pipe dream, I'm afraid. Can't sing. Can't dance. But if my instincts are correct – and they usually are – then I believe you four are going to realise the dream for me.'

Murat was given the task of leading the guided tour of the mansion's facilities. Damon scampered after him like a puppy, Mitch a short distance behind, Cary and Kenny at the back. The tour began in the basement with the indoor pool, sauna and solarium. Damon yapped on endlessly, delighted. 'Wow!', 'Double Wow!' and 'Triple Wow!' made up the bulk of his vivid commentary. The other lads were, for the most part, struck dumb.

Fortunately Murat was a little more forthcoming. Seminars were to be held in the main dining hall. And the kitchen, sitting room and library on the ground floor were all at their disposal. Then on up to the first-floor dance space, gym and recording studio. At length, they trooped outside to the tennis court. There, Murat pointed to the gardens and the woodlands beyond.

'Behind those trees you'll find a boating lake. From here on you be better to explore for yourself. But we go back inside now. Time for dinner. I have prepared something special.'

Cary felt a pull towards the water, wanting to see it for himself. Even so, he turned and dutifully followed the others back into the main hall.

Mitch collapsed into bed and not a minute too soon.

I'm knackered. Utterly knackered, he thought to himself, half crazed with fatigue.

The meal, the wine, the early start from Manchester that morning, had all taken their toll. And the comfort of the soft mattress, the feeling of cool cotton sheets against his hot, naked body, was just what the doctor ordered. The windows were open and a gentle breeze tickled the curtains and tempered the summer heat.

The duvet was thrown back and, as he turned on his side, he cast a leg over the fold. Snuggling into position, his cushioned cock began to wake up, even as he fell fast asleep.

He dreamt of Damon on a leash. Murat was leading him around the spacious dance studio, petting him, fussing him like a proud owner parading his pedigree pup at a dog show. Damon's fit, athletic body was clad only in a leather nappy. Murat wore a studded cod-piece, biker boots and peaked cap. He looked like a Tom of Finland cartoon, the epitome of exaggerated masculinity. A huge, hairy chest swept down to a slender waist and the curve of muscular buttocks; his arms and legs were as big and firm as tree trunks. The archetypal master – he who must be obeyed.

An elaborate obstacle course filled the space. Hoops and hurdles. Now standing centrally, Murat cracked a huge bull-whip as Damon performed against the clock, leaping over hurdles, jumping through the hoops. Around and around. Until at last a final hoop burst into flames. Damon was startled, refused to jump through it, until Murat cracked the whip around his ears. Then he flipped through the ring of fire to land unharmed on the other side.

A jury of three – Rab, Gayle and Gareth – each held up score cards. Maximum scores all around. Damon sat back on his haunches as Murat patted his head. From behind his back, the Turk produced a yellow dog bowl.

'Thirsty, boy?'

Damon nodded enthusiastically.

Murat hooked a thumb under the waist band of his cod-piece and yanked it down to reveal his pumped-up semi-erection. With a lopsided grin and a grunt, he began to piss into the bowl torrents of steaming amber nectar. On and on. It was impossible that this bowl could contain such an amount, yet there was no overflow.

At last, he placed the bowl before Damon who immediately lowered his head and began lapping up the contents. The jury burst into spontaneous applause.

Still fast asleep, Mitch groaned, ground his hips one last time into the mattress and soaked the sheet with his spunk.

★

'Damon. Damon! It is time to wake up now.' A large, meaty hand shook him roughly by the shoulder.

Murat's voice was bright and chirpy unlike Damon's half-dead response. 'Wha –' He clutched the alarm clock on his bedside table and turned the face towards him. 'But it's only six o'clock!'

'Breakfast in fifteen minutes.'

Simply opening his eyes seemed to take an immense effort, crusted, as they were, with sleep. Damon looked up into Murat's big, brown eyes. He was smiling.

'Come on, little one, before I tip you out of bed.'

'You wouldn't dare.'

'Do you dare me, Damon?'

Damon took a moment to think about it – a long, hard moment. Murat wore a playful expression but there was an intensity in his stare that made Damon think twice.

'No, Murat. I'm getting up now,' he said cheerfully, throwing back the sheets. Leaping from the bed, he strode bare-arsed to the en-suite bathroom. 'Fifteen minutes you said?'

Murat headed for the door. 'Now thirteen and a half. Don't be late.'

'Oh, I won't Murat. I won't.'

The hike that followed their substantial breakfast was a day-long affair, full of huffing and puffing and good-natured banter. Damon would later describe it as an exercise in bonding, bringing the whole team together to spend time and get to know each other. Gareth dominated the proceedings. Guiding the party through some of the most beautiful spots in the whole of the Peak District, he kept everyone entertained with a constant stream of crude jokes. He liked to play the lad, the beer boy, but he was far from dumb. 'Couldn't give a fuck!' that was the impression he gave.

Cary found that his eyes were constantly being drawn to the sight of Gareth's legs as they clambered up the path before him. Cut-off combat pants clung to powerful thighs and, below these, an expanse of healthy, tanned flesh. The muscles on his sturdy calves were clearly defined, flexing with every upward step.

The sun shone down from a cloudless sky as the group slowly made their way to the very top of Mam Tor. It had been a tough hike, lasting more than four hours. But now, with the countryside spreading out beneath them, the view seemed to have been worth all the effort. Gareth took a quick look round and announced that it was time for lunch. While Damon, Murat and Gayle busied themselves laying out the brightly checked picnic cloth and setting out the utensils, Cary, Mitch and Rab unpacked the food.

Gareth stood apart from the others, taking in the view. Cary wandered up to stand beside him. Gareth gave him a quick nod. 'Tired, are we, after that little stroll?'

'No, not at all,' Cary replied. 'It was just the sort of thing that my father used to put us through on Sunday afternoons when I was little.' His voice had taken on a melancholy tinge.

Gareth attempted to crack a joke. 'No wonder you've got all that stamina. Stamina's an asset – especially between the sheets!'

Cary didn't laugh. Gareth gave him a sympathetic look, then reached out and squeezed Cary's shoulder.

The moment passed. Gareth bent over and delved into the rucksack lying at his feet.

'I tell you what, Cary, my underwear is soaking from all of that exertion. You know, it's a wise man who always brings a change of pants with him on this sort of thing.' And so saying, Gareth produced a fresh pair of briefs from the bag and took himself off behind some rocks to change. 'Won't be a sec.'

Cary's eyes swept over the glorious countryside but all his mind could focus on was what lay hidden directly behind him: a circle of boulders, that looked not unlike an abstract modern sculpture, and at the centre a bare backside exposed to the elements.

'Pssst!'

The noise came from behind Cary's back. He ignored it.

'*Pssst!*'

The sound was louder now, more insistent. Cary turned. Having changed his pants, Gareth tossed them over to Cary.

'Put them in my rucksack, it's by your feet. I'm just going to wander off for a minute or two.'

Cary trembled as he held Gareth's underwear in his sticky palms. Did he give himself away? No one appeared to have seen the exchange. He stuffed Gareth's briefs in the top of the backpack and fastened the flap. Now they were hidden away just as surely as Cary's violent reaction.

Damon was busily munching on a cheese salad baguette. 'You make a boss sandwich, Murat.'

'I am happy that you like it.'

'I can assure you, Murat, my man, the pleasure is all mine.' He took a swig from a can of diet cola. 'Where do you come from originally?'

'I am from a small village in eastern Turkey but we moved to Antalya on the southern coast when I was seven years.'

'You must miss it?'

'No, not really. I can truly say I love England. Some of the times I think I am dreaming.' He swept his open hand across the magnificent panorama before them. 'Nowhere would we have a view like this, nowhere at all. It's completely unlike anything I have known. Most of the times, Damon, I feel I live on the set of a foreign film! Here is simply other; is simply different, one can't compare.'

Kenny, Rab, Mitch and Gayle had arranged themselves on a grassy bank; some sitting, some lying, all of them soaking up the sun.

'The real work begins tomorrow,' said Rab.

'Have we got a schedule, a programme?' asked Kenny.

'Naturally,' Gayle replied. 'You'll get a copy when we get back.'

Mitch lay his forearm across his face. 'And do you have a specific target in mind?'

'We certainly do, Mitch,' Rab replied. 'In three months' time you're going to perform your first concert.'

'What!' Kenny shot upright.

'Take it easy, Kenny.' Gayle's voice was soothing. 'Three months is plenty of time to get you into the right mindset.'

'What are we actually going to sing at this first gig?' Mitch was curious to know the answer.

'Cover versions mostly,' Gayle replied. 'It makes more sense. Audiences aren't so receptive to new material from a new band.'

Mitch looked thoughtful. 'And do we have a say in the choice of material?'

'Of course, Mitch,' Rab said. 'Everything is open to discussion. However, we have gone to the trouble of preparing some backing tracks to get you off and running. Initially, they'll form the basis of the dance and vocal training.'

Mitch shielded his eyes from the glare of the sun and threw a glance in Kenny's direction. 'I don't know about you, Ken, but I can't wait to get started.'

Kenny looked more than a little sceptical. 'Three months? Well, I guess the sooner we get started the better.'

That evening, whilst the others played cards in the sitting room, Cary pleaded tiredness and headed off upstairs. Murat had noticed that Cary had been strangely preoccupied and somewhat withdrawn for the best part of the late afternoon and early evening. He was somewhat relieved to find such an easy explanation. Of course Cary was tired, he thought. The past couple of days had been eventful to say the least. Still, Murat decided he would check that all was OK first thing in the morning.

Sleep was the last thing on Cary's mind, however, as he snuck up three flights of stairs and into Gareth's room. Had anyone come along he would have been hard pressed to explain his presence there, but no matter. The desired object, still damp, stained with sweat and the trace of Gareth's crack, lay on top of Gareth's open rucksack.

Murat had been right about one thing at least: Cary had been preoccupied, preoccupied ever since the moment when he had first held this garment in his trembling hands. And as the afternoon had passed into evening, he found he could hardly concentrate on anything else besides the surge of feelings Gareth's underwear had produced in him. He had never felt such an intimate connection with a relative stranger.

Trembling once more in fear and excitement, Cary plucked the briefs from where they lay and pressed them to his face, burying his nose into the crotch, breathing deep, savouring the sweet, acrid, odour. His head swam like a drunkard.

The next morning, Murat turfed them all out of bed at seven. Thus began the regular schedule of events. Breakfast at seven-thirty; work began at eight. An hour of breathing and gentle vocal exercise with Gayle was followed by step class with Gareth. Mid-morning break, followed by a strenuous dance class. After lunch, individual and group vocal work. Afternoon break with gym routine to follow. Murat was on hand at all times to offer help and encouragement when energy levels started to flag.

The dance hall was as big as a basketball court. Mirrors lined the walls. Step and dance classes both took place there. It had the salty smell of a school gym, a smell that invigorated Cary just as much as it irritated Damon. An evocative smell that produced fond memories in one and an allergic reaction in the other.

Colour Me Badd's 'I Wanna Sex You Up' had been number one on both sides of the Atlantic and it was with an upbeat cover version of this song that the boys learnt their first dance routine together.

Gayle led them through the choreography step by step, starting at the beginning and building gradually, a few moves at a time.

'Just one question?' Damon leant over to catch his breath during a brief pause in the music. 'What is it with all these pelvic thrusts!'

Kenny burst into song: 'They really drive you in-sa-y-yeh-yeh-yeh-yeh-y-ane. Let's do the time warp –'

'Shut your mouth!' said Damon.

Mitch spoke up next. 'You see, unfortunately, our Damon hasn't had too much practice with pelvic thrusts, Gayle.'

'Oh, but, Damon, the girlies love them. Believe me, they absolutely love them.'

And not just the girlies, thought Cary to himself.

But as their dance routine grew more polished, their movements more defined, Damon's opinion would be revised. He, too, would grow to love those pelvic thrusts along with the odour of the locker room.

Saturday night was to become known as speciality night in the Manor's roomy kitchen. The posh dining room would be abandoned in favour of the kitchen table. It was the one night of the week when the whole gang were allowed to forget the calorie count and pig out instead. Fish-and-chip suppers became a short-lived fashion once Murat had offered to cook them all a Turkish meal. From that point on, he was stuck with the job of Saturday chef.

Cary was in raptures once again. 'This is fantastic, Murat. You've outdone yourself again. What do you call it?'

'Dolmades. Vine leaves stuffed with rice, pine nuts and herbs.'

Gareth shovelled another helping into his mouth. 'It's like nothing I've ever tasted before.'

'It's like the food of the gods,' Damon said as he took a slug of Turkish beer.

'It's like having an orgasm in the mouth!' said Gayle.

All mouths stopped working and turned in her direction.

Whilst the others crowded around the mixing desk in the cramped control room, Kenny sat behind glass in the soundproof booth and listened to the playback. He wanted to cry. No, he wanted to burst into tears.

It was a blessed relief when the tape played out. Remi Odesanya, ace engineer, switched on the intercom. Afro-Caribbean, Remi was a blue-black, square-jawed hunk of solid muscle. The sleeves of his T-shirt strained over impressive biceps. His head was shaved bald. White teeth split his crooked smile.

'So, Kenny. What did you think of that?'

'Not to put too fine a point on it, Remi,' Kenny wailed, 'it was shit!'

Damon was the first to leap to support him. 'No, it wasn't, Kenny. It was OK. It really was. It was OK.'

Cary followed suit. 'Don't take it so hard, Kenny. It wasn't bad at all for a first attempt. You're not used to the technology, none of us are, that's all.'

'Yeah? Sure!' Kenny failed to be convinced.

'Tell you what, Ken.' Mitch grinned. 'Compared to my attempt that was a definite number-one contender!'

Kenny laughed. And continued to laugh as everyone joined in.

Gayle sat at the back of the studio, smiling to herself. This was something to tell Rab. An important development was taking place, just as they had hoped. The lads were gelling into a group, – a group of friends.

Sleep was never going to be a problem, Mitch thought to himself as he stood under the communal showers, at least not at this rate, not so long as they were in training at least. The daily programme of activities was back-breaking. By the end of the second week he could barely make it from the gym to the shower room. Now he had been standing under the steaming jet for how long? – a good ten minutes longer than any of the others.

By the time Gayle entered the changing room he was alone. Bare-arsed, a white bath towel stretched across his back, he dried himself off in the middle of the tiled floor. As his eyes caught sight of her he reflexively tensed his muscles, showing off his body to its best effect.

'Put it away, Mitch,' Gayle remarked dryly. 'I've seen bigger ones than that before.'

Mitch smirked. 'I doubt that very much, Gayle. I do doubt that.' He noted with some amusement that her eyes never left his crotch until he eventually wrapped the towel around his waist. And he had deliberately taken his time. 'Ever heard of knocking?'

'I did knock. I also called out.'

'Funny. I never heard you.' He reached for his deodorant. 'What do you want anyway?'

'Rab's here. He's come a day early. Wants to see you all in the dining room in ten minutes.'

'Not bad news I hope?'

'No. I think you'll be pleasantly surprised.'

And the good news was that they were being given shore leave, a whole weekend.

'Gayle and Gareth seem to have decided you'll all go stir-crazy if I keep you cooped up here any longer. But remember: not a word to anyone about our little project. And I do mean, *not a word*.'

Within half an hour, Mitch, Cary, Kenny and Damon were packed and ready to go.

Three

Cary was the first to return. It took him all of two and a half hours, just as long as it took to get to the nearest mainline station and back.

He had found himself standing on the platform, waiting for the 8.20 to Newcastle, when at last the truth of the situation dawned on him: he really had no place to go. What was there to go home for? Home wasn't home any more. Most of his friends from university were spread countrywide. And the oppressive atmosphere of his parental home – his father's house – was more than he could bear. So he turned on his heels and headed back the way he had come.

Red sky at night. Cary marvelled at the view from the train carriage as he arrived back at the regional station. Murat was waiting to give him a lift.

'You change your mind?' Murat asked, as he took the backpack from Cary's shoulders and placed it in the spacious boot of the limousine.

'Something like that.'

They drove back in silence.

It was around eleven o'clock at night when Gareth bumped into Cary in the kitchen.

As he pushed through the swing door, Gareth leapt back in shock. 'Bloody hell!' He exhaled slowly. 'For a minute I thought we'd got a soddin' intruder!'

'Shock you, did I?'

Gareth shrugged, acting unperturbed all of a sudden. 'Takes a lot to shock me, I'll tell you, son.'

'I don't doubt that.' Cary grinned.

He liked Gareth. He liked his bluff Northern exterior; liked his easy camaraderie; liked his effortless masculinity. Simply liked him. And he *loved* it when Gareth called him son. Loved the intimacy implicit in this particular term of endearment. Son was a word his own father would never think to use.

'What're you doing here?'

'Well, at this precise moment in time, I'm making myself some hot milk. I had planned to take a late-night dip in the pool but Murat has seen fit to drain it. He said he wants to check something technical. So that idea's bolloxed.'

'Not necessarily. There's always the lake.'

'The lake?'

'Why not? It's mild out tonight.'

'You on for it?'

'Can't sleep. Why not!'

'Great. I'll just get my togs.'

'Fuck that. Don't tell me you're shy?'

Cary had heard that question somewhere before. 'No.'

'So? Come on then. I'll race you.' Gareth was already standing in the open doorway to outside. 'Last one in the water's a wussie!'

Sky blue-pink. A full moon loomed large in the midsummer night heavens. Ghostly pale, it cast a shimmering light upon the ripples of an otherwise jet-black lake. A silent idyll about to be rudely disturbed by the two intruders who now ploughed through the undergrowth into the woodland clearing and on to the mudbank. Perched on the edge of the lake, tottering on one foot, they each pulled off first one boot, then the other. One laughing heartily whilst the other kept quiet, they continued to strip until both stood stark naked. Bare flesh basked in the warm night air. Moonbathing. And blood began to pump.

Having dumped his clothes unceremoniously, Gareth was the first to swagger into the breach. Moments later, ice cold water hit his nuts and, yelping, he dived headlong, shattering the mirrored surface. The resulting splash cracked like a whiplash against the silence of night.

Immersing his body was his best line of defence. He knew this from experience. Just get it over with, get the shock over with. Cary remained on the shore, mud oozing through his toes as he shifted weight from one foot to the other.

'Come on in, the water's fine!' Gareth lied, as he splashed about. 'Come on!'

Cary dipped in a toe, then one foot up to the ankle. Each disappeared in turn. Eventually, he was up to his calves and, steeling himself against the onslaught, he began to wade towards his trainer.

'Whose crazy idea was this anyhow?' Cary asked rhetorically, when suddenly the ground beneath his feet gave way and he plunged beneath the surface of the water. When, coughing and spluttering, his head re-emerged, only Gareth's laughter could be heard.

'That's the way to do it, son!' Gareth declared. 'Now just tread water. Get yourself warmed up.'

'I could have drowned!' Cary exclaimed.

Gareth snorted with laughter. 'Oh, stop your whinging and whining. I'm here, aren't I? You're safe enough with me.' He waited a moment until Cary got his breath back then, raising his hand, he pointed. 'See the island in the centre of the lake?'

'Yeah.'

'I'll race you.'

'You'll beat me.'

'I'll count to twenty, then I'll start. Ready? One . . . Two . . .'

Cary took up the challenge. By the count of ten he was slicing through the water at a rate of knots, cutting through the surface like a hot knife through butter and well on target. He hadn't mentioned that he used to swim for his county. Nor that he invariably won. It was all a game at the end of the day. Cary was no dumb blond.

Even as he scrambled up the bank to victory, Gareth was chasing after him.

'You little bastard!' he was shouting. 'You were having me on.'

And suddenly Gareth was on Cary's back, knocking him off balance. They crumpled together in a heap on the damp earth. Gareth wrestled him over on to his back and pinned him to the ground.

'You need to be taught a lesson, young man.'

'Oh, yeah?'

'Yeah! And I'm the man who's going to teach you.'

'When you're big enough!' Cary sneered.

'Oh? Cocky now, are we? Been taking lessons from Mitch? Thought you'd got more about you. Seems I've been too soft. But don't worry. Now I'm going to put you in your place. And do you know where that place is?'

'No, I don't, big-head.'

Gareth shook his head. 'Oh, my. You are asking for it, aren't you? Then I'll tell you where your rightful place is, shall I? It's under me.'

'Get off me!' Cary tried to wrestle free. 'Get off me!'

But it was useless. Cary was beaten. Gareth pinned him down flat with superior strength and, leaning his face in close to Cary's, he smirked in triumph.

It was only when Cary relaxed into submission that he noticed the extent of their mutual arousal. A cock sandwich. And as Gareth began to rotate his slick hips, the friction of wet dicks against wet bellies produced a jolt of energy that threatened to make him shoot his load right then and there.

But not quite. Not yet.

'Now,' Gareth asked pointedly, 'are you going to take your punishment like a man?'

'You're a fucking bully, Gareth,' Cary replied angrily, trying in vain to conceal his embarrassment and arousal.

'No. Just horny. As horny as you are by the looks of it. I feel like a monk in a monastery. My bollocks are full to bursting. It's criminal all this ripe, fertile come going begging.' He paused for effect. 'Haven't had a pull for five days.'

'How interesting.' Cary yawned, affecting disinterest like a pro.

Gareth was oblivious. 'Yeah, it is, isn't it?' He carried on enthused. 'Imagine, you and me cast away together on an island like Robinson Crusoe and that other bloke. A man has his needs.'

'Why don't you change the record or just whack off!' Cary suggested, with as little overt enthusiasm as he could muster. Tired of the game. Irritated. And more than a little unprepared for Gareth's response.

'Not such a bad idea, son,' he replied and slid a hand between their bellies. He winked, slyly. 'You can watch if you want.'

Gareth grasped both their cocks in his fist and rubbed them together languidly for all of about sixty seconds before moving to his knees. His donkey dick lurched over Cary's face. Gareth's fist grabbed a firm hold on the inflated shaft. The piss slit was temptingly visible, peeping out of his heavily wrinkled foreskin. Slowly he eased it further back, releasing an impressive mushroom head – a head that seemed to bloom as it was released from its confines. Suddenly, he slapped his dick hard against Cary's cheek. A rod of iron. Then he held it towards Cary for a closer examination.

He laughed as Cary's mouth dropped open. 'Impressed?'

All Cary could do was nod.

'Want to see it pop?'

Another nod.

Gareth spat on his fingers and doused the smooth, bulbous helmet, buffing and polishing it with the tips of his fingers till it shimmered and shone.

Looking Cary straight in the eye, he chuckled. 'Wipe your mouth. You're drooling.'

And so saying, he returned his focus to the task in hand, working his sturdy fist up and down the solid shaft. Unhurried. Slow and easy, from fruit to root. Straddling Cary's face now, he spread his thighs wider, bending both knees for comfort and support. Relaxing into it.

His breathing came more heavily, his expression more intense. He stopped the slow jerk and squeezed tight. Precome oozed from the tip and balanced like a glistening jewel on the crown of his knob. Sweeping it up on his index finger, he examined it, then held it out at arm's length towards Cary. When he spoke, his throat was thick with lust.

'Want it?'

Cary's tongue poked out timidly as he tipped up his head but before he knew it Gareth had stuffed the finger in his own mouth. Five, maybe ten seconds passed till Gareth tugged the finger free.

'Tough luck,' he snickered, then paused. 'Now I'm going to sit on your face.'

For one brief moment, Gareth held his position. Tension filled the space between them, crackling like electricity. But it would have been a feeble attempt on Cary's part to defy him. Ultimately, he would be compelled to obey his trainer's firm instruction. The situation left little room for negotiation. Gareth had set the terms. One false move on Cary's part and Gareth could easily withdraw from the game and he wasn't about to give him an excuse to quit.

Gareth swung around and repositioned his arse squarely over Cary's face. He lowered himself slowly, the crack of his arse parting ever so slightly to reveal a crop of dark curls. Within seconds, Cary began snuffling like a pig in a trough.

It was only after he was seated that Gareth relaxed, focusing his gaze on Cary's erection and resuming the task at hand, lovingly stroking his pride and joy.

His eyes drank in the whole of Cary. He was physically perfect. Just perfect. Everything Gareth considered attractive in a man other than himself. A film of sweat adding a lustre to Cary's smooth, pale skin. The only blemishes were from external sources — streaks of mud and bits of grass clinging to his body where they had rolled on the ground. Moonlight caused golden body hair to glitter over muscular forearms, thighs and calves.

Big, strong feet flexing and pointing involuntarily. The intensity of feeling as Cary worked his mouth and the vehemence with which his fists now gripped his own cock and ball sack alike as they pumped out a rhythm to beat the band impressed Gareth no end.

'You love it, don't you?' Gareth's voice trembled, his breathing laboured.

Cary could only mumble his agreement.

'Eat me. Eat me all up.'

Another mumble. Meanwhile, Cary never missed a stroke.

He was blinded by two hulking, hairy buttocks but Gareth's eyes were open wide, looking down. Nipples, small and erect, stood out proudly on Cary's hairless chest. Gareth's free hand teased and tugged on them – tugged them mercilessly – whilst his eyes traced the fine line which led down to the deep cleft of Cary's navel then blossomed out into luxuriant pubic hair surrounding a pulsing tool, engorged with blood and pointing to the heavens.

Gareth's eyes continued their downward glide over athletic thighs, chiselled knees and muscular calves. Then down to Cary's feet, scuffed with grass and damp earth.

As his fist pumped mercilessly Gareth's nuts responded reflexively. First rising and then lowering. His cock was straining fit to burst.

'I'm going to shoot my load. I'm going to empty my big bollocks. And you? You're going to watch me. You're going to open your eyes wide and watch me.' He shuddered and leapt to his feet to stand astride Cary's face. 'Tell me what you want,' Gareth demanded, clamping a sweaty fist around his throbbing shaft.

'Come over me. Come all over me while I wank off.'

'You want that?'

'Yeah, it's what I want. Do it!'

Gareth bent down and held out his palm in front of Cary's lips.

'Spit.'

Eager to please, Cary fulfilled his request in the instant, his complicity giving the distinct impression that he would have done anything, promised Gareth anything, so urgent was his need for relief. It was clear by his whole demeanour. He lay back passively, expectantly. Gareth smeared his erection with Cary's saliva and gazed down on upon him.

Hard as a rock, he resumed his jack-off rhythm as Cary matched it. His eyes focused on Cary's dick as he towered over his prostrate body, licking his lips. He was grinding his hips, thrusting them up to meet his pummelling fist.

'Learnt your lesson, have you, son?'

'Yes,' Cary gasped. 'You're a good teacher.'

'Look up to me, just a little bit, do you, son?'

'Yeah. I do, yeah.'

'Tell me then. Let me hear you say it.'

'I look up to you, Gareth.' Cary was almost giggling. 'I'm flat on my back, what else can I do?'

Gareth was out of it, thrusting his hips, keeping rhythm with his fist that encompassed his cock and primed his balls to discharge.

'I can feel it, son. Can feel all the come bubbling up inside of me. All my come, just for you. Bubbling up just because of you, you sexy little fucker. Can feel it coming. Won't hold anything back. Feel it coming up, rising up. Coming now. Come . . .'

Gareth's hand had been working his cock furiously. Abruptly, the action stopped, he froze stock still, and then with a whoop a great wad of ball juice leapt from the head of his prick and splashed on to Cary's heaving belly, tension draining away with every dose, with every thick, creamy splatter. Dousing Cary like a sudden summer storm. Dry one minute, drenched the next.

It was all too much for Cary. He was no longer thinking rationally, pure instinct had taken over. He was desperate to get the ache out of his nuts and the jism out of his system. Jerking it out, jerking it up and out. His bollocks hung heavy like fruit on a tree, aching with juice. Aching with juice that needed to be squeezed out. Jerking it out, jerking it up and out. And the big squeeze began as his balls hunkered up high, high and tight.

With one final yank, Cary's prick began to squirt. Jet upon jet of spunk shot high in the air like bolts from a Roman candle, rocketing over his chest and belly, crash-landing on to his tits and neck. Time after time after time.

At last, the pulses grew weaker. Emptied out. Rivulets of sperm dribbled over his fingers. He reached up a hand to tug Gareth's knob-sack purposefully and shake the last few drops free from the tip of his cockhead. The final drop splashed on to the corner of Cary's mouth. He couldn't help but laugh. A deep belly laugh. It felt therapeutic, all tension gone.

Gareth was laughing too. It was his turn to be impressed. Quality *and* quantity. 'When exactly was the last time you came? 1995?'

They both exploded into peals of laughter.

Then came silence. Cary sighed and, in so doing, his body seemed to merge with the ground beneath him, with nature itself. Reaching down, he dipped his fingers into the congealed puddle on his stomach. Gareth dropped on his haunches, squatting down to kiss him. Long and hard and deep. Suddenly, Cary wrestled him down, wrapping his body around him, deliberately grinding his sticky body against Gareth's. At first, Gareth struggled but then relaxed as Cary's arms wrapped around his broad back. Their lips locked together in a hard, lingering kiss.

'Better wash this muck off,' Gareth said, finally attempting to extricate himself from Cary's grip. 'We need to clean up and get you back to your warm milk!'

'Got me some of that already!' Cary's voice faded, grew suddenly poignant, whilst his grip remained firm. 'I don't want to sleep alone. Not tonight. Stay with me?' And just as quickly he slipped back into comic mode. 'Anyhow, I haven't finished with you yet. Won't let you go unless you promise.'

'Eh? Has anyone ever told you, you're a fuckin' bully?' Again Gareth tried to wrestle free.

'You're staying with me tonight. Just this once, you're going to do as you are told.'

Gareth paused in his struggle, surprised by Cary's burst of

strength. He held up his hands as a sign of submission. 'OK, you win.' He grinned. 'Just this once, Cary. Just this once.'

Saturday afternoon found Mitch in bed. He was doing one last favour – turning one last trick for a valued customer. Covers thrown aside, he lay on his back. Never again. Never again would he be in this motorway hotel room. Not that his client knew that – he had yet to inform him that their arrangement had come to an end. It was going to be difficult, Mitch knew that. He actually liked this guy.

Jack had been a regular. A thick-set, burly ape of a man in his early forties. A building worker with huge hands that bore all the scars of a lifetime's manual labour. Usual story: married with children, closeted. But he wasn't embittered or screwed up like so many johns. He was kind, always affectionate and surprisingly tender. Mitch knew that this guy could easily get laid without paying. Then again, his tastes were somewhat unconventional. That's where Mitch came in.

Feet were Jack's thing. As usual, Mitch's feet, lovingly scrubbed, had been bound at the ankles by rope then laid on a silver platter. Jack was going through his usual mantra of compliments. Reverently bathing the soles of Mitch's feet with his tongue whilst telling him how he wasn't worthy to do so. Praising each toe as he kissed them. This could keep Jack happy for hours. It suited Mitch; he loved giving pleasure and with Jack he only had to lie back and be. Nothing else. Nothing was enough.

Mitch glanced down the length of his own naked body and caught sight of the look of rapture on Jack's face. Blissfully licking and sucking and nibbling. It wouldn't be long now before Jack would kneel astride the objects of his adoration and chug a load out of his hefty scrotum, washing Mitch's feet with come and tears – for he always cried at the point of orgasm. In the past, it had worried Mitch but Jack had assured him that they were tears of happiness. But today?

What should he tell him? That was the question uppermost in Mitch's mind. He was tempted to reveal all, to share with Jack the secret of his new-found career. So far he had told no one, just as Rab had instructed, but it was driving him crazy. He had this fabulous secret and he could not share it. Why not with Jack? Why not? Jack had secrets enough of his own. Hadn't Mitch kept them? And maybe, just maybe, it would take the sting out of Jack's disappointment. Maybe it would be for the best to just tell him the truth. After all, what harm could it really do?

The gang were reunited late on Sunday evening. Damon was the last to arrive, his little silver Mini rattling up the drive towards the main entrance. The belching exhaust summoned all the others to the door. Kenny looked on ruefully as he saw what amounted to a pile of scrap on wheels, trailing a cloud of black smoke.

'I promised to look it over for him.' Kenny turned to the others. 'Me and my big mouth.'

The Mini ground to a halt at the foot of the steps and Damon bounced out and jumped up the steps, two at a time. He wore a three-quarter length T-shirt that revealed his pierced navel and emblazoned on the front was the legend HUG ME – in big capital letters.

In his own inimitable style, Damon flung his arms around each one in turn and planted a big kiss on their cheeks. He saved the biggest and sloppiest one for Murat – precisely because he knew it would embarrass him most. It did. But Kenny came a close second.

'We don't do that kind of thing up North.' Kenny grimaced, as he wiped Damon's kiss from his face.

'Then it's about time you started, tight-arse. Didn't your mother tell you it's good to hug!'

'You what! You could get locked up for less than that in Sheffield!' he barked.

'Very liberal and enlightened. Remind me to give your home town a wide berth.' Damon turned to Mitch. 'You're from the North, Mitch. Would it get me locked up in Manchester?'

'Nah, you'd probably get a round of applause and the key to the city.'

It was Gayle's turn to chime in. 'In which case, Mr Liberal, how come you're not demonstrative? A hug and a kiss is more than I got from you when you arrived back.'

Mitch grinned. 'Because kissing and hugging a man is one thing, kissing and hugging a woman is another matter entirely.'

'Really?'

'Yeah, really. You might get the wrong idea and then where would we be.'

'Wouldn't you like to know!'

As the others turned to go inside Mitch pulled Cary aside. 'Did you hear that!'

'Hear what?' Cary replied, bemused, preoccupied.

'Gayle? She's got the hots for me in a big bad way.'

'Eh?'

'I said she's dying for it. What do you reckon?'

'About what?'

'Do you think I should put her out of her misery? You know,' – his voice dropped to a whisper – 'give her a good poke?'

'Has anyone ever told you, you're a sexist pig?'

'Geddaway.' He paused meaningfully. 'You're just *jealous*.'

Cary turned pale. 'Just what do you mean by that?'

'Nothing.'

'Come on. Spit it out.'

Mitch's face clouded over. 'She fancies me, not you, and your ego can't stand the competition, can it?' He spun on his heels and walked away.

You have never been so wrong, thought Cary to himself. You aren't my competition – she is.

The daily routine was quickly resumed. If anything, it accelerated. Cary had precious little free time to worry about affairs of the heart, his mind and body were otherwise engaged. Over the coming month any number of experts were drafted in to present a whole series of workshops. Topics on offer ranged from the practical – 'How to Perform on Camera' – through survival techniques – 'How to Deal with the Press' – and into the realm of personal behaviour – 'How to Conduct Yourself in the Public Arena'.

All of the above were in addition to the regular daily programme. So it could hardly be considered surprising that by the third week, the boys were again starting to flag. Murat found Damon one evening, shortly after dinner, fast asleep on the sofa in the spacious sitting room. He didn't bother to wake him but simply carried him up to his room. Once there, he undressed him and put him to bed. There was no need for a bedtime story, just a kiss on the forehead, before turning out the light and closing the door quietly as he crept out of the room.

Cary heard a tap on his door and Gareth's head appeared around it.

'Just thought I'd check to see how you're doing.'

Cary's heart sank. The novelty had all too soon worn off. Gareth's attentions were escalating beyond a joke. The guy was insatiable. Even after countless assignations here he was again, back for more. Cary had tried to let him down easily; had tried to explain that he was a creature of mood not instinct; that it wasn't a question of lack of desire but that he was simply exhausted. Gareth couldn't seem to take no for an answer.

'How about if I climb in there with you?' Having quickly checked over his shoulder, Gareth whispered, 'I want you, Cary.' He stepped inside and closed the door behind him. 'I'm hard just thinking about you. Look.' He traced the outline of his cock with finger and thumb as it protruded out from the front of his jogging bottoms.

Cary had never failed to be impressed by the size and potency of Gareth's manhood. And tonight, despite himself, the impact it had on him was much the same.

Gareth took his first step towards the bed. 'Just feel it.'

Cary put up both hands. 'Close enough. Down, Rover!' He shook his head. 'Not right now. I'm not in the mood.'

Gareth's features rearranged into a childlike pout. '"I'm not in the mood."' He crooked an eyebrow. 'Guess what? I don't believe you!'

'Maybe after a good night's sleep, whenever that will be. Maybe then I'll be in the mood. Don't hassle me, Gareth, please. It won't get you what you want. Look, I've explained the situation. I don't want to keep having to repeat myself. Why won't you listen?'

'You were keen enough when I've asked you before.' Gareth edged ever closer to the bed.

'Yeah? But not now, OK? Work is too important.'

Gareth changed tactics. 'Don't go believing that bollocks about sex affecting your performance. I've scored more goals after a good shag than I ever did practising abstinence.'

'Gareth . . .'

'OK. But what about if I say please?' Gareth hooked his thumb under his waistband and began to ease it down over his bulging basket.

'Gareth!'

Gareth's cock sprang from its enclosure and, as he proudly displayed it, Gareth began to stroke it. 'Pretty please?'

Cary sighed in resignation, then threw back the duvet. 'OK, get in.'

Gareth was naked and alongside him in the blink of an eye.

Cary moaned as Gareth's tongue began to lick his balls. 'I tell you, Gareth, and it's no word of a lie –' he shivered with anticipation as Gareth's tongue inched towards the base of his fully erect penis '– I'll be glad when your contract finally expires.'

'Two weeks to go,' Gareth mumbled.

'Two weeks to a decent night's kip.'

'Oh, but you'll miss me when I'm gone!'

Late on Thursday evening, a day earlier than expected, Rab jumped into his customised Morgan and put his foot down. He didn't so much drive as race all the way from London to his country retreat, arriving around 11.45 p.m. All was quiet. All lights were out. Good. He wasn't in the mood for company.

He entered his private study, poured himself a brandy, then

threw open the French windows. The night air was cool and the night sky bright. Big fucking deal! thought Rab. He was not a happy man.

Linda had been playing up again. Linda, his ex-wife and biggest mistake, had taken it upon herself to prevent him from seeing his five-year-old daughter, claiming it distressed her too much. In reality, Linda was simply using little Alice as leverage to negotiate a new financial deal. Of course, her smarmy, high-class solicitor had put it a different way but it amounted to the same thing once you cut through the bullshit and legalese. Rab was sick and tired of her shenanigans, contemptuous of her and her money-grabbing machinations. At any rate, he figured she'd had a more than generous financial settlement in the first place. Especially if one considered that it was she who had effectively ended their relationship by shagging his best friend. He had never hated anybody in his whole life before. Before Linda, that is. He hated her.

Closing his eyes, he took a deep, deep breath. Then exhaled slowly, opening his clenched fists as he opened his eyes again. One day, he thought, my hot temper is going to get me in big trouble.

His private study was a place of solace and, therefore, strictly out of bounds. Rab valued his privacy. In here he had created the ideal place to relax. On this occasion, however, he didn't feel comforted, he felt trapped. The walls were oak-panelled; the open fire was unlit; on either side of the chimney breast, rows of shelves bowed under the weight of first editions that reached from floor to high ceiling. A leather sofa and armchair fringed the Persian rug but they didn't invite him to sit.

From where he stood he could see the summer pavilion. A place where, a generation before him, people had once picnicked and played croquet. He could almost see them: ghostly figures dressed in white, engaged in pleasant pastimes. No worries. Another world. What he wouldn't give to escape into that world just for one day. It called to him now in silence; caused him to wander through the open doors and across the immaculate lawn.

He lit a cigar on the way, an occasional indulgence but it

seemed deserved after a day like he had had. Lost in thought, it was only as he drew near the pavilion that he heard the stifled laughter. He stood stock still, a shiver running down his spine. Ghosts? First, a woman's voice and then a man's, floating on the breeze. Whispering, giggling and – what was it – grunting? Intruders!

He threw the cigar on to the ground, grinding it out with the toe of his shoe. Being careful to avoid any unnecessary noise, he made his way towards the muffled voices. With the greatest of care he edged his way along the wall of dense vegetation that skirted the pavilion until, inch by inch, he came upon the lattice panelling. Peeping through, moonlight cast a fractured glow over the debauchery.

Gayle Driver, her knickers around one ankle, lay on her back on a wrought-iron bench. Two fulsome breasts wobbled within the confines of her bra as she quivered and shook. Mitch's hands reached up to grasp both heaving mounds whilst he knelt between her legs and ate her pussy. Her knickers and bra were the only items of clothing on view. Otherwise, both were naked, their clothes scattered out of sight.

Rab felt an immense swell of anger surface and surge through his veins. How dare they? How dare they betray his trust? These were his first thoughts but he could barely articulate the underlying reason behind the reaction. Had Gayle chosen any other guy but Mitch then Rab might not have felt such fury. Sure, it was unprofessional – she had been appointed guardian of sorts – but Mitch? Mitch was special. Mitch was going to be his.

Clearly, they hadn't reckoned on being caught out. It was also patently obvious, to Rab's jaundiced mind, that their own agenda had taken precedent over the demands of the project or any feelings of responsibility to him or the others. Yes, he was furious that they could jeopardise the project by giving in to their own selfish desires. But something else was happening here; something beyond righteous anger; something Rab couldn't or wouldn't acknowledge. For, despite his denial, he was also mesmerised.

Mitch was up on his feet, foraging in his jeans pocket for the small cardboard packet. Just as quickly he was back between Gayle's thighs. From the box he retrieved a cellophane rectangle and tossed the packet aside. Stroking his cock with one hand he bit into the wrapper, tore the seal and with a flick of the wrist he rolled the condom over his middle wicket.

Spreading Gayle's legs wide, Mitch eased gently into her, inching his way, teasing and taunting her. A long, thick tube poked out from Mitch's forest of pubic hair; now you see it, now you don't, as Gayle first willingly consumed then reluctantly released it. Rab's eyes fixed on Mitch's muscular buttocks as they reflexively tensed and relaxed, tensed and relaxed. For Gayle's part, she was anything but passive; humping back with increased appetite, impaling herself on Mitch's dick whilst he plucked both breasts from her bra and caressed them.

His arse was a prize winner. Set high and firm, round and hairless. Two lustrous orbs reflecting the moonlight, jiggling up and down as Gayle wrapped her legs around his waist and begged him to fuck her harder.

Her painted nails clung to and dimpled those same buttocks, urging him deeper in, parting the cheeks to expose his hairy cleft. Fucking her, grinding into her, whilst Rab watched, entranced. Mitch was doing something right: Gayle was groaning ever more loudly as she strained towards her climax. Mitch reached up to cover her mouth and dampen her cries. And, gritting his own teeth, gave a final thrust . . . pause . . . then another . . . and with each single jab, he continued to spurt.

As they dressed, they smiled but didn't talk. Suddenly business-like. No great display of affection. No post-coital cuddle. Just wrinkles smoothed away. Then Mitch held up his used rubber by the knot he had tied at the end and asked Gayle if she'd like it for keepsake.

'Fuck off!' she said with a snort.

'Very ladylike,' he replied.

She looked first to his smirking face, then the dangling condom and, with pursed lips, reached out to take it between thumb and forefinger. With little ado she flung it over her shoulder and into the bushes.

'Maybe it'll take root and grow.' He laughed.

Tossing back her shoulder-length hair, Gayle snorted again. 'I hope not. I dread to think what Rab would make of a rubber plant suddenly popping up in the middle of his prize rose patch. My life wouldn't be worth living.'

Mitch laughed again. Gayle didn't.

'Maybe that wasn't such a good idea,' she muttered, looking over her shoulder. 'What does it say on the packet? Dispose of carefully?'

'No one's going to stumble across it,' he reassured her. 'You couldn't find it even if you knew what you were looking for.'

'Guess so.' She linked arms with him and they headed back towards the house.

The freshly discarded condom hung suspended on a branch, hooked by a single thorn. Mitch's load lay heavy in the rubber tip, stretching the teat. If Rab wasn't mistaken (and he was not), the contents should still be thick and creamy. He waited until all was quiet then tiptoed closer. Lowering his face he examined the desired object, inspecting the wealth of contents, repulsed and transfixed. It was deliciously full. A shame to waste all that protein, he thought to himself. Lifting it free, his fingers trembled as he undid the knot. Bringing his nose to the lip, he inhaled the pungent aroma, causing the erection in his pants to swell to bursting.

Once back in his private study, Rab poured himself another brandy and rinsed his mouth thoroughly, washing the aftertaste away, the bitter taste of betrayal. Betrayed by both of them. But Gayle had no excuse. She knew the terms of their agreement. A hands-on approach should not be taken so literally.

'So, what to do?' His feelings were irrational but none the less vivid for all that; he had little awareness that Linda's manipulations on the one hand and intense jealousy on the other were seriously affecting his judgement.

'Oh, I'll take care of her all right. Don't you worry about

that,' he announced to the empty room. And, checking for his keys, he headed for the door and a return journey. There was much to be done before he would finally confront his most trusted of employees.

Four

Gayle was history before she knew it.
    Rab returned to the mansion early the following Friday and, at his request, the four band members had been called to the recording studio. It was a little after ten when he made his appearance. Gayle and Remi, having each put the four guys through a thorough vocal warm-up and sound check were about to lay down a vocal track with Cary singing lead.

Eyebrows were raised and subtle shrugs exchanged as Rab entered. He had a young woman in tow; a serious-looking young woman hiding behind sunglasses; a woman he failed to introduce but simply gestured towards a seat at the back of the room.

'Let's hear what you lads have been up to,' was all Rab said as he sat at the control panel and motioned for the pre-recorded backing track to be played.

'They've been working on a vocal arrangement with Cary singing –'

Rab cut Gayle short with a wave of his hand. 'Less talk, more action,' he said with little warmth.

Suitably rebuked, Gayle nodded to Remi as the boys took up position behind the microphone. Behind the glass screen, the intro music was piped through four sets of headphones. In the control room the small assembled group were all ears.

Gayle glowered as Rab lit a cigar. Timidly, Remi produced a paper cup for him to use as an ashtray and passed it across the mixing desk. Remi knew that Rab was well aware Gayle had forbidden anyone from smoking in the studio and so could not help but wonder what the hell was going on. Better to just keep his head down.

Remi introduced the track. 'The song's called, "What Kind Of Fool (Do You Take Me For)".'

How appropriate, thought Rab, and he allowed himself a wry smile. 'Take it away.'

Within the soundproof booth, four sets of knees were quaking in unison. This was the first real test and Rab's approval (or lack of it) could well make the difference between stardom and a one-way ticket home. Then again, maybe not. They had come this far, after all. But, at the very least, that's how the lads were feeling as the intro led into the inevitable – an opening chorus of multi-layered harmony. All went well. Cary followed through, sweeping the song up and away into the first verse. A pattern that was repeated before the middle eight.

The break belonged to Mitch. It took the form of a rap; something he'd improvised during the week. Both funny and sexy, he delivered it with his tongue planted firmly in his cheek. Gayle almost giggled with delight at this point. The lads were not only a credit to her, they were a credit to themselves.

At last came the final verse leading into the chorus and fade. As the final notes ebbed away, all four guys held their breath.

After what seemed like an age, Rab's face broke into a smile – a smile that seemed to stretch from ear to ear. 'Well done, my boys. Well done!'

The collective sigh of relief was audible.

'I understand there's another track with Mitch singing lead?' Rab said without pause.

'Yes,' Gayle replied. '"Say I'm Your Number One".'

'OK. Let's hear it.'

Shortly thereafter, Rab thanked the boys, thanked Remi. In fact he gave thanks to everyone and his grandmother. All except Gayle, that is. And, having told the assembled group that he would meet with them all again shortly, he left the control room. The mysterious stranger following at his heels.

'What the fuck was that all about?' asked a bemused Damon as he led the other lads out from behind the glass.

'Don't ask me, I just work here,' Gayle replied tartly as she collected up her things. 'You might as well take a break until after lunch.' And with that, she made a dramatic exit.

'Ooh! Get her!' Damon said, as the door swung shut. 'Who rattled her cage?'

No one replied. No one had to. The answer was obvious.

Mitch retired to the privacy of his room and the comfort of a long, slow, leisurely wank. He was feeling smug. Smug and aroused. He'd seen the way Rab had looked at him as he had performed his number. There was no mistaking the look in his eyes. Mitch had seen it before, countless times, in the eyes of his punters. It told him that Rab had a soft spot for him – a wet spot – and a rock hard mound to match.

He slipped out of his jeans and T-shirt and lay back on the feather duvet. His head was on the pillows, a fist gripping his impressive erection. He was blissfully unaware that Cary, having removed the key from the lock of the connecting door, was watching him through the keyhole. Watching him and stroking his own exposed member.

Gayle was determined to have it out with Rab. She stormed into the library to find him puffing on a thick, pungent cigar as he poured brandy. One for himself, one for the stranger. Her nose turned up at the aroma. It offended her even further.

'Rab, we need to speak.'

'Indeed we do, Gayle,' he concurred. Handing over the second glass of brandy to his silent guest he said, 'Perhaps you could give us a few minutes alone, Jayne?'

Without a word, Jayne exited through the French windows.

'You were saying, Gayle?'

Stridently, she bulldozed ahead. 'For the past week, we have had virtually no contact. You have consistently failed to return my calls. Then, I get a curt little fax asking me to arrange this morning's session during which you ignore, if not insult, me. After that, you make a point of thanking everyone for their hard work – everyone except me.' There was a pause. Her voice suddenly softened. 'What's the game, Rab? You could always talk to me. So? What gives?'

'I'm afraid I'm going to have to terminate our professional relationship.'

Gayle was stunned. Speechless. Then she stuttered, 'But . . . but why?'

'What if I said I'm not happy with your work.'

'You've just seen them perform!' Her tone grew angry. 'You can see the progress they made. Progress they made with my help.'

'Then let's just say, I found a rubber plant growing amongst my prize rose bushes.'

His comment hit her like a slap in the face, then a bitter smile twisted her lips. 'Mitch told you? The shit! The little shit!'

Rab's voice was devoid of emotion. 'If it's any comfort to you, Gayle, he did not.'

'Then how?'

'That's not important right now. What is important is that you leave quickly and quietly without causing any more damage.'

'What's the problem here, Rab? I fucked him. It's not –' she struggled for the right words '– something to be proud of but, at the end of the day, so what? What's the deal?'

'The deal is –' his temper began to flare – 'that at an extremely fragile point in the development of the group dynamic you were actively showing favour to one member in particular. What if they'd found out? What if I wanted to make him lead singer? Would they put two and two together and make five, do you think?' His voice grew cold once more. 'You have compromised me. And that is unforgivable. That's the deal, Gayle.'

'What am I going to tell the boys?'

'Nothing. I took the liberty of asking Murat to pack your

bags. They should be in the boot of your car. You're going to leave quickly and quietly without any fuss.'

'And if I refuse?'

He ignored the question. 'Of course, you won't be leaving empty-handed. Your salary will be paid for a further six months after which you'll receive a glowing reference and a generous cash bonus. In the meantime, you are welcome to look for other employment.'

She nodded. He turned his back.

'You know your own way out. Goodbye, Gayle.'

Up the winding staircase, Cary and Mitch were oblivious to the machinations below. Both had their hands full. Cary's lips were tender, tingling, swollen with lust, his mouth awash with saliva as he imagined himself feasting on Mitch's hunk of prime beef. At regular intervals, Mitch had been basting his meat with his own spit. Cooking it to perfection, bringing it to the boil.

Cary changed hands. His wrist ached. He'd been whacking on himself for an age but holding back; holding the come in his nuts, awaiting the right moment, the right timing. Mitch lay back, his eyes closed, indulging himself and loving every minute of it. To pop or not to pop, that wasn't the question – only when. How long should a good thing last?

Almost imperceptibly at first, Mitch began to buck his hips upwards to greet his industrious fist. Had Cary been able to climb through the keyhole at that moment he would have. Instead, he used his mind's eye to project himself into the scene. He imagined himself climbing astride Mitch's solid thighs, then lowering himself so that his anal ring would twitch against Mitch's bulbous cockhead before opening up to consume it. And sitting back, he would inch his way down the circumference until firm buttocks touched base with big, hairy, come-filled bollocks.

Mitch moaned. Then again. A little louder each time. His fist and hips working in perfect unison. Heaving. Not just leading but yanking the horse to water. Working his way towards orgasm with a fury, with a violence, that was almost frightening. Cary looked on, his own fist working in rhythm. He saw the pronounced definition of the muscle on Mitch's belly scrunch up, watched Mitch's feet point involuntarily towards his spy hole and then the first spasm hit.

Mitch let out the groan of an animal in pain as a stream of creamy come sprang from his crimson helmet and shot high in the air. Cary's own cock, distended with blood, actually hurt it was so hard. Hard as granite. A couple more jerks and he too was firing on both cylinders, feeling the spunk force a path through his aching tubes, up and out. He covered the door in a second gloss coat.

Mitch held his cock still as it squirted out its ample quantity of ball-juice. It lathered his hand and the ridges of his stomach were awash. And though his hand was now motionless, his body jerked and convulsed in the grip of each powerful aftershock.

At last, he sank back into the mattress, a sublime look on his face – like the cat who got the cream.

'Yeah,' Mitch sighed. 'Take that, you bastard. Take that.'

Cary lifted his eye from the keyhole, pressed his forehead against the door frame and in so doing missed the punchline. Mitch had blown a kiss in the direction of the door.

An hour later the boys regrouped around the oak table in the dining room. They were joined by Rab and the stranger. The air hung heavy with the weight of unspoken questions.

'OK, guys. I'm afraid you're going to have to brace yourself for a shock,' Rab began.

'Oh, well,' Kenny cast his eyes down, 'it was good while it lasted.'

'No, Kenny! Not that kind of a shock,' Rab reassured him and checked with the others before continuing. 'No. I'm afraid we've suffered something of a loss. Gayle is no longer project coordinator. In fact, she's left the project altogether.'

Reactions on the faces around the table ranged from shocked through stunned to disappointed and back again.

'Now, perhaps you're angry and disgruntled. I'm sure you

have a lot of questions. But if you are angry, be angry with me. It wasn't Gayle's idea to go, it was mine.'

'But why?' Mitch blurted out.

How predictable of you to jump to her defence, thought Rab. Admirable, really. But all he said was, 'Do you trust my judgement, Mitch?'

'Of course I do.'

'Then believe me when I say I have only your best interests at heart.'

'And she's gone without saying goodbye?' Cary shook his head in disbelief.

'We thought it better.'

'Then you thought wrong!' Damon's eyes welled up with tears. 'I liked Gayle. She was with us from the beginning. We've just said goodbye to Gareth, now Gayle's gone. Who's next?'

'I know you liked her, Damon. And believe me, I know she made a big contribution to the development of the team.' Rab spoke gently. 'But consider this: maybe she has taught you as much as she can.' He paused to let the thought sink in. 'I know you're going to miss her, but she's gone now. From now on I'm going to take personal care of you myself.'

'Every day? You'll be here during the week?' asked Kenny.

'Every single day, at least for the next month. You can count on it. And so will –' he deferred with a nod of the head '– Jayne Hanvey. Say "hi", Jayne.'

The stranger finally removed her sunglasses and smiled. Her eyes were violet, piercing, unmistakable.

'Hi!' Jayne said.

Mitch was the first to respond. '*The* Jayne Hanvey? The infamous Jayne Hanvey?' Silly question. Violet eyes confirmed it even though her other trademark – long, blond hair – had been replaced by an elfin chestnut crop.

'The one and only,' said Rab.

'I know this might be a dumb question but who is *the* Jayne Hanvey?' Kenny said perplexed.

'Take no notice of him, Jayne,' Damon said with a look of

mock disapproval. 'He's from up North. They're still waiting for the wireless to be invented.'

'Up yours,' Kenny retorted.

Cary interjected. 'Jayne was lead singer/songwriter with M.N.S.'

'Marks & Spencer's?' Kenny asked without guile.

'No! "Midsummer Night Scene".' Damon took a deep breath. 'Formed in Sydney, Australia in 1993 by Jayne Hanvey and guitarist, Leon Arris. Five top ten hits in their home country before breaking worldwide with the platinum album, "Living Room". Split in 1997 to pursue other artistic ventures. I *loved* that band.'

'Thanks for filling in the background, Damon.' Rab nodded towards him then continued. 'She's been just as successful since the band broke up – as the brains behind a new wave of young artists. She's probably the most successful producer/songwriter in Britain today. You wouldn't necessarily know her name, Kenny – not unless you read the specialist music press. But I assure you that if anyone can get this band off to a flying start it's Jayne.'

'And I do want to work with you guys,' Jayne added. 'The performance you gave this morning knocked me out. Believe me, you have all the makings of a monster hit band. We just need to let the rest of the world in on the secret.'

Four faces beamed.

Jayne continued. 'You may or you may not know that for the past few years I've been head of my own small but very successful indie record company? Well, I've just licensed my operation to a major. We've been looking for a new act to kick off the coalition and I believe you fit the bill perfectly.'

Four mouths dropped open.

'First things first,' said Rab. 'You need a name. Jayne suggested "Bigfun". It seems appropriate enough to me. Any objections?'

Four heads shook. Still speechless.

Rab continued. 'Jayne also feels the band needs an identifiable lead singer to focus attention and give the band a unique sound.'

Mitch folded his arms across his chest and threw a self-satisfied smile in Jayne's direction.

'We decided it should be Cary.'

Mitch was stung. His smile remained in place but was now forced, frozen, fossilised.

'Thank fuck it isn't me!' Kenny sighed with relief.

'Congrats, Cary,' Damon said, clapping him on the back. 'You get to shoulder the burden.'

'Of course, you'll all get the opportunity to do the odd speciality number as time goes on,' Jayne added. 'But it makes it easier in the early stages to sell a band with an identifiable front man.'

Rab could see through Mitch's façade. He was pissed off. Pissed off in a *big* way. This situation would need careful handling. But he was up to it. Rab was nothing if not expert at delicate negotiations.

'It's time to move on, lads,' Rab added finally. 'Onwards and upwards and into the recording studio. It's time to start work on your first single.'

Mitch dropped his towel as he closed the door to the sauna. A wooden pail, half filled with water, and a ladle stood beside the glowing coals. Kicking his flip-flops aside he eased a ladleful over the burning embers and as scorching steam filled the air he swirled his towel to disperse it. Quickly, he spread the towel over the third tier of wooden seating and climbed up to lie flat on his back. Alone at last, alone with his thoughts. Right now it was all he wanted.

It wasn't to be.

The door to the sauna clicked open and shut. Mitch kept his eyes closed.

'I was hoping I'd find you in here.' There was no mistaking Rab's Scottish drawl nor its ability to caress the ear. 'Are you asleep, Mitch?'

'No. Just relaxing.'

'Good. I wanted to have a wee chat.' Rab arranged his towel on the second tier and sat down at right angles to Mitch.

'Couldn't it wait till another time?' Mitch's hand wandered to his groin and tugged the heavy foreskin on his slack cock.

'No time like the present.' Droplets of sweat began to form on Rab's forehead.

Mitch sighed. 'OK. What is it?'

'Would I be right in thinking that you are less than pleased about the events of today?'

Mitch's hand cupped his moist, relaxed ball-sack. His fingers pulled back to ruffle his pubic hair. 'If you mean in involving Jayne Hanvey in the project, the answer is I'm delighted. Her track record is second to none.'

'That isn't what I mean. You were close to Gayle?' Rab's eyes swept over the length of Mitch's lean, muscular body.

'I wouldn't go that far. Liked her, yes. Sad to see her go, yes. But that's life.'

'That's very understanding of you, Mitch.'

'Didn't you know, it's my middle name. Just call me Mitch "Understanding" Mitchell.'

Rab spread his hairy thighs wide as he brushed the flat of his palm over his firm, tufted pecs. One sweeping action sent a shower of sweat down over his belly and on to his fat, circumcised cock and weighty balls. 'So, you're not disappointed that Cary got lead, not you?'

'Oh. So that's what this little chat is all about. A pep talk? Well, thanks, Rab. But I can roll with the punches when I have to.'

'You make it sound like a battle.' Rab toyed with his thickening length.

Eyes still shut, Mitch was oblivious. 'Do I?'

'I'm on your side, Mitch.'

'Yeah?'

'Yes. It was purely a business decision. Cary has a broader appeal. You? You're more of a specialised taste. But at the end of the day it's the combination of all four of you that makes the band what it is. No one member is more important than any other.'

'Was it Jayne's decision?'

'Other people suggest. The final decision always rests with me.'

Mitch ran his fingers over his taut stomach and dipped into his navel. 'I see.'

'Do you?' Rab stopped playing with his dick abruptly. It was almost fully erect. He covered his lap with a corner of the towel, discretion being the better part of valour.

'It's a big investment. You want the maximum return on your money. It makes sense.'

Rab felt an ache deep in his nuts; pleasure and pain, but a feeling that was not at all unpleasant. 'So you're not angry?'

'Disappointed . . . Yeah, sure. But not angry.'

'Good.' And here Rab hesitated briefly. 'You know, I'm very fond of you, Mitch. I don't want you to think of me only as your boss.' He reached out a hand and brushed his thick fingers against the stubble on Mitch's head. 'I want to get close to you. I want us to be friends.'

Mitch grinned from ear to ear, then sat bolt upright. 'I like you too, Rab,' he replied brusquely. 'Phew! It's fucking hot in here. Must go shower.' And without another word he was up and out of the sauna.

Five

Kenny was noticeably green around the gills. He had already decided that he was not experiencing butterflies in his tummy but rather a herd of wild elephants in steel toe-capped pit boots doing the conga up and down, and round and round his stomach. Having visited the toilet ten times in the space of half an hour he was certain he would be going again any minute.

Fresh from the shower, Damon was feeling as high as a kite. He stood in the middle of the dressing room. The hand-towel wrapped around his waist barely covering his embarrassment, he looked around at the other three and made his declaration.

'I feel just like one of The Village People!'

Kenny raised his head from his hands and moaned. 'The who?'

'No, not The Who, The Village People.' Damon slipped into encyclopedic mode. 'Formed by Jacques Morali in 1977 as a vehicle for his song writing. First British chart entry, "San Francisco (You've got me)", got to Number 44. Biggest hit "YMCA", Number 1, 25th November 1978.'

'What's he on about now?' Kenny asked the others in exasperation. 'I wasn't even born then. How am I supposed to know?'

'Just let me finish.' Damon paused until he had the group's

undivided attention. 'Thank you. As I was saying, I feel just like one of The Village –'

'We heard you the first time,' said Mitch, as he buttoned up his shirt. 'So, you feel like a has-been?'

Damon ignored him with a purse of the lips and turned to Cary. 'You must have seen that tragic film they made? Directed by Nancy Walker, released in 1980? It always gets shown during those worst films of all time series.'

'*Can't Stop The Music?*' Mitch interjected.

'That's the one. And you know that bit where they're all freaked out backstage before the final gig?'

Mitch adopted an American twang. ' "Leather men don't get nervous".'

'That's right!' Damon giggled. 'Well, that's just like us.'

'But didn't it bomb?' asked Cary as he pulled on a sock.

Damon was taken aback. 'What?'

'It *bombed*,' said Mitch. 'The film bombed at the box office. It was a total commercial and artistic flop.'

'*Can't Stop The Music?*' Cary groaned. 'Well, that film sure managed to put a stop to their music. The band never recovered! They were a laughing stock.'

'Yes, well, I'm not thinking of the film, I'm thinking of the gig that ended the film. The crowd went wild,' Damon said with a pout of indignation.

'Yeah, but wasn't that crowd getting paid? That lot out there aren't,' Cary said ruefully.

'Thanks for the encouragement, Damon,' Kenny said as he headed for the little boys' room.

Just then, Rab's head popped around the door. 'All set?' he asked with a grin. 'Fifteen minutes and counting.'

Just a short walk down the hall, on the far side of a locked security door, the club was pulsating. A sea of heaving bodies raising hell, exclusive DJ dance-mixes fanning the flames. The name of the venue was Throb – London's most happening gay nightclub – and it was here that Bigfun were about to make their public debut.

Rab had had a few qualms about launching the band at a gay event. It was potentially risky but Rab had his reasons, establishing a loyal fan base being one of them; courting healthy controversy being another. But despite these, he had thought the band might have some reservations. He was pleasantly surprised when no one turned a hair. Damon simply pointed out that it was gay men who, more often than not, set the trends that everyone else follows. It was, therefore, a canny move. No argument.

Fortunately, securing the venue had proved to be no problem. The club was owned by an old friend of Rab's, Stutz Wagner, who had used his considerable clout to ensure the success of the event. Together, he and Rab had concocted an impressive VIP guest list. Now it seemed that everyone invited had made the effort to be there. The balcony had been given over exclusively to cater for the cream of the media movers and shakers. Even now, Stutz was being his most charming self, keeping everyone entertained. Always the host with the most – the most expensive champagne and caviar and the most handsome young waiters to serve the crowd. Thus, Rab was left free to care for his own boys.

From this vantage point the gods could look down on the assembled masses. Muscle boys and drag queens, leather men and disco-bunnies, adding colour to an already vibrant decor. Something for everyone. Caged dancers wriggled and humped beneath the strobe lights; a variety of themed bars offered a well-stocked selection served up by hunky barmen in macho drag; and thrusting out into the crowd, a semi-circular stage shrouded by silver lamé drapes.

To cap it all, there was an unmistakable buzz in the air. Sheer energy. A sense of expectation that was almost palpable.

Kenny led the others out of the dressing room, down the corridor, towards the security door. Suddenly, he stopped short. Turning up his nose as if recoiling in shock.

'Oh, shit! What is that fucking horrible smell?'

'Someone must have dropped a bottle of amyl nitrate,' Mitch

replied without missing a beat. 'Some people get off on sniffing it. Gives them a real buzz.'

'People smell that for fun?' Kenny was incredulous. 'It smells like crusty old socks!'

Mitch threw the lock on the security door. 'I don't mean to alarm you, Ken, but there are guys who also get off on sniffing those too. The crustier the better.' And without waiting for a reply from a speechless Kenny, Mitch led the band out on to the stage.

Four lads huddled up in a scrum; a group hug, back slapping, exchanging words of support, just as Rab had encouraged them to do. Meanwhile, Rab looked on from the wings. He had given each one a hug back in the dressing room, now he knew he had to let go. This was their moment. Stand or fall, there was nothing he could do about it. It was out of his hands and into theirs.

He felt tears spring into his eyes. Tears of joy? Of sadness? He couldn't be sure. He only knew they had all worked so hard for this moment. What if it didn't come together? This was a possibility which did not bear thinking about.

Finally, the boys broke free and turned to take up positions. The moment of truth had arrived.

From the tape deck came the rousing strains of 'Land of Hope and Glory' silencing the audience to an expectant hush. As the backing tape kicked in the curtains opened to reveal all four boys in a line with their backs to the audience. Cold blue light cast a luminous glow over the frozen tableau. Each lad dressed in a suit of midnight-blue, crushed velvet. Each lad waiting for the cue to face front.

At length, the tune faded. Then came the smoky voice of the club DJ. 'You wanted the best and you've got it! The hottest boyband in the land – Bigfun!'

Almost imperceptibly, four feet began to tap in rhythm with the beat of the intro. Building inexorably. An explosion of brilliant white light greeted them as they spun around in unison. Four voices in effortless harmony sang out the opening line: 'I wanna sex you up!' The crowd roared its approval.

Rab looked on from the wings with Murat at his side, a surge of excitement pulsing through his veins. His pleasure in the boys' performance might have been vicarious but even so it was no less real. As he watched Cary strut around the stage, the other three complimenting his performance with their own, Rab found himself full of wonder. Just what was it that happened when the lights came on? Something magical. It was as if a light inside the lads switched on, switched into overdrive, every time they stood in the spotlight.

It wasn't only Rab who was impressed, the audience were intoxicated. Sure, they had had their share of alcohol and party substances but the sole focus of attention was now on the four figures singing and dancing up a storm. The first song reached its climax and was met with thundering applause.

As Cary came forward to introduce the band members, the audience surged forward. A row of bouncers stood their ground easing the crowd back. A small group down the front were singing 'Get them off' to the tune of the football chant 'Here we go'.

Mitch spoke directly to them: 'I hope you're talking about our knickers and not the band!'

It got a big, big laugh.

The set was relatively short with only six songs, six cover versions, including their shortly to be released first single, 'Victim Of Pleasure'. 'Pleasure' was the only cover version of the six that had not been a hit the first time around. Jayne had been adamant that the band should record it; to her mind it was a hit song simply waiting for a hit performance. As such, it was the perfect vehicle to launch the group.

At this event, it was as equally and enthusiastically received as the other more well-known numbers. With a combination of sex appeal, a raunchy dance routine and one hundred per cent commitment, the band didn't simply perform the song – they *sold* it.

After the show, the invited guests congregated together in the Green Room. Champagne flowed and the clink-clink of glasses was accompanied by a hubbub of animated chatter.

Stutz wandered over to Rab's side and whispered conspiratorially, 'Clive Foxx would like a word with you. He's *very* keen on the band.'

'So? Why can't he come over and tell me that himself?'

'Get off your high horse and go talk to him, Rab. He's talking America and the world!'

Rab felt obliged to follow up the suggestion but somehow felt resentful. He didn't like power games and this felt like exactly that.

Not to put too fine a point on it, Clive Foxx was an ugly, arrogant old lush. He was also a big wheel in the entertainment industry – had been for years – though it was clear that his success could hardly be attributed to personal charm. Foxx's creative hairdo consisted of a ponytail incorporating not more than the bare minimum number of wispy strands gelled back and braided. His hand, festooned with gaudy gold rings, clutched a glass of red wine. The wine sloshed around in the glass as his short, fat frame tottered unsteadily on Cuban heels.

As Rab introduced himself, Foxx threw an arm around his shoulder, a flamboyant gesture of friendship that struck Rab as less than sincere, particularly when said hand then slid down to cup his left buttock.

'Love the band!' Foxx declared. 'They were fabulous. Absolutely fabulous. And such *handsome* young men. Very, very handsome. We must work together.'

'I'm glad you enjoyed the show. They've worked extremely hard for this event. I have to say, I was very proud –'

Foxx interrupted him in mid-sentence. 'Listen. I'm serious, Rab. We *must* work together. These boys of yours could be bigger than big. But there is just one thing I have to know.'

Rab was mildly annoyed at having the conversation so rudely commandeered but he masked it well. 'Yes.'

Foxx leant towards Rab's ear and whispered conspiratorially, 'Which of the boys are gay? Do tell!'

Rab felt himself stiffen. No, he thought to himself, you do not need to know that. But all he said was, 'To be honest, Clive, we've never discussed the matter but to the best of my knowledge, none of them is.'

'What a waste,' Foxx replied, with a leering smile, 'because I'd be quite happy for all four of them to tie me down and rape me.'

Rab couldn't believe what he was hearing. And what was worse, much worse, was that Foxx talked as if Rab himself would fully understand, if not actively approve.

'And as for that one' – Foxx nodded over in the direction of Mitch, his mouth almost salivating – 'what my friends wouldn't give to shoot their load over a body like that!'

Rab's eyes scanned the room looking for the quickest escape route. Clive carried on regardless.

'Do mention my interest to the boys. I could do a lot for them. Of course we would have to change their image a little, find them some new songs –'

Rab interrupted the flow, just a little too briskly. 'Sorry, Clive, but I must just, erm, attend to some other business. I'll get back to you later. Promise. And I will discuss your proposal with the boys. You can be sure about that. Absolutely sure.' And with an insincere smile Rab made his escape.

If Foxx wants to wait let him wait – until hell freezes over, Rab muttered through gritted teeth as he stomped off in search of Stutz and a few well-chosen words.

Damon was holding court amidst a circle of admirers. Kenny stood alongside him, a little reticent, smiling benignly. A perfect foil to Damon's larger than life personality, Kenny fitted effortlessly into the role of glamorous assistant.

'I just love performing,' Damon enthused to a group of young recording executives. 'I don't know quite what comes over me but one whiff of the crowd and I switch into performance mode.'

'Me too,' muttered Kenny.

Damon threw Kenny a smile then returned to his audience. 'Of course, I have trodden the boards on many occasions. I was the star performer at the Madge Mogg School of Tap and Song, you know? Well, you may not have heard of her but I can assure you that she's a legend in the East End.'

'One year, I was in the chorus of the panto in Barnsley,' Kenny added. 'I was a Munchkin.'

'And I'm sure you looked very nice in tights, Kenny,' teased Damon.

'I've got good legs, me.' Kenny smiled.

'And don't let anyone tell you otherwise.'

Mitch was working the crowd and delighting in his celebrity. Murat had pointed out who was who and it was Murat alone who noticed how skilled Mitch was at using the information to his best advantage.

As for Murat himself, he was keeping a low profile. He sat strategically by the door. It gave him a broader field of vision and he had taken it upon himself to oversee the proceedings. Had any of the guys got into any sort of trouble he would have stepped in and sorted things out as tactfully and diplomatically as he could. But if muscle was necessary he was prepared to use that too. Taking care of the boys was a labour of love not a chore; a responsibility he took seriously.

Cary was over the moon; way over the moon, as if he had landed on a different planet. He drifted through the party, accepting compliments graciously, but not really connecting with anybody. This was an alien world and it would take time for him to adjust. The atmosphere was just a little too thin to be comfortable.

After putting in a polite appearance he took himself off for a solitary wander backstage, exploring the building along miles of corridors and past countless doors. At last, he found himself down in the basement. The only sound was the hum of a generator. The only light was minimal emergency lighting. Before him was a door, a door to the cellar. He shouldered it open then felt around for the light switch.

A single, naked bulb hung from a cord in the middle of the room. As it burst into life, Cary had to shield his eyes until he grew accustomed to the change. The room was stocked from floor to ceiling with crates of wine, beer barrels, boxes of spirits, cartons of cigarettes. A piss-artist's paradise. Suddenly, from over his shoulder came a gruff exclamation.

'What the fuck are you doing in here?'

Cary turned. It was one of the burly bouncers who had fringed the stage just a short time before. His twin stood behind him. Their menacing glares melted as they recognised the face of the intruder.

'I'm sorry. I . . .' Cary shrugged. He didn't know what else to say.

'No one is allowed down here without permission,' the twin said by way of explanation. 'Security. You understand?'

'Sure,' Cary replied. 'Then I'll just be going.' He made to brush past and out of the door when the first bouncer put the palm of his hand firmly against Cary's chest.

The second bouncer blocked the exit. 'Not so fast, if you don't mind. We're going to have to search you.'

Cary studied his assailants. They looked like two chips from the same block. Both had auburn hair cropped to no more than a hint of stubble; both had three-day beards. They were dressed in the standard uniform: tuxedo, bow-tie and dress-shirt ensemble, their shirt collars straining to contain thick necks. Square jaws and cleft chins jutted out menacingly above bodies built like power-lifters. They could indeed have been twins.

'But –' Cary stammered '– I only walked through the door a minute before you guys.'

'We only have your word for that now. Don't we?' said the first.

'I hope you're not going to make this difficult,' said the second.

Like a well-rehearsed double act, the first picked up where the other left off. 'I wouldn't make Eddie angry if I were you. You wouldn't like him when he gets angry.'

Then came the order, punctuated with a sneer. 'Up against that wall and spread your legs, there's a good bloke.'

★

Over in a far corner of the bar, Rab was brooding. He could not help himself. He felt like Daniel cast into the lion's den. His back was literally up against a wall. He had dealt with all kinds of businessmen, been involved in all kinds of business, but never before had the terms of the negotiation involved the exchange of body fluids. Stutz had had little truck with Rab's complaints. 'What did you expect?' he had said. 'Since when was talent enough?' And, as if he needed to, he had pointed out that Foxx could be a mighty ally or a powerful adversary. 'Be very careful,' Stutz had warned him.

Being careful was the last thing Rab wanted to be. He wanted to smack Clive Foxx right in his smug little kisser. Rab's temper flared easily but in this case he wasn't just angry, he was furious. Why? He was old enough to know the potential hazards of the game. Foxx wasn't the first letch he had met and he surely would not be the last. No. It was the subtle inference that Rab was no better than he; that he would collude with the exploitation of the lads for his own ends.

All around him, the room was buzzing but Rab was lost in his own little world. Lost, that is, until Mitch snapped his fingers in front of Rab's face.

'C'mon. Wake up, sleeping beauty!'

Slowly, the scene came back into focus for Rab. 'Having a good time?'

'Mega! I've just been chatted up by Clive Foxx. He says he wants to work with us. Market us in America and all. Have you talked with him yet?'

'Yes. What do you think of him?'

'Him? Bit of an old tosser but seemed harmless enough. Why?'

Rab gave a contrite smile. 'He's far from harmless, Mitch.'

'Yeah, but it's the business, isn't it. You've got to be tough.'

'Oh, he's tough all right. Tough as old boots.'

Mitch frowned. 'You don't seem very enthusiastic.'

'Don't think I can afford his kind of commission.'

'Eh?'

'He wants your arse, Mitch.'

'What?'

Mitch's thoughts spun off into the outer stratosphere. America was a big deal. Was this for real? All he would have to do is what he had been doing these past few years – putting out. But then he looked at Rab's face and knew that that simply wasn't an option any more. Rab would lose all respect for him and this mattered. Rab's respect mattered.

Mitch cleared his throat. 'Well, he can go fuck himself, the dirty old bastard! If we make it in America, we'll do it by ourselves. We don't need the likes of him.'

Suddenly, Rab smiled. Clasping Mitch's face in his powerful hands he drew him forward and planted a big, wet kiss on his lips.

'I hoped you'd say that, Mitch, my boy.' Rab smiled into Mitch's face.

'Gerroff me!' Mitch laughed, wiping his mouth in mock disgust.

'I'm really proud of you, you know that?'

Mitch winked at him. 'Don't know about you but I've had enough for one night. Why don't we get out of here? Any chance of a lift to the hotel?'

'Sure, just follow me.'

'OK, boss. You lead, I'll follow.'

The two beefy bouncers had Cary over a barrel. Stark-bollock-naked and literally bent over a barrel. One parted Cary's buttocks as the other inserted a thick, lubricated finger deep within Cary's puckered arsehole. Down in the cellar, it was certain, no one else would hear his groans.

'Nothing up here, Phil. Guess he's clean,' Eddie told his cohort.

'Yeah, but what do we have down here?' The first bouncer reached down to grasp Cary's erection. 'How could he have hoped to slip that big thing past the two of us?'

Cary whimpered as the second bouncer removed one finger and replaced it with two more.

'I reckon he fancies us, Eddie. What do you think?'

The first bouncer unclipped his dicky-bow and began to pop the buttons down the front of his crisp white dress-shirt.

'I think you might be right, Phil.'

Cary had been playing along so far. Now it was time for the award-winning part of his performance. 'Listen, guys, I'll give you anything you want. *Anything –*' Cary's monologue was cut short at that precise moment as the three fingers stuffed up his arse were twisted around forcing him to emit a growl of pleasure.

The two meat-heads did a double take at each other and cracked up laughing.

In the back of Rab's limousine there was more than enough room to stretch out and unwind. He kicked off his shoes and relaxed back into the plush leather upholstery, plucked a bottle of champagne from the ice bucket and popped the cork. Rab poured as Mitch held two tall glasses out towards him. The mini-disc was playing *Tosca*, Rab's favourite version of his favourite opera. Callas, DiStefano and Gobbi, dating back to 1953. Mitch wasn't much of an opera fan but on this occasion an exception was easily made. He thought it brought a touch of class to the proceedings.

Tonight could well be the night, thought Mitch, as he settled down beside his boss.

'Cheers.' They clinked glasses and drank.

'So it's back to the hotel, is it?' asked Rab.

'Couldn't we just drive around a while?' Mitch replied. 'My head's still buzzing.'

'Sure. Sounds like a good idea. I could do with some space to clear my head.'

Rab picked up the intercom handset and instructed Murat to do just that.

'And the partition? I feel like I'm in a goldfish bowl. Murat can see everything. Can't we have a bit of privacy?'

With the press of a button a second partition rose into place, a solid partition.

'Better?' Rab asked.

'Much.'

Rab took another sip from his glass. 'How are you feeling now, after all the excitement?'

'Horny.'

'Horny?'

'Yeah, I feel like getting my dick out and letting you suck it till it pops.'

Rab was momentarily taken aback. Mitch's comment came out of left field. But Rab followed it up with raucous laughter.

Mitch frowned. 'What're you laughing it? Don't laugh at me.'

Rab quickly recovered his composure and grinned. 'I wasn't laughing at you, Mitch. It's just' – he patted Mitch's knee – 'you sound pretty cocksure of yourself. What gives you the idea that I'd take you up on the offer?'

'I know you want me, Rab.' Mitch remained subdued. 'I've seen the way you look at me.'

'Oh, yeah? And exactly what way would that be?'

'Like you're gagging for it.'

'Really?'

'Yeah, *really*. And that's OK 'cause I want you too. Tonight. If you want, you can have me tonight.'

Rab struggled to stifle his amusement but there was no need. Mitch smothered his mouth with a kiss as he fought with the buttons on the fly of his own black 501s and yanked his mammoth organ free.

Rab looked down, his breath was now coming in short, sharp bursts.

'Do you like what you see?'

Rab nodded.

'So what are you waiting for?'

Rab pounced on the proud, stiff, juicy cock that teased and taunted his appetite. The degree of his enthusiasm surprised even Mitch. Rab's fist grasped the base of the thick shaft and squeezed tight while his mouth worked with pneumatic force, up and down the length, pummelling Mitch's organ, making mincemeat out of prime sirloin. Mitch clutched the back of Rab's head and tried to temper the rhythm but it was useless. Rab was like a man possessed.

Just as suddenly as he had begun, Rab yanked his mouth free to speak. 'I want more than this.' He pulled Mitch's T-shirt free of his waistband and began to cover his stomach with kisses. 'I want to smell you and taste you and drink you. I want to eat you all up.'

Mitch was giggling and squirming. Rab's kisses tickled.

'Forget the hotel. Come home with me. Spend the night with me.' Rab was pleading. There was an unmistakable edge of desperation in his voice.

A shiver of concern rippled through Mitch's body. A shiver that was almost stifled by the overpowering demands of his loins, but not quite. Mitch paused for thought, considering his options. Just what was he getting himself into? Too late, Rab fell once again on his stiff, aching cock. Mitch looked down, watching Rab feast with renewed appetite. Bound by desire, Mitch found he had no option at all.

'Like I said, you're the boss.' Mitch lifted the handset off the hook and held it to Rab's ear. 'Better give Murat some new instructions.'

Down in the cellar of the club three naked bodies were about to do battle. Naked except for shoes and socks that is. Both big, beefy bouncers kept their white socks and shiny, black shoes on. The rest of their clothes were neatly folded over the back of a chair.

Cary wasn't looking at their shoes, he was otherwise distracted. He trembled as the Brothers Grimm waved their massive erections in his face. Phil spat on his palm and caressed his length, causing it to glisten as he stroked the surface with a slow, practised hand. His cock was a prize-winner. Long and stout with a couple of large, pulsing veins clearly defined. Eddie's was the image of Phil's. He, in turn, tugged on his heavy, wrinkled spout of foreskin, stretching it towards Cary's salivating mouth.

Eddie smiled a big smile. 'Suck on me. Wash my foreskin with your tongue.'

'Then will you let me go?' Cary said with a false nervousness.

He could tell that they were perfectly aware that he wanted to stay.

Phil looked at Eddie. 'We might. Then again —'

His brother-chip finished the sentence: '— we might not.'

Cary strained his neck towards those powerful thighs, mesmerised by Eddie's poker-stiff penis as it twitched upright before his very eyes. He looked at it reverently as Eddie lowered it towards his outstretched tongue.

But before he could reach it, Phil plunged his cock down Cary's gullet, fucking his face. Showing no mercy. Grunting, determined, with one purpose. He fed Cary his length and Cary feasted in turn. Flesh, burning flesh, bucking and wrestling and fucking his throat. Gliding rapturously into Cary's moist, cavernous need. Cary was loving the fullness of Phil's cosh as it pumped fit to burst. Unable to speak, to think. Only able to milk the object of his heartfelt desire, his nose bashing up against bushy, auburn pubes.

'Oh, oh, yeah, blondie! Open your throat, you little fucker. Get ready for Round Two.'

No sooner had he pulled out than Eddie replaced him.

'That's it, pal. Suck on that. Take the full measure of it. Open wide. Wider . . .'

Without further warning, Phil started to worm his way back in alongside Eddie. Easing the blunt end of his fat, juicy organ between Cary's lips, he inched his way ever deeper, stretching Cary's mouth to capacity. Twin cocks battering the one hole whilst Cary struggled to accommodate and contain them both.

At long last, Eddie pulled out. 'You're a talented boy, you are. That mouth of yours is wasted on singing.' He spat on his palm. 'Now let's see if you're as skilled at the other end.'

Phil continued to fuck face while Eddie mounted Cary from behind. His thick, latex-covered link eased into Cary's aching hole like a penny into the slot.

'Perfect fit, Phil,' Eddie groaned to his accomplice. 'Look. Just perfect. This guy's a professional.'

'Shut up, Eddie. Just fuck him, will you? I can't hold off much longer.'

The fuck sandwich began in earnest with Eddie providing one thick slice and Phil the other. Cary was lost somewhere in between, furiously jerking on his own erection. Eddie displayed all the bedside manner of a dog in heat, Phil more akin to a rabbit, but what they lacked in artistry they more than made up for in enthusiasm.

Phil was the first to lose it. 'I'm going to shoot, Eddie. It's going to come.'

'Let me see, brother. Pull out, let me see.'

And in the instant shot an abundance of spunk over Cary's head that then skidded along his back and finally splashed on to Eddie's undulating belly.

'Yes . . .' Eddie growled. 'Yes! That did it, that did it.' And he was out of Cary, removing the condom and violently jerking the last few strokes towards a blinding orgasm. The first bolt of jism flew from Eddie's penis and landed on the tip of Phil's.

'Yes! What a shot!' Eddie was well pleased.

Cary had watched the dollop of cream land, and now watched it slide off of Phil's shiny helmet and drip on to the cement floor as he himself squirted his load and followed suit. Had he had a bucket under him, it would have sounded like milking time down on the farm.

When all grew still, Phil sighed. 'That was brilliant.'

Eddie could do nothing but agree. 'You're right there, bro.' He slapped Cary's arse. 'How about you? How do you feel, pal?'

'Fucked,' said Cary, 'Well and truly fucked.'

Six

Mitch followed closely behind as they both entered Rab's apartment. The front door opened on to the upstairs landing with the hallway leading to bedroom and bathroom. A winding, open-plan staircase led down to the lounge with private balcony, a dining room and kitchen. Mitch wandered around, taking in the opulence of chrome and leather and glass, admiring the stylish framed prints that adorned the walls; a typical bachelor pad. It was impressive, very.

Mitch cocked an eyebrow. 'Only one bedroom? Where does Murat sleep?'

'He has his own studio flat in the basement. It's small but comfortable. He needs his own space, I need mine.'

'He's a very handsome man.'

'I can't argue with that.'

'So . . . Do you . . .?'

'Do we what?' Rab gave a knowing smile. 'Have more than a professional relationship? Do you care?'

'Only if he's the jealous type. I wouldn't want to get on the wrong side of those muscles.'

'Then you have nothing to worry about.'

Rab excused himself, just long enough for Mitch to make his way up to the bedroom, strip and slip under the duvet on Rab's king-size bed. He heard footsteps outside and lay back expectantly. A bedside lamp cast a warm glow. Ready and waiting, Mitch rubbed his crutch as Rab's rugged frame filled the doorway.

'What do we have here?' Rab grinned. 'One sexy young fucker, methinks.' He came towards Mitch.

'Wait,' Mitch insisted, his head resting back on his arms.

'No, now!' Rab demanded lustily.

'Nah,' Mitch replied. 'I want you to turn me on.'

'From over here? And how could I best do that now?' Rab's eyes sparkled.

'Give me a striptease . . .'

'But we've no music?' Rab protested.

'Make your own. Sing to me,' Mitch replied.

What followed was a hilarious bump and grind rendition of 'It's Now or Never' with Rab demonstrating all the grace of a bull in a china shop. He was drunk on champagne and lust and he threw himself into it with gusto, lowering his jacket over one shoulder, tugging at his braces, pulling off his shoes and flinging them at Mitch. He unbuttoned his shirt, pulled the tail from his waist band, played peek-a-boo with his nipples. Down to pants and socks. Socks off, he swirled them around his head, then jettisoned them into space.

Turning his back, he pulled his pants down over firm mounds of hairy flesh, teasing them up and down, up and down, and down, down, down to the ankles. Kicking them aside, he swung round, two hands barely containing his ample proportions. Then he threw those hands wide, to stand proud and erect.

He really was a striking figure of a man, built and solid and hairy. His succulent penis was so large and fat and juicy that it fair made Mitch's mouth water just to look at it. It strained towards him, no foreskin to obscure the moist purple glans, and stared straight at Mitch with its one eye, and a tear that overflowed and dripped down on to the carpet.

'Now, did that do the trick by any chance?' Rab asked, arrogantly.

'Well, it's clear why you were never going to be a pop star at least.'

Mitch threw back the duvet and all was revealed. His own erection sprang from its enclosure. 'What do you think?'

'Better than a round of applause.' Rab chuckled. 'And now for the encore.'

Rab climbed on the bed and knelt beside Mitch. For the first few moments he simply marvelled at the exquisite beauty of Mitch's rod. He lowered his head, bringing his face up close, so that he could examine it minutely. Mitch had shorn his thick pubic hair short and neat, the edges sculpted with the same care as he took over his goatee; big balls hung low in their slack, shaven sack and his painfully erect organ stood proud between thumb and forefinger, a pearl of precome perched on the tip of his swollen cockhead.

Delivering his manhood into Rab's hands, Mitch looked on as Rab lovingly rolled the pink latex ring over the crown, making sure to squeeze any air out of the teat. It was a tight fit, Mitch's tubular cock stretching the rubber to the max. Then Rab turned around to face the bedhead on all fours as Mitch stuffed two lubricated fingers deep inside his aching hole, stretching him wider, preparing him as best he could for what was to come.

When his cock finally bulldozed its way inside Rab it proved as tight a fit as the condom, stretching his sphincter to its limits. Still, Rab was determined to accommodate Mitch; he forced himself to relax, loving the feeling of fullness. Mitch revelled in the delicious sensation of being welcomed inside his enthusiastic lover; of feeling his cock so lovingly embraced by another. He looked down and watched his powerful length slide in and halfway out of Rab's pulsing orifice, a sight that struck him as totally horny.

No words were necessary, only action. Mitch drove deep but slowly, loosening Rab up gradually, building up a head of steam. Rab began to push back as Mitch lunged forward, cramming in as much as he could, encouraging Mitch to drive ever deeper. Soon Mitch was flogging Rab's arse more ferociously than he would normally have thought possible. Rab didn't just take everything Mitch could give, he was actively begging for more; slamming back to meet Mitch's thrusts, urging him to spill his seed without delay.

When Mitch came he held still; all his energy was directed into the condom, blasting his spunk into the teat and with each subsequent spurt he began growling, with authority, that he was the boss in bed and that Rab should never forget it.

Rab had fallen asleep in his arms, head on Mitch's chest, suckling his nipple. It was two o'clock in the afternoon by the time Mitch awoke in an empty bed, yawning and stretching. Rab clambered back in beside him, bare arsed, two mugs of tea and a big plate of toast to hand.

'Mind my feet, they're cold,' Rab warned him. 'A side effect of stripped floorboards, I'm afraid.'

'Give them here,' Mitch bid him, rubbing his own feet against them. 'Fuck! You weren't joking!' he exclaimed, but with that familiar twinkle in his eye.

Munching on his third piece of toast, Rab chuckled. 'The condemned man ate a hearty breakfast! Fuck me, Mitch, this is too sweet. Why can't life always be like this . . . this good.'

'Some of us have to earn a living, that's why. Don't they say, "Time waits for no man".'

'If things work out to plan, give it three years and you could join the ranks of the idle rich.'

'You're filthy rich and you're not idle!'

'You've got a point there.'

Mitch brushed some crumbs from the edge of his moustache. 'Guess I'll have to be going soon.'

'Must you?'

'Well, eventually.' Mitch grinned. 'You're a fantastic fuck, Rab, even if you can't sing and dance. It just has to be said.'

'Thank you kindly, Mitch. You can stay as long as you like.'

They continued eating in silence. By the fourth piece of toast Rab was feeling a little more analytical.

'Mitch?'

'Yeah?'

'Would you sleep with Clive Foxx?'
'Is that a question or a request?'
'A question.'
Mitch took a slurp of tea. 'No.'
'Why not?'
'Apart from the obvious? He's repulsive! Why would I?'
'He could be a big help to your career . . .'
'Yeah?'
'You slept with me . . .'
'Some comparison! You think too much, Rab. It gives a bloke headaches when they think too much.'
'But where's the difference?'
'I like you, that's a good place to start. I wanted you, that's another. Then again, on a level of pure self-interest, if I had said no to you, you would have accepted it; there would have been no consequences. But with him? He is one nasty piece of work. Plus I don't come that cheap.'
'There's a lot of bastards out there who would hurt you, Mitch. A lot of bastards, and I'm not one of them.'
'Don't you think I know that?'

Three weeks after the band's public debut the first CD single was officially released. DJ-only mixes had been distributed some two weeks earlier and feedback had been excellent. 'Victim of Pleasure' was a Hi-NRG stomper in time-honoured tradition but with club remixes by the likes of Sister Handbag and T-EYE-T all bases were covered. Bigfun looked set to have themselves a serious floor filler. All they needed now was a crossover chart success.

To coincide with the release of the single, Rab had put together an arduous promotional tour that was to cover the length and breadth of Britain. The band had no qualms, they were 100 per cent committed. Wasn't this what they had been working towards all along?

The tour bus sailed up the motorway. Two weeks into the tour and Damon still delighted in the comforts on offer within their little 'hotel on wheels'. He was standing in the kitchen area serving himself from the espresso machine as he sneaked a look down the central aisle. The other lads were watching a movie on video. Remi was up front talking to the small crew of technicians. Murat stood beside Damon, preparing lunch.

'This is the way to travel, isn't it, handsome?' Damon looked up into Murat's beautiful, brooding face and he batted his eyelashes provocatively.

'Damon. Please stop teasing me. I get embarrassed.'

Damon's expression rearranged itself into a petulant pout. 'But I'm bored, Murat. What else is there to do?'

'Drink your coffee. We'll be there soon.'

'Yeah. Another day, another shopping centre.' Damon affected boredom with practised ease.

'Is it really so bad?'

'Nah!' Damon grinned. 'Not at all. It's a lot of fun really.'

Indeed it was. A non-stop tour of shopping centres, local radio stations and nightclub PAs country wide. It was Rab's idea to reach the parts other bands didn't or couldn't be bothered to reach. And after two weeks it was starting to garner significant reaction. Publicity had been good, as had word of mouth. Now their first single was poised to make its appearance in the lower reaches of the charts. Things were building slowly but surely; all in line with Rab's master plan.

As the credits on the video rolled, Kenny nudged Cary. They both removed their earphones.

'That was a great movie, wasn't it? I love a good action film.'

'Yeah. But then again, anything with Alec Brewster in it is worth watching. That guy is so watchable.'

'Don't know why he finds it necessary to get his kit off all the time, though. It's embarrassing. It's like, any old excuse and he drops his pants. Can't imagine why.'

Cary raised his eyebrows. 'Can't you? I'd have thought it was obvious. It's called 'box office'. Even if the film is a dud his arse isn't.'

'That's pathetic. Don't tell me you'd watch a film just 'cause Alec Brewster's arse was in it?'

Mitch's head suddenly appeared over the back of their seat. 'I would even if he wouldn't.'

Cary smiled despite himself.

'C'mon, Mitch. It's just an arse. What's so special about his?' Kenny protested.

'If you don't know, Ken, I can't explain it to you. Let's just say it's a question of taste. And it would seem that the film-going public in general would want to taste his arse more than most.'

'But –'

The debate was interrupted by Damon as he appeared alongside them, pointing out of the window. 'Time to get your glad rags on, girls, we've reached destination number one hundred and thirty-nine on our action-packed itinerary.'

Diamond Meadows was the shopping centre to end all shopping centres. Touted as the largest in Europe, its crystal dome could be seen in every direction for miles around. It rose up out of an industrial wasteland. A less than glamorous location but ideally situated at the heart of the motorway network. Miles and miles of easy parking and a vast array of merchandise attracted customers from far and wide. Today was no exception. The place was packed.

Every Saturday, Kuddle Radio's 'Diamonds and Purls' show was transmitted throughout Northern England right from this very spot. Hosted by Peter Purls, a Radio One has-been, it was aimed at the 18–30 market. A hodgepodge of chart music, sport, third-hand celebrity gossip, reviews and guest performances was slung together at a fast and furious pace. The likes of Bigfun were its bread and butter – chewed up and swallowed with a mighty gulp, then on to the next mouthful.

Damon stood backstage watching the local celebrity DJ go through his routine. He was not impressed.

'The only good thing that can be said about the show so far is that it isn't televised.'

'Oh no,' Kenny groaned. 'He's off on one again.'

Damon carried on regardless. 'We are indeed fortunate that Peter "Mega" Purls and his amazing, creative hairdo cannot be seen over the airwaves since he would have any sane person reaching for the off switch in a trice.'

'Shut your gob. I like him. He's dead popular around here,' said Kenny.

'Yes,' replied Damon smartly, looking Kenny up and down. 'His influence on you is noticeable. Two peas from the same pod.'

'Will someone shut him up before I lamp him one,' Kenny retorted.

'Button it, will you, Damon?' Mitch intervened. 'You know how uptight Ken gets before a gig.'

'Oh, pardon me for breathing!' Damon replied indignantly.

Cary and Mitch cracked up laughing.

Damon was peeved. 'And just what's so funny?' he said, arching his eyebrow. No one replied. No one needed to. All four were laughing now.

The stage, such as it was, was a raised rectangle in the centre of a busy café space. The patrons of numerous eateries spilled out on to a communal area strewn with tables and chairs. Potted palms and an array of green foliage aimed to give the space a pseudo-tropical air. It was the first time the boys had played to an audience who seemed more interested in their burgers than the band. Until the music began to play, that is.

As the opening strains of 'Victim of Pleasure' boomed through the speakers the startled audience were suddenly all ears and eyes. The dance routine was as raunchy as the lyric, which had Cary singing about being a 'slave' to love in no uncertain terms. Mitch was grinding and flexing his body in a totally outrageous way and loving every minute of it. Damon picked out a group of teenage girls and aimed all his considerable energies towards them. Kenny kept an eye on family and friends who had travelled down en masse to see him perform. They were on their feet whooping and clapping, generating a completely positive vibe.

A few old grannies toddled away in disgust but these were quickly replaced by a horde of enthusiastic newcomers.

The boys were only meant to perform the one song but when Peter Purls tried to move the show along he was drowned out by the clamour of the audience demanding more. Purls had no option but to capitulate and give them what they wanted. 'I Wanna Sex You Up' brought pandemonium to the proceedings. After which, the boys had to be escorted off-stage by the security team. Peter Purls looked visibly shaken and for once in his life he was truly lost for words.

As the tour bus pulled out of the car park, the mood of the group was triumphant.

'Did you see that blonde babe down at the front? Couldn't keep her eyes off of me,' Damon remarked with enthusiasm, much to everyone's surprise. 'She was awesome. Like a younger, better looking version of Pamela Anderson.'

Cary spoke up, quick as a flash. 'Is that the one I saw stumbling out of the opticians earlier on?'

'You should have slipped her your telephone number,' Mitch added. 'You never know, she might have made a man out of you.'

'Somebody ought to,' said Kenny.

'And how would a big Yorkshire bone-head like you know what makes a man a man?' Damon was outraged. 'I could certainly teach you a thing or two.'

'I'm sure you could. Unfortunately, I don't want to learn how to make my own frocks.'

Damon's response was short and to the point. 'Fuck you, arsehole!'

Much, much later, back at the hotel, Damon stretched out in the bath. Having fulfilled the commitments of the day he intended to pamper himself; to luxuriate beneath the perfumed bubbles. The warmth of the water soothed his aching muscles and washed the tension away. He may have been small but he was perfectly formed. Slim but not thin; shapely but without bulk. And his long, thick, circumcised penis looked all the more enormous by comparison. He ran a palm over his smooth, hairless chest, absentmindedly tugged on one tiny pink nipple and sighed.

The daily round of interviews with the local press had led into the nightly round of club PAs. Three had been visited tonight. Two straight, one gay. And at all three the band had been astonished to see the same small group feature prominently at the front of the crowd. A group of fans, no less! And amongst them the blonde babe.

When had he noticed that Murat was annoyed? Why hadn't he seen this coming? Why had he found it necessary to be such a little prick-tease? Murat had grabbed him and kissed him in a darkened doorway at the first opportunity. It was only as he had felt the slick wetness of Murat's tongue forcing its way down his throat that Damon had been obliged to pull away and plead heterosexuality; that it had all been a game. Murat was not pleased. Damon didn't blame him. He didn't blame him at all.

But it was the blonde babe who was now very much at the forefront of his mind. His pulsing erection pointed out of the water like a periscope, straining towards the ceiling. Seldom had his young dick been swollen so hard. Fist curled around cock.

He did not hear the outer door open and close. Nor the feet padding towards the bathroom. It was only as the bathroom door creaked that he opened his eyes and let go of his raging hard-on.

Murat stood in the doorway, grinning. A white T-shirt pulled tight across the bronzed muscles on his chest. He leant against the door frame, folded his arms across his chest and stared. Coarse black hair covered his sturdy forearms and poked out of the round neck of his top. With forefinger and thumb he stroked his dense moustache. Finally, he spoke.

'You have another admirer.'

'Really?'

'Yes. The beautiful blonde woman from today is sitting downstairs in the bar. I told her I tell you she is here. You want me to tell her you come?'

'Tell her I'll be there in ten minutes.'

'She sits alone in the corner with a big cocktail and two straws. I think she wants you bad.'

'Make that five minutes.'

'And me? I have nothing to do. Maybe I can stay and watch?'

'You want to watch?'

'I happy to watch. I happy to join in. Which you want?'

'Not this time, Murat. It might put me off my stroke.'

'Next time?'

'Maybe. Look, you better go down. She might get tired of waiting. Tell her I won't be long.' Damon reached for a towel as Murat turned to leave. 'Oh and Murat?'

'Yes?'

He turned quickly and Damon felt Murat's eyes sweep over his naked body as he stepped out of the bath and reached for a towel.

Damon blushed from head to toe. 'I'm sorry I can't give you what you want.'

'Give me what, Damon?'

'Y'know . . .' He looked away. '*Sex*.'

'You misunderstand, Damon. I want much more than sex.'

Damon looked at him quizzically.

'I want friendship.'

A big smile lit up Damon's face. 'You got it, Murat.' He stepped out of the bath and, taking a few steps forward, reached up and stroked Murat's cheek. 'You got that.'

Back in his Earl's Court apartment, Rab was tucked up in bed reading the latest series of financial reports which his accountants had prepared for him. Hardly his favourite bedtime reading but necessary nonetheless. He had explained to the lads that some things simply couldn't be done by fax and phone and so he was forced to stay in London for a few days on business. Hopefully, for only four or five days at most. Four if he maximised his time, hence his reading in bed. He could then rejoin the boys on tour a little further down the road.

For the duration of the tour so far, Rab had been maintaining a polite distance. The effort to keep his hands off Mitch was almost killing him but he had convinced himself it was the only professional thing to do – for the moment, at least. Then there would be those times when his eyes would be inexplicably drawn towards the object of his lust only to find Mitch staring back, a provocative smirk on his face, rubbing the sizeable bulge in the crotch of his jeans. The guy was incorrigible. Maybe it was just as well he had been called back to town. He could do with the breather.

But then again there was also the matter of Linda to attend to. She continued to insist on being difficult and Rab had been summoned to yet another meeting with the lawyer to discuss strategy. One that invariably involved more money.

His lids grew heavy and, somewhat reluctantly, because it would mean having to pick it up tomorrow, he put the final report aside, turned off the bedside light and snuggled down for the night.

It had been his habit since childhood to spend the time just before sleeping in quiet contemplation of the events of the day. Earlier he had rung Damon to see how the gig at Diamond Meadows had gone.

'Mega,' said Damon with his customary enthusiasm. 'We've got ourselves a bunch of fans, Rab. Real fans. They're following us around. I feel like a proper pop star.'

Their brief conversation had ended with Damon reassuring Rab; telling him not to worry, everything was hunky-dory, Murat was doing a great job at managing the tour.

'He's such a sweetheart, Rab. Wherever did you find him?' Damon had asked but it wasn't really a question, just a compliment in a question form.

It was just as well too. How would Rab have explained the nature of their meeting to Damon? It would not have been easy.

And as he relaxed, his body melting into the mattress, Rab's thoughts drifted away from the pressures of the day towards the memory of his initial meeting with Murat. The memory came as a welcome distraction. In his mind's eye, Rab could still visualise that late afternoon, the sun beating down on the dusty streets that he had wandered aimlessly, looking for all the world like just one more anonymous tourist. Feeling more like a runaway. Turkey offered him anonymity. Freedom from his responsibilities. Freedom from his wealth and reputation. And it was here, at the age of thirty-four, that he hoped he would resolve his inner turmoil for good and all.

It was down by the waterfront that he had first stumbled across Murat. Another new hotel was being built. Murat stood amid the heat and dust, stripped to the waist, carrying some kind of hod. Even at a distance he looked awesome – like a heroic statue – sculpted muscle with a lush coating of body hair.

As Rab drew closer he noted the thick, blue-black moustache, the close-cropped hair mussed with some white powder, rivulets of sweat, dirt and sand glittering on his broad back. Last, but certainly not least, he noticed the builder's cleavage peeping out of the back of his low-slung trousers.

Rab stared unabashed. Shielding his eyes from the glare of the sun, he stood transfixed. How long was it before Murat turned his face towards him and flashed that shit-eating grin? Seconds? Minutes? His teeth shone brilliant white in stark contrast to his natural tan.

First a brief wave, then the builder jumped down from the scaffolding and walked slowly towards him. Within himself, Rab felt a surge of fear so primal he thought he would pass out on the spot. Part terror, part desire. Would the guy kiss him or kill him? But he stood his ground as Murat offered him one big, calloused hand. And as their hands met, Rab felt no ordinary handshake. Murat's middle finger stroked Rab's palm; an age-old signal.

'You English?' Murat asked.

'Scottish.'

'Where you stay?'

'I'm renting a small apartment.'

'I finish work now. You want to go for a drink.'

The words spilt out of Rab's mouth before he had time to censor himself: 'There's beer back at my place.' Instantly, he thought he'd overstepped the mark. But to his surprise, the builder simply grinned once more.

'One moment, please. I get my things.' And without waiting for an affirmative response, he hurried back to his workplace.

By the time Rab ushered Murat through the door to his apartment they had had time to exchange names and enough small-talk for Rab to learn that his new companion had a fairly decent grasp of English.

'I like to practise on the tourists,' Murat told him, adding, 'Men *and* women.'

Rab did not doubt that for a minute.

He took a couple of bottles of beer from the fridge whilst Murat looked around. The apartment had seemed fairly basic to Rab: clean and comfortable; white walls, tiled floors, simple furniture and the usual mod cons. But his guest seemed overawed.

Murat's head appeared around the doorway to the bathroom, his face beaming. 'You have a shower! I love to shower. And –' he sniffed his armpits '– I sure need it. Can I?'

'Clean towels are on the side. Help yourself,' Rab replied, as Murat disappeared. He heard the shower gush into action through a crack in the open door then returned to the kitchen in search of the bottle opener.

Minutes passed. Rab re-entered the lounge with bottles in hand. He called out, 'I have your beer.'

'Please to bring it in here.'

The sight that met Rab's eyes as he pushed wide the door almost made him drop both bottles. A glorious back view. No shower curtain pulled across, just full naked exposure. Murat's head was bowed under the downpour, tight cropped curls soaking wet. His powerful frame was breathtaking: a thick neck leading to cords of muscle forming his shoulders; arms bulging all the way down to massive hands; the expanse of his back swept down to a tiny waist, then broadened out over buttocks, firm and weighty; chunky thighs and shapely calves led down to the biggest surprise – small feet. They were tiny in comparison, though perfectly formed. No larger than a seven, they had looked much bigger in boots.

Rab carefully placed both bottles on the glass shelf over the sink. 'Would you like me to scrub your back?'

'Please,' Murat croaked, his throat tight.
'I'll get my clothes wet. Maybe I'd better undress?'
'Yes.'
T-shirt and shorts were quickly discarded. 'You want me to wash your chest also?'
'Yes.'
Rab stepped on to the shower mat, feeling a fine spray fall on his naked skin. 'And your dick? We shouldn't forget your dick.'
The reply came from deep within Murat's throat. 'Do what you want. Do with me what you want.'
Rab's stiffness poked into Murat's fleshy buttock the second he stepped close in behind him but he didn't move, only sighed. With soaped-up hands Rab spread both palms over Murat's back: gentle hands, lathering creamy suds over smooth, hard muscle, working free the dirt of the day and watching it swirl away.
Murat turned his head to watch them both in the bathroom mirror: him pliable, passive, not resisting nor encouraging as Rab worked his fingers into Murat's bushy armpits and around to cup his solid pecs. Soaping through the mass of blue-black chest hair, Rab toyed with nipples as hard and sharp as tacks.
Hugging Murat now from behind, one hand followed the trail of hair down from nipple to navel. His index finger poked a way in and Murat laughed delightedly. Rab's other hand traced a line down to first find, then tease, Murat's deep, hairy arse-crack. There was no going back once Rab grabbed a tight hold on Murat's hulking erection.
Murat sprang to life, swung around and ground his mouth down upon his tormentor. Rab whimpered with pleasure, whilst stroking Murat's velvety cock; a cock of gigantic proportions, matched with bollocks the size of duck eggs. Big wasn't the word, *huge* was.
'Fuck, Murat' – Rab wrenched his mouth free – 'your dick! It's like a baby elephant's trunk.' A slight exaggeration. But only slight.
'You like?' Murat asked with a broad smile.
'Oh, yes. I like.'

'You want me to fuck you?'

Rab's raised his eyebrows. 'I want you to fuck me. Yes. But' – he could barely keep the edge of concern from his voice – 'that thing would split me in half.'

'Trust me,' Murat replied, as he turned the shower handle to off and reached for a towel. 'I be gentle.'

Murat lay Rab down on the bed and watched him stretch out like a cat. Hoisting his legs high and wide, Rab spread his arse for Murat's inspection. Drawing close to within inches, Murat gazed at the virtually hairless cleft. At its core was the object of desire, a tight, flawless little rosebud.

Murat's fingers prised Rab's arse-cheeks even wider, then with long, slow strokes he lapped the crack with the full length and breadth of his tongue. Being careful not to touch the kernel, he savoured the moistened flesh. When at last he hit the spot, a shock wave ran through Rab's entire body and his tight, little anus tremored against Murat's tongue.

'Oh, big man.' Rab sighed. 'That feels *so* good.'

Time passed. Minutes? Hours? Murat worked remorselessly, loosening Rab up to take the full length of his tongue, before inserting one thick finger, then two, then three. Stretching him wide. Wider. A steady stream of saliva drenched his hole, ran between his cheeks and dripped down on to the striped bed-cover. Greased up for the final penetration, Rab's own fingers urgently spread his cheeks wider as Murat reached out to pluck a condom from the bedside table.

The transparent latex stretched to encompass Murat's mammoth tool, but not without difficulty. At last he succeeded. Then, with mounting pressure, he slowly teased the bulbous cockhead against Rab's pulsing ring, urging him to relax. Rab complied. With a gentle push Murat entered, just over the rim of his purple helmet. His eyes were closed, his luxuriant eyelashes fluttering. No sound escaped his throat as he persevered towards their mutual goal, gently nine-inching his way to the hilt, whilst Rab held his breath.

Rocking into him, almost imperceptibly at first, Murat increased his rhythm until the thrusting began in earnest. Bollocks slapped against Rab's rump. Rab's hands, in turn, clawed at Murat's backside, urging him ever deeper.

'Fuck me!' Rab's voice cracked the silence. 'Fuck my hole, big man.'

'Yeah? My big cock is in you. Deep in you. I see it go in' – Murat paused for effect – 'and out. You love my big cock, don't you? Don't you!'

'Oh, yeah. Oh, yeah. I've wanted this so long, so fuckin' long!'

Sweat dripped from Murat's forehead on to Rab's shoulders. Rab bucked and ground his arse upwards as Murat lunged, mercilessly, into him, both working on instinct. Wordlessly grunting like animals. Wild animals. Thrashing about on the bed. Murat marking out his territory, pinning Rab to the mattress, crushing him with his full weight, stabbing his horn deep into the belly of his prey.

The air hung thickly with the stench of sex. Whetting the appetite. Lust like hunger. Lust like thirst. And the need, the compulsion, to sate the appetite.

'Come inside me, big man. Empty yourself inside me.'

'I going to come inside you,' Murat gulped. 'You get your reward.'

'Whenever you're ready. Just love me with your big fat dick.'

'Oh, yeah. Oh, yeah.' Murat nodded furiously his agreement. 'I ready now. Here it comes. I going to come. I going to . . .' And with one final thrust the dam wall burst. The first spurt threatened to bust his big balls, a torrent of come rushing wave upon wave into blistering rubber as Rab clung on to Murat's firm, beefy buttocks.

'Don't pull out, big man,' Rab begged him, rocking his head back on the pillow, like a lost thing. 'Don't.'

And whilst Murat held firm Rab felt the rumble in his own balls. A roar growing fiercer and fiercer and fiercer until, without so much as a touch of his hand, a thick jet of sperm shot over his quivering belly. And with each subsequent spurt, Murat simply looked down and grinned.

'Yes. Yes. Yes.'

★

Rab was in his own bed, drifting somewhere between waking and sleeping, aware of his erection and the sweet friction produced by the bedcovers. But he wasn't about to disperse the energy and wank it away. He would leave it, and fall asleep with that delicious ache still in his loins.

Murat. His own dear friend. It hadn't taken long for their lust to mellow into friendship. The passionate aspect of the relationship had never gone; they remained, for want of a better word, fuck buddies. But they were never going to be lovers in any real sense. It wasn't that kind of love. Perhaps it would have been better, and less complicated, if it had been? He'd never know. As it was, Rab slipped into a blissful sleep with Mitch's face very much at the forefront of his mind.

When Kenny arrived at the breakfast table next morning somewhat the worse for wear, he was more than a little surprised to see the glamorous blonde flanked by Murat and Damon. All three were tucking into a full English breakfast. All three were visibly glowing. She looked ravishing. Her make-up was model perfect. Her hair fashionably tousled. The only thing that looked slightly out of place was the red, low-cut, spray-on mini-dress that allowed her impressive cleavage to dominate the room.

'Pull up a chair,' Damon bid him. 'I don't think you've met Cassandra, have you?'

Cassandra looked at Kenny. She managed to smile and pout both at the very same time. 'Hello, Kenny.' Her voice was husky, seductive and, against all appearances, remarkably posh.

'Morning,' he nodded, unimpressed.

'Cassandra wants to set up our fan club.'

'And what does Rab have to say about that?'

'He doesn't know yet. I'll talk to him about it later.'

Kenny frowned. 'Anyroadup, isn't it a bit early to be talking business?'

'Hmph! Obviously somebody got out of the wrong side of bed this morning.'

'Well, that's where you're wrong, see.' Kenny paused then

shook his head woefully. 'I never got to bed as it happens. Stayed up all night catching up with my mates.'

'I got to bed reasonably early.'

Kenny threw a look at Cassandra. 'I don't doubt it.' He changed the subject. 'So what do you do for a living, Cassandra?'

'Call me Cassie. All my friends do.'

'So what do you do for a living, *Cassie*?'

'I'm a student.'

'Studying?'

'Law.'

Kenny almost choked on his cornflakes. Somehow he just could not picture her in long black robes and a fuzzy wig.

Seven

After all their hard work, 'Victim of Pleasure' just managed to miss the Top 40. It peaked at 41. Jayne was furious and blamed poor distribution. This was something that would get 'sorted' before their next release, she assured them, or heads would roll. She was as good as her word.

The second single, 'I Love To Love', made the Top 20 in England, Top 5 throughout Europe and Number 1 in Germany. It was a triumph of Rab's marketing strategy. Behind the scenes he had an empire at work on the band's success. Familiar with selling a more orthodox commodity, Rab had no problems with adjusting his sales methods. Selling was what he did best and Bigfun were, in real terms, no less a product than, say, computers. He simply ensured that he was working alongside specialists in the field – Jayne, for example – though most of the actual mechanics were kept hidden from the band. That was his job, their job was to be creative.

Rab was more than earning his commission. Offers were flooding in left, right and centre. Teen mags were clamouring for photos, the music press were demanding interviews, and TV was offering a wide range of promo opportunities. Despite adopting a sales strategy that veered markedly towards the hard sell, few people in the industry balked. Bigfun were big news.

Things were happening, and happening all at once. All the band had to do, Rab reminded them, was to keep on keeping on. And he would take care of the rest.

Damon opened his eyes, yawned and turned to Murat.
'Is it Thursday?'
'Yes, it is.'
'Then it must be Cologne.'
The flight from Brussels had been fairly uneventful and an early start meant that Damon had fallen asleep as soon as the plane took off. Murat was seated at his side and had leant him a broad, convenient shoulder to snooze on. Now they were coming in to land and the announcement to that effect had roused Damon from dreams of Cassie.

They had been hopping from one major European city to another at breakneck speed. Ten cities in ten days. Cologne, at least, offered some free time.

'Get me outa here!' Kenny unclipped his seat belt as the plane coasted to a halt and the engines grew still. 'Let me kiss the ground.'

Damon looked over the back of his seat. Kenny was scrambling over Cary's lap in his rush to reach the exit.

'He'll be turning Catholic next,' Damon piped up.
'I suppose you are never nearer to God than when you're in a plane,' Cary added thoughtfully.
'Very philosophical, Professor Clarke. Is flying a religious experience for you too?' Mitch asked.
'No. But you are.'
'How come?'
'You're the thorn in my side; you were put on this earth to test me,' Cary replied.
'And will you pass the test?'
'That remains to be seen.'

It was three o'clock in the morning before Rab and Mitch entered Aktion! They had spent the previous two hours trolling the numerous gay bars, at Mitch's insistence. Rab was not about to let him go unescorted. No way. He knew the scene here only too well and so, reluctantly, he had offered to act as tour guide for the evening. His only proviso had been that they go to Rab's kind of bars, not the disco bunny variety.

For his part, Mitch was glad Rab had agreed to chaperone him. He felt safer with someone who knew his way around. Take the dress code, for example: he was happy to let Rab take charge and tell him what to wear so as not to look out of place.

Bears were big in Cologne. And what does a well-dressed bear wear? According to Rab it was a wool workshirt tucked into faded Levis plus a wide belt with a big buckle; heavy hiking boots; a Pendleton shirt jacket; and a baseball cap to complete the ensemble. Nothing out of the ordinary for Rab but for Mitch it was a new experience, a fun experience, like fancy dress. He found he felt comfortable in Rab's clothing.

Now dressed alike, Rab and Mitch fitted Aktion! perfectly. A daddy bear and his little bear cub.

The club was decked out like a dungeon. Black walls, black ceiling, black floor, black furniture and subdued lighting. Prison bars caged the barmen in place behind the counter. Handcuffs and chains provided the only decoration. The clientele were more colourful. Some were dressed in army combats, some in regulation bearwear and still others in leather. Full beards were common, as were bushy moustaches and chest hair. Bodies were strong and masculine. Some had weight and were proud to show it. Everything about these men seemed several hands bigger than usual.

As Mitch aimed to push his way through to the bar Rab caught his elbow.

'You order. I need a piss.'

'But I can't speak German!'

'How much German do you need? Repeat after me: "*Zwei Bier, bitte*".'

'*Zwei Bier, bitte.*'

'Perfect. Now go do your duty.' Rab turned and left him to it, as he headed for the gents.

The toilets were a hive of activity. Both cubicles were

occupied and judging from the grunts and groans that came from behind closed doors they had more than one occupant – maybe many more. Meanwhile, outside, in the corner of the cramped space, two guys were crouched down blowing a third.

Not six feet away, Rab relieved himself at one of only two urinals, all the time watching the fervent activity of the threesome from the corner of his eye. With a final shake he zipped up and turned, taking the few steps necessary to get a closer look. He leant in to the broad back of the goateed guy standing and looked down. In the glare of fluorescent light, two mouths fought for the privilege of licking and sucking on the most meat at any given moment; both faces were clean-shaven and both bore a look of complete and utter rapture.

The goateed guy had a long, thick, circumcised cock that tapered slightly at the end. A sheen of spittle glistened as he gripped the base and lowered it, directed it, stuffing it first in one hungry mouth then the other. At length, he threw a look over his shoulder and smiled at Rab, then reached back to cup Rab's groin.

Normally, Rab would not have been in the least perturbed by these events, would, in fact, have warmed to the touch of the stranger's hand, but in the circumstances he found himself react reflexively, jerking his crotch out of reach, as if he had been struck by a mild electric shock.

No good. It was impossible to lose himself to the moment, he was too busy analysing. Mentally he was aroused but his head stubbornly refused to send the message down to his dick. No response there. Zip. Zilch. And thinking to himself all the while, 'What kind of a place have I brought Mitch to? What have I done?'

The answer was: nothing; nothing that Mitch wouldn't have done by himself. Though, at the time, Rab could not see this, love being blind.

As Rab approached the bar he found Mitch in conversation with a bearded guy in American motorcycle cop uniform. The 'cop' had hooked an arm casually around Mitch's waist and was giving him serious eye contact as they laughed and talked together. When Rab arrived at their side the cop clearly regarded it as an unwelcome intrusion.

Rab reached between them with difficulty and lifted his bottle of Becks from the bar.

'Mine, I presume?' he asked Mitch pointedly. He raised the bottle to his lips, took a swig as his eyes scanned the room. 'C'mon. Let's take a look around.'

Mitch gave the cop the briefest of kisses and followed as Rab led the way.

'Thought you couldn't speak German?'

'No need. Everyone speaks English.'

'Talked to everyone, did you?'

'And then some. You were gone ages. Had fun?'

Rab ignored that comment. 'So, what did the cop want?'

'What do you think?'

'Cramping your style, am I?'

Mitch stood stock still and turned to face Rab. 'Look. I really, really like you, Rab.'

'But.'

'But you don't own me.'

Rab lowered his eyes. 'No, you're right. I'm sorry.' He felt suitably chastised.

'Hey!' Mitch punched his shoulder. 'Lighten up. The night is young' – he winked – 'and I'm enormous!'

To the left of the toilets was an area for dancing. Coloured lights flickered maniacally. Rab and Mitch arrived at the edge of the dance floor just as David Van Helsing's club remix of 'Victim of Pleasure' began to play.

'What?' cried Mitch above the blistering beat. 'Magic moment or what?' And with that he stepped into the midst of the heaving mass, just another anonymous playmate on the dance floor.

Cary entered Aktion! at that self-same moment. Blond hair tucked under a black baseball cap; black leather jacket over white T-shirt; torn blue jeans and biker boots. His entrance did not go unremarked. Not just fresh meat but sirloin steak.

He had left Kenny, Damon and Murat back at the hotel some

hours earlier. They were going to go to a sauna then on to a restaurant. Cary had other priorities. The desire to connect had driven him from one bar to the next. Flirting, always flirting but never really biting. He needed another drink, more Dutch courage and maybe even a guy from the Netherlands. Why not? He had already snogged a Belgian, a Spaniard, an Egyptian and countless Germans. Cary smiled, confident of his ability to attract; he felt on top of the world, felt like sex on legs. What is more, his song was playing, the place was buzzing. Magic.

Rab had been brooding as he watched Mitch flirt around the dance floor. Despite his best intentions, he could not help feeling compromised. OK, if that's the way you want to play it, he thought, as Mitch rejoined him, everything's up for grabs.

Mitch pointed a finger towards a mesh curtain of camouflage green that hung ceiling to floor cordoning off a section at the far end of the room.

'What's that?' Mitch asked.

'Backroom. Want to explore?'

'Sure. I'm game.'

They made their way across. Rab fumbled for an opening and, as the curtains parted, disco lights illuminated a bare arse, bent over. Two latex-gloved hands parted the cheeks. As Rab let the curtain drop behind them all inside was pitch black as before.

The 'cop' sidled up to Cary. 'You speak English?'

'Sure.'

'Good.' The cop flashed a killer smile. Perfect teeth framed by a bushy, chocolate-brown moustache. 'English or American?'

'English. And you?'

'Dutch.'

Cary allowed himself a sly smile.

The Backroom was a labyrinth of dimly lit corridors and darkened enclaves. Rab and Mitch lost each other shortly after entering and by the time their eyes had adjusted to the dark they were at opposite ends of the maze.

Anonymous hands reached out and touched the most intimate of places as body brushed against body. To Mitch it had a dream-like quality; a wet-dream-like quality, surreal and highly charged. He brushed away hands that felt for his zipper – 'No you don't, not yet, I'm having too much fun' – as he continued to explore.

Rab, on the other hand, allowed himself to be pulled into a scrum of muscular, hairy flesh. As the centre of attention, he felt hands unbutton his shirt, unbuckle his belt, unzip his jeans and slide them down to his calves. Then all hell broke loose. Teeth found his nipples, a mouth consumed his semi-erect cock and, as hands parted his arse cheeks, a long, wet tongue probed his anus. Rab let out a deep, prolonged growl.

The 'cop' was making no bones about his interest in Cary. 'You want me to fuck you? I have a big cock and I love to fuck.'

'Are you always this direct?' Cary asked with some amusement.

The cop shrugged and replied matter of factly, 'We have only one life to live, so let's live it.'

'You have some place to go?'

'No, my partner is back at the hotel. What about you?'

'Likewise,' Cary lied.

'So then' – the cop took his hand – 'follow me.' He led him towards the backroom.

Mitch flitted from one guy to another, grabbing a crutch here, a dick there, tweaking nipples, stealing the odd kiss. He was in his element, a prick-tease extraordinaire, pulling away just when the other guy's enthusiasm threatened to get out of hand.

Rab was caught up in a group kiss. Three mouths melding, tongues probing and all the while his cock was being blown to perfection. Hands coursed over his exposed flesh, ripples of pleasure tipping him closer to the edge and beyond, into oblivion.

★

The cop wasn't much into foreplay. Having found an empty alcove, he had turned Cary towards the wall and yanked his jeans down. Coarse fingers lubed up his arsehole. Cary placed one hand against the wall and reached behind with the other in order to check that the guy had protection. He had. Just as well. A cock that size could cause serious damage. Cary took hold and guided the plug into the socket.

Mitch felt his way along the wall, trying as best as he could not to trip or fall over the numerous hives of activity. Too late, he stumbled into a pitch-black alcove and felt himself crushed up against two bodies in furious motion. It didn't take long to realise that one was being seriously fucked by the other. He reached down and felt a cock exposed to the air. He curled his palm around it; the thrusting of hips meant the prick was fucking his fist. He released it, letting his fingers drift up to the hem of a cotton T-shirt. His hands slid underneath it and travelled upwards to knead and caress two hard pecs before finally tugging on nipples that were fiercely aroused.

Cary was straining against the tug of the anonymous stranger, the stranger who was teasing the front as the cop pounded his back. He turned his mouth, straining to be kissed, searching for a mouth in the dark. He smelt perfumed breath before he tasted minty kisses as their lips and tongues finally clashed.

Over in the far corner, Rab felt that unmistakable surge in his nuts that told him he was about to blow. Two mouths continued to feast on his hairy chest as a third licked his balls. He crushed the heads down on to his nipples and thrust out his hips, his prick swollen fit to bust, and then he let fly over the head of the bollock sucker. '*Oh, ja,*' came from the mouth buried in his groin. '*Oh, ja, Oh, ja!*'

The cop had pulled out and was furiously wanking over Cary's backside, while the hands at Cary's nipples reached down to grab Cary's twitching organ. Cary's response was immediate. He sprayed the wall like a fire hose on a burning building as the cop followed suit over his buttocks.

When the wave of orgasm had finally subsided, Cary found himself alone with the cop, who was gently wiping the come from his arse-cheeks. 'Let's get you cleaned up,' he said. 'My name's René, by the way. Can I buy you a drink?'

Mitch caught up with Rab at the bar.

'Drink?'

'Nah. Let's get off,' Mitch replied, yawning at the same time.

'Had enough?'

'Can never have enough, Rab. I'm just working up an appetite.'

'So.'

'So.' He grinned. 'Your bed or mine?'

It was in Cologne that Rab first met Cassie. Her plane arrived early the next morning; she had flown over specially to share Damon's precious free time, and he was there to meet her with a big bunch of flowers. They took a taxi back to the hotel and when they finally emerged from his bedroom there was only one evening left. Rab and Kenny were seated at the hotel bar when the handsome couple entered.

'Well, I can't question his taste,' Rab said as an aside. 'That girl looks like a million dollars –'

Kenny completed the sentence. '– worth of plastic surgery.'

'Hi, Rab. Hi, Kenny. Mind if we join you?'

Kenny patted the bar stool alongside him. 'Please take a seat. I'm sure you must be worn out, both of you.'

Damon ignored him. 'Rab, you haven't met Cassie yet, have you?'

'No. But it's an honour and a pleasure.' Rab turned to Cassie and held out his hand. 'Any friend of Damon's is a friend of mine.'

'And of course you've met Kenny?' Damon's face soured.

'Yes. Hello, Kenny.' Once again she treated him to a pouting smile. 'But even if I hadn't I'd feel as if I know you. Damon's told me all about you.'

'That must have been an experience and a half.'

'Yes, it was. He thinks the world of you, you know?' She shot a sideways glance and squeezed Damon's hand.

Kenny was caught short. 'Oh . . . Oh, really?' He blushed crimson. 'Well, of course I like him too. We just tease each other something rotten. You'll get used to it . . . Cassie.' He shrugged, smiled, and gave Damon's arm a playful punch.

Cassie had disarmed Kenny with kindness. The moment was not lost on Rab.

Rab knew of Damon's suggestion that Cassie should form and front the fan club. And even though she didn't know it yet, this glamorous girl had just passed the interview with flying colours. She had got herself the job.

Eight

It was Jayne Hanvey's idea to have the boys write their own material. If the band was to have any longevity, she argued, it was a necessity. But it was Cary who had provided the stimulus. He'd been quietly and consistently working, with Remi's aid, towards producing a four-track demo. When he presented it to Jayne she was astounded, and felt absolutely certain that one song in particular, 'With All My Heart', was a sure-fire hit single.

Cary played the piano well and some guitar and had been kicking around ideas ever since he first tinkered on the keyboard. It seemed the disciplines of childhood were finally about to bear fruit. This was one thing he could thank his father for, at least.

Consequently, 'With All My Heart' became Bigfun's third single and raced up the charts in Britain quicker than anyone could have imagined. The record company were taken by surprise and the presses were forced to work overtime. 'Heart' took a mere three weeks to hit the top slot. Six weeks later, the single repeated its success on the other side of the Atlantic. Bigfun were poised to become the new media darlings.

A private reception was rapidly arranged for the band at the record company headquarters to celebrate their breakthrough. As Jayne held court, the champagne flowed once again. It pissed

Kenny off no end because he would have preferred a good, old-fashioned pint of John Smith's.

'Will you quit grumbling!' Damon complained in turn.

'What's all this about?' Rab was now alongside.

'Nothing,' said Kenny. 'I was just saying I'd prefer a pint.'

'He has such an uneducated palate, Rab. Take no notice of him,' Damon said.

Kenny was not amused. 'I'll re-educate your palate with my fist if you don't shut it, buster.'

'And prove what? That only real men drink beer? When you're big enough, Kenny.'

'Can't you two just get along with each other for five minutes?' Rab asked with an amused twinkle in his eye. 'Today is a day for celebrating in case you hadn't noticed.'

'He started it.' Kenny was now in a huff.

'If you want a pint, you shall have a pint. I'll see to it.' And Rab disappeared to put in the order.

'Satisfied now?' Damon asked with more than a hint of sarcasm.

'No. Not until I get your head on a stick.'

'Charming.' Damon was indignant. 'Is that all the thanks I get for trying to drag you up out of the gutter by the boot straps?'

Kenny didn't bother to give him the benefit of a response.

In a corner of the room, Jayne and Cary were deep in conversation. She had taken a real shine to him. The feeling was mutual. Funny how opinions change, he thought to himself. When he first saw her he had felt intimidated. Her look was so striking, so severe and she seemed incredibly self-possessed. Now he was familiar with her keen sense of humour and kind heart. More than this, he admired her for being up front about her partner – her female partner – Jo. Jo worked as Jayne's PA. They were almost inseparable and quite clearly comfortable with the arrangement.

Jayne poured Cary another glass of bubbly and leant towards his ear. 'So are you finally going to tell me who the lyric is about?'

'I told you, Jayne. It's a figment of my own creative imagination.'

Jayne snorted. 'Excuse me! 'Heart' fairly *drips* with longing. And it's certainly struck a chord with the masses.' She lowered her voice to a conspiratory whisper. 'Go on, you can tell me . . .'

Cary cast a sideways glance in Mitch's direction. Mitch was standing by the buffet table, being effortlessly charming to some junior executive or other. Cary paused. 'No one you'd know, Jayne.'

'Spoilsport!' She groaned in defeat.

Gayle Driver sat behind the executive desk in her spacious Docklands office, preoccupied. She lit a menthol cigarette and blew a stream of smoke out of the corner of her mouth, never once taking her eyes off of the magazine cover that lay in front of her. Smoking was an occasional indulgence she allowed herself, a secret vice she kept hidden from the eyes of the world and it was strictly limited to moments of extreme stress. This was one of those moments.

'Exclusive! Bigfun in the bath!' boasted the headline. The four boys were pictured like soccer players in a communal tub amidst a volume of bubbles. Slap bang in the centre was Mitch, grinning, his thumbs pressed up against the cork on a champagne bottle. It didn't seem to matter where she turned these days, the boys were sure to be found, on hoardings as she commuted to work, in the morning paper, whenever she switched on the TV or radio. She simply couldn't escape them, they were everywhere.

It isn't fair! she told herself, stabbing her cigarette butt into the ashtray and grinding the life out of it. She had tried so hard to put that mess behind her but it seemed hopeless. It was all beyond her control.

She could hardly believe the turn of events that had led to her present position. The wheel of fortune had spun like a top, leaving her dazed and confused. Things had taken on their own momentum. Once the initial pain and embarrassment of Rab's marching orders had passed she had resolved not to fold under the weight of self-pity. Instead, she took up the offer of a month in LA at the insistence of an old girlfriend who was fast establishing herself as a scout for a top Hollywood talent agency.

As luck would have it, Gayle had just happened to be in her girlfriend's office when the call came through from their British associates. A Breakfast TV company were desperate for a Brit to step immediately into the role of celebrity gossip monger for a slot on morning television. Gayle got the job and within days made her debut before the camera. It was only a two-month stint but it kept her fully occupied. Somehow it had brought her to the attention of her current boss and a dream job with a long-term contract that seemed to herald a new beginning.

But no. No, it was actually part of her new job to keep abreast of all that was happening in the media. Gayle was now a cog in that particular machine. Lifestyle publishing was the buzz word. She had been appointed to the post of assistant editor of *Grrrl!* magazine. Lifestyles of the rich and famous were her speciality. That and 'Secrets of the Stars'. She believed she had been recruited through a series of lucky accidents – being in the right place at the right time. What other reason could there have been? What other reason indeed. She didn't have a background in journalism but, as she well knew, what you know is not as important as who you know.

Her connection to Bigfun could have made her a fortune, except there was no connection any more, was there?

Kenny and Mitch entered the communal showers together and, despite there being five free shower heads, they stood side by side, chatting amiably. The searing hot jets of water turned their pumped-up muscles red. Kenny was meticulous in his ablutions, thoroughly soaping every part of his brawny anatomy; from one set of rosy cheeks to the other. Mitch was impressed. Kenny's body had been going through a significant process of development. And as Mitch watched him, he matched him stroke for soapy stroke.

A good five minutes bathing were matched by a vigorous rub-down which Kenny rounded off by applying some kind of cream lotion to his skin. Naked and proud, he lathered a handful over his firm pecs; one foot was placed up on the seat beside Mitch, his cock only inches from Mitch's face. The action of his hands roughly manipulating his chest muscles set his loose bollocks jiggling. Close enough for Mitch to reach out and steady them. Of course he didn't. Instead, he let the moment pass, but not without registering that something was decidedly off kilter. If he hadn't known better he would have said Kenny was coming on to him. Not that the idea offended him, it had just somehow never presented itself as a possibility before.

Reaching into his bag, Kenny produced a clean pair of socks and settled his sturdy rump on the wooden bench beside Mitch.

'It'd be great if you joined this gym too,' Kenny remarked, all upbeat and chatty.

'Why, just 'cause I live around the corner?'

'Of course it's really convenient for us both but, more important, we could train together.' Kenny pulled on the first sock.

'What's come over you? There was a time when you had to be dragged kicking and screaming into the gym. Now look at you. You're turning into a muscle monster.'

'Yeah? Well, maybe I decided that size is important.'

'Then you're a man after my own heart.'

'Good,' Kenny replied, hoping his face wasn't as red as it felt. He looked over his shoulder towards the closed door and, with a slight tremor in his voice, his eyes focused on Mitch's chest, he said, 'Are those tits as hard as they look?'

'Why, Kenny,' Mitch grinned, 'if I didn't know better I'd say you were flirting with me.'

'It was just a question.'

'Why don't you feel them and find out?' Mitch teased.

Kenny's breathing was laboured but he didn't move.

Mitch continued. 'Go on then, Kenny. Live dangerously. You know you want to.'

'I'm not coming on to you, Mitch,' he responded vehemently.

Mitch was far from convinced. 'Yeah? Then you're walking a very thin line!'

Kenny checked the door again. 'Want to come back to my place for a beer or what?'

Kenny's sitting room was spartan and arranged with almost military precision. White walls were hung with framed muscle posters.

'Who's he?' Mitch asked, pointing to one particularly horny athlete.

'Oh, him. His name's Tom. He works out at the same gym.'

'Where do I sign the membership form?'

Kenny rubbed the back of his neck. 'I'm so stiff.'

'Me too. That poster has some effect.'

'No. I mean stiff from the training.'

'Fancy a massage?' Mitch asked without batting an eye.

'You do massage?'

'Sure. It's one of my specialities. I'll do you, then you can do me.'

'I don't have a clue what to do. You'll have to educate me.'

'Just my luck, yet another wee virgin. Leave it to me,' Mitch assured him. 'We'll take things nice and slow. Let's start. Better get out of those clothes.'

Kenny closed the bedroom curtains as he stripped down to dark blue briefs. Climbing on to the double bed, he lay tummy down whilst Mitch undressed himself and then straddled Kenny's firm buttocks. Kenny was warm to the touch, his skin made supple and moist by the lotion he had liberally applied not half an hour earlier. Mitch's hands swept over Kenny's broad back and muscular neck, down over the curvature of his biceps to the tips of his fingers and back again to the base of his spine.

Five minutes, it had taken Mitch. Five minutes to loosen Kenny up to the point where he could allow the first of a hundred murmurs and moans to escape his lips. Working deeper on the big muscle grouping around his shoulders, Mitch felt for the knots of tension and worked hard to loosen the ties. His fingers kneaded the resistant flesh until it became pliable. This simple act brought about a significant release of tension; this was self-evident from the blissful look on Kenny's face, his expression growing ever more serene. It would seem Mitch's fingers were multitalented.

Mitch flipped Kenny over on to his back and stared at the pyramid of material that constituted the crotch of his briefs. A huge pole forced it up and out. Mitch left it well alone as he worked over Kenny's tits. Deep penetration, fingers sinking into flesh. Then down to the thighs and calves. He folded them over his lap and stroked the tender inside. Kenny sighed, his eyes closed but fluttering behind the lids.

Mitch took hold of the right foot, working thumb and fingers into the ball.

'Oh, yeah,' Kenny gasped. 'That feels fuckin' wonderful.'

His feet were large, broad and well cared for. Trim white nails, a peppering of hair over his toes. Mitch brought Kenny's foot to his mouth, tracing a line with his tongue along Kenny's inner sole and finally his lips embraced Kenny's toes. Kenny buried his head in his pillow and tried to stifle his squeals of delight.

'Enough, enough!' he cried finally and Mitch let the foot fall. Kenny's pupils had dilated to the point where the iris had all but disappeared and he fixed those eyes on Mitch, brimful with longing. He eased his crutch an inch or two from the bed and nodded towards the straining material. Mitch knelt by Kenny's waist and hooked his fingers under the elastic.

In the instant he peeled down the waist band, Kenny squirted his first. A luxuriously long squirt, an outpouring of creamy spunk drenching his belly. With each pulse of his organ, another dollop spurted. Mitch counted the spurts. Ten. His tits and stomach were awash with come.

'It's OK. Everything's OK,' Mitch reassured him as the well ran dry. Reaching out a hand, Mitch let the tip of his forefinger dip into the milky pool of steaming jism that gathered in the valley between Kenny's pecs.

'What are you doing?' Kenny asked, bemused.

'Writing my name across your heart,' Mitch replied.

Later, when they had cleaned up and then cuddled up under the covers, Mitch asked Kenny for some form of explanation.

Like, where on earth had this turn of events sprung from? Kenny was a little reticent at first but then finally began to open up.

'Would you believe me if I said that I simply wanted to try it?'

'Sure. But there must be more to it than that.'

Kenny thought for a moment. 'The older I get the more I find myself looking at men.'

'And wanting them.'

'You get the picture?'

'Sure do. But why me?'

'You're the only gay guy I know.'

'Thanks for the compliment!'

'I didn't mean it that way.'

'Anyway, I'm not the only gay guy you know.'

'Really?'

Kenny had no idea; not a clue as to who was gay, who wasn't and who could be considered reasonably suspect. Naive wasn't the word. He was equally naive about homo sex, had only the vaguest notion what it could involve. Arse fucking was a completely alien concept. Kenny would later admit he had thought that the most they might do would be to pull each other off. Mitch would be the one to open not only his eyes but also his arse for good measure; would soon put him straight on the pleasures of men, one to another. Kenny's gratitude knew no bounds. They spent the weekend in bed rutting like rabbits. His tight, sweet little ring-piece swallowing Mitch whole.

In a little over forty-eight hours Kenny progressed from novice to expert in one giant leap for mankind. Fucking and sucking became second nature. Once he got his toes wet he took to it all like a duck to water. A thirst for knowledge only matched by a thirst for kisses. Thwacking Mitch's poor, bruised knob time and again. Wanting always more. Begging for it. Literally begging for it.

By Sunday night Mitch had to crawl back home. His plums had turned to prunes.

★

When the call came through, Gayle had been somewhat surprised. Then surprise had turned to anxiety as she wondered why the big chief had summoned her to a private meeting. Clive Foxx rarely met anyone personally.

It was Clive Foxx, the media tycoon, who was the owner of *Grrrl!* along with any number of other mainstream publications. When she had found herself head-hunted for her present job Gayle had been astounded to hear that it was under his direct instructions. She could hardly believe that such a key player could take a personal interest in her. Then again, up until this point, she still hadn't met the man to have it confirmed from his own lips. Maybe it was just so much blather by the recruitment officer.

His private offices were on the fourteenth floor of the building, accessed by his own lift, though, if the truth be known, he was seldom to be found there. With so many fingers in so many pies, he left the day-to-day matters of running his various businesses to his minions. Word was that he demanded total obedience, but for this his subordinates were rewarded handsomely. The more cynical members of staff referred to their contract as a pact with the Devil, but never too loudly. Not if they knew on which side their bread was buttered.

When the time arrived, Gayle dressed to impress. Power-dressed in a smart two-piece suit and designer blouse, silk stockings and tastefully accessorised, she looked like the classic young female executive. Her hair was pulled sharply back and piled on top of her head; her make-up was subtle and immaculate.

Foxx's private secretary was clearly expecting her and, with a professional smile and efficient manner, she ushered Gayle through to the inner sanctum. Foxx's office was an exercise in style over content, spacious and uncluttered. Gayle imagined it reflected the taste of some high-priced interior decorator. There was no personality in evidence here, not unless Clive Foxx was totally vacuous.

He entered without fanfare yet it barely detracted from the consummate theatricality with which he threw wide the connecting doors from his private chambers and strode in. He crossed the room purposefully and with a fixed smile he offered his hand. It was fleshy, limp and clammy to the touch.

'Finally, we get to meet!' he announced with a flourish. And without waiting for a response he asked, 'Tea? Coffee? Or would you prefer something stronger?'

'Do you have peppermint –'

He waved his hand. '– tea? No problem.' He pressed the button on the intercom and related his instructions to the secretary.

'Please take a seat, Gayle. I can call you Gayle, can't I? I know of you, of course, but I feel as if I know you, I know so much about you. Please call me Clive. I don't stand on ceremony. And please do sit down!'

Even as she sat, she was beginning to feel uneasy. Her chief was being a tad too solicitous. It wasn't what he said so much as how he said it – dripping, as it was, with smarm.

'Now you're probably wondering why I asked you up here. The answer is simple; to congratulate you on all the hard work you're doing. I can see my judgement was spot-on once again. You're a credit to the organisation.' He paused dramatically. 'And that's why I've decided to increase your salary.'

Gayle hardly knew what to say. 'Well, thank –'

Foxx held up his hand to silence her.

'Nothing to thank me for, my dear.' And again that creepy smile. 'It's no more than you deserve.'

The sentence was punctuated by the buzz of the intercom. Foxx's face dropped, mildly peeved that his moment in the limelight should be so rudely interrupted. It was his secretary.

'Sorry to interrupt, Mr Foxx, but Mr Foster is on line two. You said to tell you if –'

'Yes, yes, it's quite all right, Miriam.' The smile had returned once again to Foxx's face. In fact, he was positively glowing. 'I'll take it on the other line.' He turned to Gayle. 'If you'll just excuse me for a few minutes? Please do make yourself at home.' And with that he made his exit, stage left.

Make herself at home? What? Kick off her shoes? Put her feet up? Gayle didn't think so. And anyway, this was no place to relax. The minutes dragged by. She was halfway down her cup of peppermint tea before he returned.

'Now where were we?' he asked as he took his seat once more.

'You were say –'

'Ah, yes! I'm going to give you a substantial pay increase. I understand you've bought yourself a new flat?'

Gayle nodded but could barely disguise her consternation that he had knowledge of this.

Foxx's laughter was high and thin. 'Oh, I don't miss much, Gayle. It was very expensive, I understand, but a wise investment, I don't doubt, so long as you can maintain the repayments. Believe me, I don't underestimate what a drain this must be on your bank balance. That's one of the reasons why this rise in salary seems so . . . appropriate. Of course, the increase does come with certain . . . conditions.'

Oh, yes. Here we go, thought Gayle. Finally, we're getting around to the hidden agenda.

'You will, by now, be familiar enough with my organisation to know that I expect one hundred per cent commitment from my work force? I have to know they can be trusted, Gayle. This is of vital importance. Without trust' – another pause – 'well, I'm sure I don't have to spell it out for you.'

Gayle simply wished he would get to the point. He did, soon enough.

'We have something in common, Gayle. You see, I know all about your involvement with a certain boyband.'

'All about –'

'Yes, my dear. *All* about. I know you helped create them. They're a credit to you. Really, a credit. But you were robbed of the fruits of your labour, I understand?'

'If you mean –'

'Precisely, Gayle. You were unceremoniously dropped when you had outlived your usefulness. By rights, you should be earning millions, not the comparatively paltry sum you earn here – substantial though it may be.'

'Well, I wouldn't say —'

'No. But I would, Gayle. I would. You and I, we're allies in a way. I'm sure there's no love lost between you and Rab Mackay and the same could indeed be said for me. In fact, I fully intend to expose him for the arsehole he is.' Foxx seemed to savour the word. He repeated it for good measure, 'Yes, *arsehole*. Not exactly the Queen's English but wholly appropriate nonetheless.' The look on his face was enough to curdle milk. He checked himself, regained his composure, smiled again. 'That's where you come in. With your inside knowledge and the advantages of my empire, I'm sure we can ensure he gets his just desserts.'

Foxx pressed the intercom button once more and spoke to his secretary. 'Have Milo bring the Roller around to the side door.' He turned back to Gayle. 'I think that's all I have to say for the moment, my dear, but I'll speak with you again very soon.'

Gayle had been dismissed. She placed her tea cup on the glass coffee table and stood to leave.

'One last thing, my dear.' His beady eyes swept up and down her body, from head to toe and back again. It made her skin crawl. 'The get-up.' He shook his head. 'It might be OK at *Cosmo* but this is a teen and twenties magazine. Have a word with my secretary on your way out. I've made you an appointment with our style consultant. He's going to give you a makeover. But don't worry, I'm also giving you a budget for clothes.'

Gayle was speechless.

'Mustn't forget you're representing Clive Foxx when you're out in the big wide world.'

As she rode the lift to reception, Gayle realised that he hadn't allowed her to finish a single sentence. Now she wondered if she would ever find her voice again.

Nine

Cassie had invited a privileged group, drawn at random from the list of fan club members, to review and select the tracks for Bigfun's first album. It had been Cassie's suggestion but, as always, subject to Rab's consent. In the event, he had been enthusiastic in his approval. It struck him as a very clever marketing strategy. That Cassie made the suggestion didn't surprise him in the least. Membership in the fan club was booming and feedback was terrific. She had more than proven herself to be a babe with brains.

All the tracks could be used eventually in one form or another, she had argued. Perhaps as extra tracks on the CD singles, or maybe as an EP. But why not let the fans decide the content of the album? If they didn't know what would appeal to the fan base no one would. Plus when the story was eventually released to the press it would generate the best kind of PR.

It was for this reason that a mixed group of twenty spent the best part of a weekend at a London recording studio. Rab made the formal introductions and once the band and their fans had had the opportunity to mingle and chat, the programme began in earnest. Remi explained the finer points of the recording process, Jayne spoke about her role in selecting and producing the material, and the boys gave a little background to each song.

Thereafter, the chosen few listened enthusiastically and repeatedly to twenty-five new songs over the course of two days. After much heated debate, the final selection was agreed upon. This would mean that seven of the fourteen tracks were written by Cary, three by Mitch, one each by Damon and Kenny, plus two cover versions. It was a decision that everyone seemed happy with. Sunday evening came around and, with the fun and excitement of the decision process over, the fan club faithful somewhat reluctantly made their separate ways back home. All, that is, except one. He was a cute little guy called Andy: short at 5 foot 4 or so; dark brown hair cut in a flat-top, a neat moustache, his bottom lip punctuated by a small triangle of facial hair; and a lithe, lightly muscled body. He said he was thirty but shave off the whiskers and he could have been eighteen. He had a thing about his age – and over the weekend kept bringing attention to it, saying things like, 'I'm so young!' It began to piss Rab off no end – though not enough to ignore his obvious charms. Rab was nothing if not pragmatic.

Andy claimed to be the band's number-one fan – didn't they all? But Andy took it one step further by spending almost all of his time making eyes at Mitch. When he wasn't busy making eyes, he was hanging on to Rab's every word. Flitting between the two of them like a manic moth drawn to separate flames and unable to choose between the two. It wasn't so surprising, therefore, to find him hanging around by the studio gates once everyone else had gone.

Exiting the gates, Mitch spotted him. 'Hey, Rab, look, there's that Andy bloke. Wonder what he's waiting for?' he said with a smirk on his lips, though it was pretty obvious given the way Andy was toying with the not-unimpressive bulge in his tight leather trousers. Rab raised his eyebrows, and indicated to Murat to pull over.

Rolling the window down, Rab leant out. 'Need a lift somewhere, Andy?'

'Yeah, sure. That'd be great, Rab,' he replied, his face lighting up, while his fingers left the outline of his swollen cock and stuffed themselves deep in the pockets of his bomber jacket. 'I'm heading over towards the city.' Rab opened the door and, quick as a flash, Andy was squeezing in past Rab to position himself right in the middle. The car pulled off again. Seated between both of them on the back seat of the limousine, Andy looked first at Mitch and then at Rab. Both reached out and began to fondle his chest, leaning into him. Andy didn't know whose face to suck first. Three-way kisses and roaming fingers, then it was back home to Rab's apartment and his big, big bed.

Entering the bedroom, Mitch knelt down in front of Andy and began to pop the buttons of his leather trousers, easing them down over his muscular thighs. He watched Andy's cock inflate, the bulge pressing against the white cotton of his French-cut briefs. Pressing his face against the mound, Mitch could feel Andy's boner, rigid and warm against his cheek. He wrapped his mouth around it and exhaled warm air through the straining cotton. Rab stood behind Andy, his hands running over Andy's tits, and felt his cock pressing up against his lower back as he ground against it. Reaching down he pressed Mitch's head tight into Andy's crotch making him gag. Meanwhile Mitch had taken hold of the pants and was now peeling them off. As Mitch pulled back, Andy's prong burst proudly into view. It was neither big, nor small, but it was very pleasing to the eye and painfully stiff. Mitch noticed how his dick was darker than the rest of his body – though he would later learn that it wasn't the sole exception for his ring piece was equally tan, tasty and begging to be explored. Having dropped to his knees, Rab was only too happy to oblige in that direction. Mitch's tongue took immense pleasure in exploring every inch of Andy's shaved cock and balls whilst Rab licked between his arse cheeks with long, luxurious strokes.

Andy was in seventh heaven, his cock and arse being worked over at one and the same time. His body first lurched forwards as he thrust his cock into Mitch's hungry mouth. Then backwards, feeling Rab's hot tongue ram ever deeper inside. He couldn't decide what he wanted more, so Rab decided for him. Gripping both arse cheeks in his hands, he opened them up like a book, positioning his thumbs on either side of Andy's sphincter. He gave one last slow, wet lick, and then began to insert one of his thumbs slowly. Andy's body shivered with pleasure, and he pushed backwards to impale himself on Rab's thumb. First the left one and then the right, and then both together. Andy's hole was insatiable, his thrusting becoming ever more urgent, loosening himself up for the more sizeable penetration he clearly craved. Finally he accommodated four fingers and thumb up his arse to the knuckle, his rosebud opening up like a flower, KY Jelly working its magic.

Rab reached under the bed to get one of his regular butt plugs and eased it into Andy's arse. Andy moaned in pleasure at the tightness of the fit, and moved to sit on the edge of the bed, grinding his arse down into the mattress to accentuate the feeling. Mitch and Rab stood one at either side, kissing deeply, while Andy sucked first on one blood-engorged member and then the other. He even tried to cram both in his mouth together, but given their respective sizes, it was a pretty impossible task.

Mitch was the first to quit, lying back on the bed while Andy squatted over him, kissing and playing with each nipple. Rab crawled between Mitch's legs, and set to work licking his cock and balls with long loving strokes, combining this with running his tongue between Andy's crack and pressing the butt plug with his hairy chin. Both Mitch and Andy bucked beneath this added pleasure. Rab removed the plug and continued sucking on Mitch's cock, while working Andy's arse again with both thumbs, opening up his hole wide to receive Mitch's meat. Rab dressed Mitch's cock with rubber and prepared to clothe his own.

Licking a trail of spittle from cockhead to arsehole, Rab led Mitch's cock with his tongue, guiding it into Andy's welcoming hole. With a single thrust Mitch was all the way in. No easing of passage. Andy was hot and hungry, and the sooner the better. Rab reached back and began to jack on his own cock while he marvelled at the sight of Mitch's cock slipping in and out of the tight arsehole. Leaning in, he could smell the mixture of sweat and musk. Sticking out his tongue he could lick Mitch's balls as his dick continued to enter and exit. He spat on Mitch's exposed member helping to lubricate it on its return journey. Meanwhile, his thumbs continued to massage the edges of Andy's ring.

With a plop Mitch suddenly pulled out. Andy arched back and seconds later Rab's cock was inside him up the hilt. Fucking like a champion, Rab ground his meat right up to the balls, feeling them slap against Andy's arse and, keeping his movements brief, just pumping harder and harder. Wanting to shoot out his frustration and tension.

Mitch broke his concentration. 'Hey, Rab, how about giving me a go?' Rab pulled out, somewhat reluctantly, while Andy repositioned himself slightly to allow Mitch's still hard cock to take over.

On and on they went, all three of them. First Mitch doing the fucking, and then Rab. It was like a competition between them. Who could fuck the longest, the hardest, the deepest. Andy was more than content to take it all. It was what his hole had been made for. Fucking, or more correctly, being fucked. And he was enjoying it. Every last inch of it. It was a long time since he had been fucked so expertly, and now the pleasure was doubled – not just one hot guy, but two. A celebrity fuck fest. If his friends could only see him now! Unless they had seen it with their own eyes no one would believe him.

Over the course of the next ten hours Andy came three times – and this included a period of some six hours' sleep. Rab's most potent memory would be of a bed of crumpled pillows and duvet cast aside in a heap, Andy sprawled on his back, jacking off whilst feasting on Mitch's meat; he was totally cock focused, opening his throat, swallowing up to the base, cramming in as much as he could; Mitch was kneeling at his head, watching Andy's throat swell to accommodate his length and thickness. Andy's cock was hard as rock and straight as an arrow, the circumcised head being the same width as the shaft. And when he came, he erupted in long powerful spurts that shot high in the air, defying the laws of gravity.

Later, lying back on the bed, with Rab sucking on one nipple, Andy on the other, it seemed to Mitch like the closest thing to bliss. He could savour the memory of how after they had both fucked Andy to cream, Mitch had been able to turn around and fuck Rab while Andy had watched. In that moment, he had never felt more powerful.

Finally all three rested, empty. Cuddled. Slept. Andy sandwiched between the other two. When Mitch reluctantly opened his eyes after too little sleep, sunlight through the curtains illuminated Andy's diminutive body laid on top of Rab's sturdy frame. Both appeared to be fast asleep. Rab on his back, Andy sprawled across him, his head nestling into Rab's hairy chest. Mitch couldn't help but smile, it was such a sweet picture. The look on Andy's face was one of absolute contentment.

It was half past two in the afternoon when Andy finally took his leave. Mitch escorted him to the Underground. Meanwhile, Rab stayed behind in the kitchen making a late breakfast. Andy headed off for Bethnal Green and home, breakfast and bed. They didn't exchange addresses. Just another Sunday afternoon in the big city.

The whir of the coffee grinder and the smell of fresh orange juice and chocolate croissants filled the apartment upon Mitch's return. Rab stood against the kitchen work surface dressed in his white towelling bathrobe. His hair was wet from the shower. Mitch snuck up behind him and slipped his arms around his waist.

'Smells good.'

'Uh-huh. Me or the food?'

'Both.'

Mitch sat on a high stool at the breakfast bar as Rab served up.

'He got off OK,' Mitch mumbled as he bit into a croissant.

'Good.'

'How was that for you?'

'Last night?'

'What else?'

'Kind of fun.'

'Kind of!' Mitch stared at Rab incredulously.

Not that Rab hadn't enjoyed this sexual interlude, but for him it had been more a form of compromise. He had felt he had to make to keep Mitch happy. Variety seemed to be the spice of Mitch's life and Rab was more than aware of his roving eye. Threesomes struck him as preferable to letting go. But only just.

'You think it could have been better?' Mitch asked.

'I'd have been just as happy with you alone.'

Mitch frowned suddenly. 'Oh, no, Rab. Not again. Can't you change the record for once?'

'There's something wrong with me wanting you all to myself?'

'Yes – No – Look we've been through all this before!'

'I don't own you. I know I don't own you, Mitch. I know that. But it's just sometimes –'

'Nobody owns me, Rab.'

'What about commitment? I don't mean to cramp your style. I'll settle for what you can give me. But it doesn't stop me wanting more.'

'I've always been straight with you, if you'll pardon the pun. I like you, Rab. I like you a lot. I just –' Mitch fell into silent frustration.

'Yes?'

'I'm just not ready for a long-term commitment.'

'But will you think about it?'

'Rab, please.'

'It's all I'm asking, just for you to think about it.'

Damon was in a cranky mood. He sat at the table in Harrods' café and stared off into space. Murat and Kenny sat opposite him and shared a weary smile.

'I'm bored!' Damon's expression was vivid.

'Since when has spending money been boring?' Kenny had little sympathy. 'Just remember how things were twelve months ago. I bet you were a damn sight more bored when you were skint. How many twenty-one year olds have a checking account at Harrods without their daddy's permission? You should think yourself lucky.'

'I don't mean I'm bored with shopping.'

'You mean you're bored with life?' Kenny shot a look in Murat's direction. 'My heart bleeds.'

'No.' Damon's eyes finally swivelled in the direction of Kenny. 'I mean I'm bored with hanging around. When are we going to do something again? When are we going to tour.'

Murat took up the gauntlet. 'Rab wants to wait until the audience is begging for you.'

'They're begging already. We've had five top-ten hits in a row. What does he want? Another five? Ten? Fifteen?'

'Everything is under control. Rab has big plans for you.'

'See?' Kenny added.

'I don't doubt it. I just wish he'd let us in on them more often.'

'Come on, Murat. You must have a clue. What's next?' Kenny offered his most winsome grin.

'My lips are shut.'

'*Sealed*, Murat. And whose side are you on anyway?'

'Everybody's.'

Damon glowered in triumph and shook his head. ''Fraid it's not possible. Come on, Murat. Spill the beans.'

'Please, Murat,' Kenny pleaded.

'OK. But not a word about who told you.'

'Naturally,' said Damon. He rested his elbows on the table. 'Go on then. We're all ears.'

'Rab thinks –'

'Yes?'

'He thinks you can reach more people with a film.'

Kenny gulped. 'What? You mean like a proper movie, not just video?'

'It stands to reason, Kenny.' The cogs began to whir behind Damon's eyes. 'Our video's are never off MTV and all those other pop video channels. They made us what we are. A film? It's just a natural progression.'

Kenny got the message. 'And people who are desperate to see us live but can't –'

Damon nodded furiously. 'Will pay to see a movie.'

'Bingo!' said Murat.

★

The top table was laden down with food, wine and celebrities. Cary was seated on the right of the speaker, an honoured guest at a charity dinner. This was one part of celebrity that he actively enjoyed. Not the part that meant him having to present a public face – that was becoming increasingly tiresome – but simply having the opportunity to make a difference merely by being present; to do good in the world. Mitch called it his Lady Di complex. Well, fuck Mitch.

Once the dinner was over he would be obliged to rub shoulders with the paying guests, sign autographs, have his picture taken, all that jazz. It came with the territory and that was OK. He was more than happy to do it in these circumstances, helping those who couldn't help themselves. It wasn't a chore, it was a pleasure.

The surprise of the evening had come earlier at the reception. Pre-dinner drinks and polite chit-chat had been interrupted by a voice from his past.

'Why, if it isn't old Nobby! Nobby Clarke!'

The booming voice had been accompanied by a clap on the back that was so forceful Cary almost tipped his drink over his conversation partner. The voice was unmistakable and brought with it such powerful memories that Cary was suddenly transported back to his old senior school soccer pitch.

Large as life and twice as handsome, Dean 'Robbo' Robinson now stood alongside Cary. Six foot one of stocky masculinity topped off with a Latin complexion. The broken nose, the shaved head, the scar that cut through his right eyebrow and those small, sticky-out ears should not have added up to drop-dead handsome but somehow they did. The sports hero of the sixth form had matured into a hunk to die for.

Cary had been privy to some of the changes, albeit at a distance, of course. He had read the sports pages, checked out the photos of Robbo in action. Now after a meteoric rise through the divisions he was playing soccer for one of the big London clubs. A tabloid favourite, Robbo's antics on and off the field would put even Gazza to shame.

'No one has called me Nobby in years,' Cary replied as they shook hands. 'Do people still call you Barley Water?'

'If they did I'd smack 'em!'

'You've not changed much then?'

Both men cracked out laughing.

'It's great to see you, Cary,' Robbo said. 'I've been planning to contact you for ages. Then my agent told me you'd be here so . . .' Robbo grinned from ear to ear. 'We're the only two lads who really made the grade from Oaklands, aren't we? Both of us rich and famous!'

'Yeah. Wonder how old Springfield feels about that.'

'Oh, aye. Mr Springfield. I'd forgotten about him. He always said I'd be dead famous one day.'

'No, I think he said 'dead and infamous' – as in serial killer or international terrorist.'

'That guy was such an arsehole. I bet he's sick as a parrot with the way things have turned out.'

Cary raised his glass. 'I'll drink to that. Cheers.'

'Cheers.' Robbo lowered the pint glass from his mouth, emptied. 'Piss call,' he said. 'See you later.'

'Hope so.'

'Know so. My seat is next to yours on the top table.'

All the way through dinner, Cary's mind kept wandering to a cutting he had on his pin board at home, a cutting carefully taken from the centre pages of a Sunday tabloid some months back. It was of Robbo in the shower after a training session. His hair had been longer then and the water had transformed it into a mass of tight little curls. Hairy buttocks were proudly displayed with just a hint of pubic hair on show as he twisted his trim waist in order to look directly into camera. Full of himself. And that smile was on his face, the same big, laddish grin that now captivated Cary as they talked on and on.

'How come we didn't hang around together back then?' Robbo finally asked.

'Is that the beer talking?'

'Nah. I'm serious.'

'I was the latecomer,' Cary reasoned. 'I didn't come to Oaklands till the start of the sixth year. You were well established, everybody liked you. I was the outsider, I doubt you'd even remember me if I hadn't played soccer.'

'You were good.'

'Maybe.' Cary smiled. 'But I was out of your league in more ways than one.'

Robbo swallowed a burp. 'When all this is over' – he indicated the banqueting hall – 'you fancy going on to a club?'

'Sure. Why not?'

'What about your entourage?'

'What entourage? Don't have one. I like to travel light.'

'Just checking,' Robbo said as he took another swig from his pint glass.

'Just a word of warning.'

'Yeah?' Robbo's ears pricked up.

'If you tell anyone my nickname was Nobby, you *will* be dead and infamous. It's taken me this long to get the paparazzi to spell my name right.'

'Trust me,' Robbo said with a wink. 'I can keep a secret, Nobby lad.'

Having done their duty, they jumped in a taxi and sped off to the club. Not any old club, a private members club catering to a very select crowd. And off the beaten track – they wouldn't get hassled there, Robbo assured Cary. They were seated in a private booth and got down to some serious catching up.

Robbo sank another pint. He could drink like a fish (but to no noticeable effect) and was good company. He told the funniest stories and was not afraid to laugh loudest. When it finally seemed like it was time to be making a move homewards he became suddenly thoughtful.

'Don't you ever feel lonely?' It was a direct question that deserved a direct answer.

'Sometimes. Maybe often.'

'They say it's tough at the top and they're right. I don't know who I can trust these days. Everyone seems to want to be my friend.' Robbo shook his head as if to shake the feeling. 'But you've got the other guys in the band.'

Cary thought about that. He considered carefully before he replied. 'You know, Robbo, we – the band – we're more like family than friends. It's like, I love them like brothers. Which means, I guess that I love them some of the time and at other times they annoy the hell out of me.'

'I'd settle for a brother.' Robbo lowered his eyes and finished his pint.

'Time to go?'

Cary and Robbo made their way to the front door of the club. The fresh air hit them both like a sledge hammer.

'Shall I hail a taxi?' Cary asked

'Mind if we walk a bit?'

It had been raining, the streets were shiny wet. They walked along the empty street in silence.

'I need a piss,' was all Robbo said as he made a sharp right turn and disappeared down an alleyway.

Cary waited. He didn't like it. He felt alone, vulnerable. There was no one to be seen and only the distant sound of a police siren to be heard. Street lights dazzled the wet pavement. Cary shivered. Moments later he heard Robbo's voice bleating.

'Cary, Cary lad, come here. I need you, mate.'

It was with some trepidation that Cary turned the corner and entered the dark alley. Light from a street lamp barely managed to illuminate the scene. Robbo was standing, his head resting against a red brick wall, his hands hanging limply by his side.

'I've got to piss, Cary.'

'Yeah, so?'

'I can't get my fly open. It's stuck. Be a pal, eh?'

'You want me to unzip you?'

'Yeah.'

'Will you want me to get your cock out and hold it for you as well?'

Robbo grinned. 'Would you, Cary? That'd be great.'

Cary couldn't believe his ears and didn't move.

'*Please*, Cary. I'm going to piss in my pants!'

Cary hesitated briefly and then complied. He pulled the zip past Robbo's shirt-tail, foraged around in his Y-fronts, imagining the whole time that at any moment a stream of drunken revellers would pile down that same alley. Fortunately, they weren't disturbed.

As Cary's fingers first touched tubular flesh Robbo grunted his appreciation. Cary's sweaty palm wrapped around the considerable girth of Robbo's dick, filling his fist with its corpulence. A wave of disbelief and excitement swept over Cary and he suddenly felt woozy himself. Wrestling the mammoth object free from the folds of cloth, it was unmistakably semi-erect.

Robbo had a tough time peeing, especially on account of the transformation from uncooked sausage into rod of iron. Fingers straining now to meet around its girth, Cary aimed it as best he could but it stoutly refused to point towards the ground. Still, Robbo groaned in gratitude.

'Thanks, pal. What a pal.'

Finally, shaking the last drips from his foreskin, Cary somehow managed to poke the thing back inside and zip Robbo back up. His heart was beating like a hammer; he now knew the true meaning of 'weak at the knees'. Resisting the overwhelming desire to initiate some cock play had zapped all his strength. What *was* going on?

Up close now, Robbo grinned a beery grin. He placed a huge hand firmly on Cary's shoulder. It was as if he had read Cary's thoughts.

'Do I have to spell it out?' His voice trailed off as his eyes misted over.

Cary's voice cracked. 'I think so, Robbo.'

Thick fingers crept up Cary's inner thigh and, discovering the stiffness, Robbo sighed heavily. Without a word spoken he took Cary's hand and placed it upon his own swollen mound.

Cary exhaled slowly. He watched his hot breath emerge in the form of a white stream that dissolved into the cold night air.

'This isn't easy for me. Hell, I have a rough, tough image to protect.'

'You can be yourself with me, Robbo. I'm not going to betray you. We've both got too much to lose.'

Robbo smiled, reassured. 'Will you come with me, Cary? I need you to come with me.'

Their eyes locked. Robbo's voice was rich with meaning. The pulsing in Cary's pants was matched by a hammering in his ears.

'Come with you where?'

Fifteen feet into the alley there was a door in the wall. As Robbo pressed against it, it swung open. Hand in hand they passed through the doorway and into the shelter of a walled garden. Arms around each other they stumbled several feet towards the trunk of a chestnut tree. Robbo supported himself against it and faced Cary, his hot breath stroking Cary's face whilst Cary trembled in anticipation.

The night air seemed to have cleared the cobwebs away; every sense was heightened to Cary. He could smell the damp earth, dead leaves, creosote; he could feel the blood pump through his veins, his heart beating against his chest; he felt he could measure the seconds as they ticked slowly by.

Robbo hesitated. Cary cupped Robbo's bulge and he let out a tortured groan. His heavy hands clasped Cary's shoulders and pressed him down on to his knees. Cary grappled once more with Robbo's fly, desperate now to taste his fat-headed manhood. And, pulling the huge organ from its hole, he sank his mouth upon it up to the tonsils. It tasted strongly of piss and beer and precome and he luxuriated in the rich mix of flavours.

'Oh . . .' Robbo said with a sigh. It was all he managed to say.

Cary thought about this big daddy of a dick. Bigger than Gareth's, the trainer at the Manor. Thicker. Much thicker. It took a considerable act of will to prise himself off it and flip Robbo around but Cary managed it. Robbo stood, disorientated, gasping. Cary unbuckled Robbo's belt from behind.

'Drop your trousers, Robbo. I gotta fuck you. You understand? It's got to be,' Cary whispered intensely, piercing the damp air.

Robbo didn't argue but did as he was told, bracing himself against the tree. To his shock and surprise it wasn't Cary's dick but his tongue that urgently worked its way into his crack. The sensation was exquisite. Cary squatted down and, as his expert tongue worked its magic, he couldn't help picturing in his mind's eye the sumptuous arse he saw each and every day on his pin board. He could hardly believe he was actually tasting it, biting it, loving it. Robbo could barely believe it either, this tongue reaching parts no other tongue had ever reached. He felt intoxicated but not from the beer.

Cary stood with difficulty and snickered as he rubbed the cramp from the back of his legs. Robbo waited expectantly until he heard Cary tear a cellophane wrapper. The next moment, lubricant was lovingly teased against his receptive sphincter.

Robbo looked over his shoulder. 'I don't have much experience at this sort of thing, Cary. Please, bear it in mind.'

'That makes two of us, Robbo. I'm something of a novice at this myself. Looks like we're going to educate each other.'

'I wouldn't let just anybody fuck me.'

'I wouldn't fuck just anybody.'

'You honour me.'

'The pleasure is all mine.'

'Not all.'

'Hopefully not.' Cary positioned his cockhead up against Robbo's anus and felt his buttocks tighten. 'This might hurt a little bit, Robbo, but just try to relax. Take a deep breath and relax.' And tentatively, Cary eased his way into Robbo's puckered hole.

Robbo gasped as Cary breached the entrance to his cavern and, after the initial pain of penetration, came an intense and welcome feeling of submission.

'That's the worst over with,' Cary whispered. 'I'm inside you now. Relax and enjoy the feeling.'

His smooth, naked thighs clapped against the back of Robbo's bare legs as he began to judder and thrust ever deeper into him. It felt good to be the fucker not the fucked for a change. They seemed to fit together so well, nice and tight. Cary reached around to grasp Robbo's hardness and began to jerk it in time with his thrusts.

'Fine big cock you've got there, Robbo. Make it come for me. Make it come.'

Robbo was gone, overwhelmed by the intensity of his lust, lost to the world. He didn't want to think, he wanted to enjoy. He wanted to give himself over as Cary fucked him like a bull. No finesse, just a desperate need for release. All those nights, all those long nights he had yanked on his pud thinking of Cary. Here was his wank fantasy come true. And now he was about to blow.

'I'm gonna come, Cary. I'm gonna . . .'

Cary hunched full over him. Robbo thought his legs would give way under Cary's weight but he somehow managed to hold his ground as Cary cupped his free hand to catch the jism that gushed forth. Without missing a stroke, he raised the cup to Robbo's lips and forced him to drink deep; forced him to suck and lick the last traces of his own come from Cary's sticky fingers.

Cary groaned. 'Oh, yes. Taste good? Taste fresh? Now I'm going to give you mine in return!'

And with this he pulled out, tore off the condom and shot load upon delicious load of thick man-juice over Robbo's bare buttocks. Spasming and gasping, on and on. Finally, quaking on unsteady feet, he hugged Robbo tight from behind, pouring a wealth of tender lip kisses over his ears, neck and collar. 'Boy. Oh, boy. Oh, boy,' was all he could manage to say.

'Does this mean we're brothers now?' Robbo finally asked.

'Yeah. I guess so. Some people have blood brothers. You and me? We go one better, we're spunk brothers!'

'Do you want to stay the night?'

'As long as it's not too far.'

Robbo nodded his head towards the house at the end of the garden. 'Apartment on the second floor. How did you think I knew about this place?'

Ten

Amidst a blaze of publicity the album went triple platinum. But by this point the band were already into their next big project. The following eight months at least would be taken up with the making of *Bigfun – The Movie*. Having been given the opportunity to make their big screen debut the boys had chosen a light-hearted piece of alternative comedy, tailored especially for them.

The development of the project as a whole did not run without hiccups. Kenny wasn't happy with the rough script. 'I never get to speak,' he complained on more than one occasion. Damon tried pointing out that his value might be on the decorative, rather than the acting, front. Kenny would have punched him had Cassie not stepped in between them at just the appropriate moment. Re-writes were suggested as a compromise.

Mitch complained about the title. He proposed an alternative, that they call the film *Cary On Up My Back Passage* and that Damon should get the Kenneth Williams role. Damon threatened to get his revenge when Mitch least expected it and Cary simply made the counter suggestion that it should be a silent movie with Mitch in the lead.

Cary was dissatisfied with the lack of a love interest. Sure there were any number of young women throwing themselves at the band in the film but the band members remained aloof. Mitch suggested that he should have a wild fuck scene with Alec Brewster but Cary pointed out that he meant on camera, not off.

Damon wanted only to keep everyone happy and felt that the best way to achieve that was to wind them up in much the same way as always.

By this point in time the band were so hot that the limited budget did not, in turn, limit the involvement of any number of guest stars. Everyone, it seemed, wanted to hitch a ride on the Bigfun bandwagon. When interviewed prior to filming, during the album hullabaloo, Mitch was asked who he most wanted to act with. Without hesitation he had answered: Alec Brewster. Within days of the story appearing in print, Brewster's agent was on the phone offering the actor's services.

Like the rest of the gay community, Mitch had eagerly awaited the release of the psychological thriller that had promised Alec Brewster's full frontal debut. Indeed, it turned out to be the film's only selling point. *Kiss of Death* lived up to its name: a thriller that didn't thrill, an epic flop at the box office. In an incredibly patchy career it was just one more Brewster dud, soon forgotten come the next hit action role. However, it did manage to make a profit when transferred to video, largely because the audience had access to freeze frame. Alec Brewster's cock had flashed by in mere seconds of screen time but on video one could enjoy it at length. Length being the appropriate word. Mitch couldn't believe his luck when he heard of Brewster's interest. At last he would have the opportunity to check out his hero, up close and personal.

In the event, Brewster did not disappoint. He was even more stunning in the flesh than he was on screen, if that could be possible. Charisma dripped from every pore. His dark Italian ancestry was self-evident. A hirsute hunk of brown eyes, olive skin, slicked-back, black hair and mighty muscle. Mitch was dripping in his pants before they had even finished shaking hands.

'Hiya, Mitch!'

'You know my name?'

'Who doesn't. I'm a big fan of yours.'

'That's my line!' Mitch actually blushed. 'But you're a star.'

'Guess that makes us about even.' Alec smiled his movie screen smile. 'I have all your CDs.'

Mitch feared that his knees would buckle under him. 'And I've seen all your films.'

'All of them?' Alec crooked an eyebrow quizzically. 'Then you have my sincere condolences.'

'I'm really looking forward to working with you.'

'The feeling's mutual.' Alec gave Mitch's hand a final squeeze and it was only then that Mitch noticed he had kept hold of Alec's throughout the length of their introduction.

Over in a corner, Damon looked on amused. They made such a lovely couple. The two of them almost creaming over each other. He couldn't help but wonder who would be the first to make the move. Either way, there was an inevitability about events to come.

Alec and Mitch were to shoot their initial scenes on location. It was September at the height of an Indian summer. The weather was unusually favourable for offshore Ireland, which was just as well given that there were few other comforts to be had. Whoever had chosen the location had taken the term 'wilderness' in the script a little too literally – it was on one of the Blasket Islands off the south-western coast and miles from anywhere. They were effectively marooned for a whole week of filming. To make up for that, the surroundings were fabulous. A broad expanse of sea blending into the distant horizon. Next stop, America.

Their home was an abandoned farmhouse and outhouses, which had been roughly refurbished. It offered few comforts, save for basic plumbing, a gas stove and portable gas or battery lamps. Furnished with wooden tables, chairs and floorboards. No plaster on the walls. Just the bare essentials. Rustic stone, hewn from the countryside, had been plonked in the middle of a field.

And this was to be their base for the week. More horrific than romantic. Mitch and Alec were allotted sleeping space in the converted barn, while the film crew and caterer took over the main farm building.

That first night, Mitch and Alec took a walk down to the beach. Walking along the gravelly strand, Alec showed Mitch how to bounce flat stones across the surface of the calm sea. And so they played like two boys together. Later, back at the farm, they sneaked a spliff by the soft mellow light of one of the gas lamps; two shadows dancing on the dry stone walls like sniggering ghosts. Alec Brewster took great delight in pointing out that Mitch didn't inhale and, with a deep drag, showed him how it should be done.

'Can't believe you never smoked dope before.'

'And it's not the only thing I haven't done,' Mitch replied with a smile.

'Oh yeah. Why do I find that hard to believe?' Alec chuckled. 'What else then?'

'Wouldn't you like to know, eh?'

Setting up the two camp beds side by side, Alec laughed. 'No expense has been spared for this set-up. Wait until I tell my agent back home. What the fuck made me agree to this?'

'Chance to work with us was too good to miss,' Mitch replied, all sweetness and light. 'We'll give you some credibility.'

'In your dreams, buddy. In your dreams!'

Two men sleeping in the one big room that first night on location. They should have considered themselves lucky: the other crew members were cram-packed into two. But still it came as cold comfort to Mitch once the light was extinguished. Strong winds whistled around the outer walls of the farmhouse, and now it began to rain, the drops splashing noisily against the windows. And the floorboards creaked! He snuggled deep into his sleeping bag and prayed for sleep to come.

Ten minutes into the dark, when all grew still, the rustling began. Almost imperceptible at first. Mitch lay alongside Alec trying, initially, to work out where the sound was coming from, and then, once located, trying to work out if it really was what it sounded like. Alec had begun pulling on his dick. On and on and on the noise escalated, Alec pulling on his dick. Didn't he care that Mitch could hear him? And all the time Mitch was longing to be so much more than a silent witness. How easy it would have been to reach over and lend a hand. Ah . . . but he couldn't! He couldn't give the game away. Alec was sure to go ballistic. And worse, the game, if it was a game, would be over for good and all.

It seemed an age before Alec finally groaned and shot his load. Mitch held his breath. Alec seemed oblivious. He mopped himself up with tissues, stuffed the tissues under his pillow and, within minutes, snored contentedly whilst Mitch lay wide awake.

Sleep lasted less than the blink of an eye. A cold flannel hit Mitch like a whiplash. Alec showed no mercy.

'Get up, you lazy bastard! It's time to join the land of the living. And breakfast will be served in ten minutes.'

Mitch ambled across to the kitchen like he was on his last legs. He joined the rest of the crew at a long breakfast table, pulled up a chair and sank down.

'Are you expecting someone to bring your breakfast to you, Mitch?' Alec's voice came from the serving hatch.

'Yeah, Alec. Thanks. That would be nice,' Mitch said with a yawn.

'That would be nice!' boomed the voice of the movie star. 'Move your fat ass over here!'

The kitchen erupted in something akin to schoolboy laughter. Mitch took it on the chin.

Alec Brewster was a dream to work with by anyone's standards. A consummate professional and an all-round good guy, well liked by the crew. He had no airs or graces. But to Mitch he was something else – an idol to be worshipped and adored. He was simply in awe of Alec. It had a calming effect: Alec's humility despite his success tempering Mitch's tendency towards arrogance. And it was clear that Alec liked Mitch from the way he would often kid around with him. Humour born of affection.

The journey to the chosen location involved a ramshackle jeep trip over potholed roads fit only for horses and farm vehicles. Getting there and coming back were the most arduous parts of the day's schedule. Filming was effortless in comparison. Mitch seemed to spend most of his time lounging about, waiting to be called for shooting. Still, it allowed him plenty of time to bask in the glow of Alec's charisma whilst he regaled the crew with his insider gossip; Hollywood anecdotes, the like of which would never see print. Not without a major libel suit.

Returning after nightfall, brought an exhausted sleep but Mitch woke in the small hours with a sack full of come and a desperate need for relief. On bare feet, he padded quietly along the dark passageway to the toilet which was located out in the yard. Inside, the light had been left on and the glare made his weary eyes smart. He stumbled sleepily to the stall and, pushing against the door, was met by an even greater shock. Resting back astride the bowl was Alec Brewster. Legs apart, he cupped his balls in one meaty hand whilst the other leisurely stroked his thick shaft. Their eyes locked. Mitch was wide awake.

Alec didn't flinch but kept pulling on his cock. He gave Mitch a quick glance and then returned to the business in hand. On automatic, Mitch locked the door behind him and rubbed his crotch. Alec ignored him. Mitch bent forward to kiss him on the lips but was roughly pushed away.

'That's not what I want,' Alec said, reaching forward to tug on the flesh poking out of Mitch's shorts. 'That is!'

Mitch dropped his pants around his ankles as Alec parted his lips to douse a big glob of spit expertly on to the fat head of his flushed penis. Standing fully erect Mitch gripped his dick and began to jerk in time with Alec's strokes.

Alec Brewster's cock had long been admired. His big balls had dropped with a resounding clang long before the rest of his classmates, while the rest of his body sprouted coarse black hair all over and grew increasingly hard and muscular. Even soft his knob and dog's bollocks were mammoth, but stiff and full they were awesome. Glassy eyed, in a dreamlike trance, he fixed on Mitch's sturdy prick and yanked, urgently, on his own. Pearls of precome doused the tip of Mitch's cockhead. Meanwhile, Alec was oozing a healthy wad of his own natural lubricant. Dripping with saliva now, Alec's thick fingers found his own hole and entered in, jerking up inside himself as his other hand jerked down.

Mitch was enthralled by this awesome sight. Here before him, Alec Brewster, film star, was lost in wanking himself senseless. Performing. Loving the fact that Mitch was watching him, and turned on by Mitch being turned on by him. And why not, he had absolutely nothing to be ashamed of. Mitch's breath grew heavy and he could feel the tickle deep in his groin, the tickle that would herald his orgasm.

Suddenly, face contorting, Alec lifted his eyes directly to Mitch's and shot his first spurt, manfully over his left shoulder, hitting the wall. Smirking with self-satisfaction, his cock popped like a soda fountain; up and over his chest in a seemingly endless stream. Then Mitch felt his own gyp surge up and out, like a rocket from its launch pad, crash-landing on Alec's cheek, on his throat, on his taut, furry belly, over his sweaty balls and chunky hands. He offered Mitch a big grin but no words were spoken. Squeezing out the last clot of his own sperm he stood and plonked a big clumsy kiss on Mitch's mouth. The lustful and enthusiastic response amused Alec no end. Then it was back to their room and separate beds.

Next morning, it was something of a relief for Mitch to find himself outdoors once again. The weather was warm and, as the day progressed, the sun grew ever hotter. Left alone with his thoughts, he withdrew into silence, content to watch the rest of the crew set up the shots and to observe Alec at a distance. As the time passed, his eyes grew heavy through lack of sleep.

Suzanne, the make-up artist, took a long, lingering look in Mitch's direction.

'What you looking at, Suzy?'

'You. I'm looking at you.' She shook her head. 'You look worn out, Mitch. Is the going too tough for you?'

'I'm not getting enough sleep, Suzz,' he replied with a yawn.

'We can't have that!' she said. 'I'm a make-up artist, not a bloody miracle worker.'

Laughter broke out once again. Alec laughed loudest.

Damn! thought Mitch. He looks like a million dollars and I look like a fucking wreck. There's no justice.

Then Alec smiled at him, only for him, and suddenly everything seemed OK.

A short while later, during a break from filming, Alec beckoned Mitch to follow him down the beach. Once out of earshot of the rest of the crew, Alec reached deep into the pocket of his faded jeans and produced a sachet of white powder which he discreetly showed to Mitch. He then took out a small silver spoon and dipped it into the sachet. He held it out in Mitch's direction and smiled.

'You say you're tired? I have exactly the thing you need.'

The film received an Easter release to a fanfare of publicity and a spectacular premiere in one of the big West End cinemas. Rab had spared no expense to make this an occasion to remember. Red carpets, stretch limousines and batteries of floodlights. It was just like Oscar night. The run-up to the event had been accompanied by newspaper articles on the making of the movie, interviews with cast members and glossy photo spreads in the fashion magazines. Cassie has organised a competition through the fan club so that at least one third of the audience was made up of partisan viewers. The effect was not lost on the ears of the journalists present.

The reviews would be largely favourable; comparisons with the Beatles' *Help!* were inevitable. It was short on plot but high on comedy and music. No one was going to win an Oscar on the strength of their performance but it did the job; it was quality entertainment. And the fans loved it. They only stopped screaming when the house lights went up and it was announced that Bigfun had already left the auditorium.

★

The reception, at a large London nightclub, was an exercise in self-congratulation. And a chance for the liggers to mingle with the stars and bask in reflected glory. It seemed like everyone that was anyone, or thought that they were someone, was there. Current media luvvies mixed with jaded rock stars, while rake-thin supermodels hobnobbed with the financial string-pullers from the City. Mitch was in his element.

Kenny leant back against the bar as Cassie and Damon appeared at his shoulder. Cassie gave him a big kiss on the cheek leaving a bright red smear of lipstick. 'See, that wasn't so painful, now was it?'

'Not for you, maybe. I was so nervous that my bladder will never be the same. I was sat there with my legs crossed all the way through the bloody thing and there wasn't enough leg room.'

'Oh, doesn't he go on,' said Damon, with a pained expression. 'I suppose it would be too much to expect you to be pleased?'

Cassie slipped an arm around Kenny's waist and gave him a squeeze. 'You really were very good, you know.'

'He was, wasn't he,' said Damon. 'Makes you wonder what all the fuss was about when he read the script.'

'A man has to stand up for himself in this life. If it had been left up to you, I'd have played the third extra on the right.'

Damon leant forward and planted a kiss on the unsmeared cheek. 'Oh, you underestimate me, Kenny. If it had been up to me you would have been the thirteenth from the right.'

Gayle made a less than spectacular entrance through one of the side doors. She had been at the party at least fifteen minutes before anyone recognised who she was. This was mainly due to the fact that her appearance had changed so drastically. Her unaffected, no-nonsense dress sense had been replaced by designer creations that made her look like she had rummaged through Madonna's rag-bag and failed to find a bargain. It was clear the white-lace get-up and Pre-Raphaelite hairdo were supposed to make her appear the height of teen fashion but at first glance she looked more like Glinda, the good witch from *The Wizard of Oz*.

As Damon crossed the floor towards her, the atmosphere was charged with embarrassment on both sides. He hardly knew how to behave or what to say. Just be yourself, Damon, he thought to himself, and opened his arms to give her a big hug.

'Does this mean the prodigal has returned to the fold?'

'I think not, Damon, my love. Just an invited guest. Forgiveness can only come from God.' She threw a glance in Rab's direction. Rab, in turn, seemed to be studiously ignoring her presence. 'Though it has to be said, I'm as surprised to be here as you clearly are to see me. I didn't expect to get a personal invitation to the movie launch but I was hardly about to turn down the opportunity.'

'Cary says you're working for *Grrrl!*?'

'He knows?' She paused, surprised. 'I'm actually the assistant editor.'

'Yes, he keeps up with all the media developments. A side effect of him checking they get his name right, I think.' It was Damon's turn to pause. 'We've been half expecting an exposé of the band – "The Woman Behind Bigfun" – that kind of thing?'

'Kiss and tell? Give me some credit, Damon. I have to think of my reputation too. I was the one who got dropped from a great height.'

'The order of the boot.'

'With steel toe-caps, if I remember correctly.'

'Just so long as you know that it was nothing to do with us.'

'Still, you didn't do too badly without me.'

Damon winced, almost imperceptibly. 'You sound almost disappointed.'

'I don't begrudge you anything, Damon. You deserve every success.'

'C'mon, come and talk to Kenny. He's been dying to see you. I think he just wasn't sure how you'd react if he got in touch.'

Damon took Gayle by the elbow and led her across the room. 'Oh, and you'll have the great privilege of meeting the sweetest girl in all the world.' As they approached, Cassie smiled and

Kenny blushed and gave a little wave. Just then, Mitch sped by them.

'Hi, Gayle. Uh, bye, Gayle.' And with that Mitch disappeared out of the door in hot pursuit of Alec Brewster.

'Take no notice, Gayle. He doesn't have time to talk to anybody these days except his *hero*.'

As always, Murat was keeping a watchful eye on proceedings. He didn't miss much. He didn't miss the pained expression on Rab's face as Mitch and Alec made their exit; he didn't miss the hurt look in Rab's eyes or the way he half turned away and took a stiff drink from his whisky glass.

If he could have made things better he would have, but what was there to do or say? Rab had chosen not to discuss the details of his relationship with Mitch, neither good nor bad. Of course Murat knew they had a relationship of sorts – he had been the one to drive them home often enough – but everything else was left to conjecture. Even so, Murat accurately read the signs, noted Rab's mood swings and felt the friction in the air as Mitch became more and more wilful, but still he resisted the urge to confront his boss and, in doing so, sacrificed the possibility now to console him.

Up on the roof, Mitch and Alec shared a farewell snort. Mitch pressed his middle finger up against his tingling nostril and rubbed it gently as the surge of adrenalin rushed through his veins. He looked out over the twinkling London skyline, threw back his head, and laughed out loud.

'I'm on top of the world, Alec.'

'And so you should be, buddy. You're a big star now. You're a success.'

'You really think so?'

'Man, I know so. When the reviews come in you're going to be singled out for praise, no doubt about it.' Alec brought a match to the tip of his cigarette. 'Seeing you up there on the big screen' – he sucked the nicotine into his lungs – 'you just set it alight.'

'Honestly?'

'When the camera loves you it loves you. And believe me, the camera loves you.'

'I couldn't have done it without you, Alec. Not without your advice and all. I want you to know how grateful I am. Truly, truly grateful.'

'Enough already!'

'But it's true. I'm going to miss you, buddy.'

'That's my line!'

'I mean it. I'm really going to miss you.'

'You don't have to miss me, Mitch.'

'Eh?'

'You could love me.'

'And what about your wife and kids?'

'In the words of the immortal bard; "Ah, there's the rub."'

'Exactly.'

'But if you ever think of packing in this pop thing and giving Hollywood a shot –'

'You really think I'm good enough?'

'I'm sure my agent would be only too happy to represent you.'

'I don't know, Alec . . .'

'Face it. You're the one people will want to watch on that screen up there. The other guys? They're OK, but you? You've got what it takes to be bigger than the other three put together. Don't squander that talent, Mitch. Celebrate it!'

'I'm part of a team. I can't just go do my own thing.'

'Why the hell not? You think they wouldn't if they had the choice? Thing is: they don't, you do.' Alec passed the half smoked cigarette to Mitch. 'I could ask my agent to put out feelers for you? How about it?'

'I don't know, Alec. It's all happening too fast. I need to think about it.'

'Fine. Fine. Just don't leave it too long. Strike while the iron is hot, that's my motto.' Alec stepped in close and gently wriggled his warm, wet tongue in Mitch's ear. 'And you, boy? You're hotter than hot. Let me hose you down. What do you say? One last time for old times' sake . . .'

Eleven

Monday morning and the spectacular view from Gayle's office was overshadowed by one single ominous presence. Des Foster, *Grrrl!*'s own investigative reporter, paced to and fro before the picture windows and consulted his notepad.

'Let me get this straight,' Foster grunted, licking the tip of his pencil with his furry tongue like a cartoon private detective. 'You want me to dig up as much dirt on the lads from Bigfun as I can find?' His stomach rumbled and churned, his temples throbbed. He really should have resisted that second bottle of gut-rot with the curry last night.

Gayle nodded slowly, completely self-possessed. 'That's correct. Make sure you leave no stone unturned.' She had to be in control, in control like the thermostat on a fridge-freezer. It was the only way she could mask her revulsion in the face of this sleazeball. He looked like an unmade bed crossed with a burst mattress. 'Of course, if you find there isn't any dirt to dish . . .'

Foster tapped the bridge of his nose with a podgy, nicotine-stained finger. 'We all have our little secrets, Gayle. Don't we?'

Gayle blushed, then shuddered. Having him use her first name made her stomach turn, implying, as it did, an intimacy that didn't exist. And just what did he mean by using the royal 'we'?

Foster continued. 'They must have done things in the past

that they are ashamed of, things they wouldn't want the world and his wife to know about. Just like you and me, eh? No one is immune, Gayle. No one.'

She shrugged off the implication. 'How long will it take?'

'How long is a piece of string? Consider this an ongoing project. You'll be the first to know when I turn something up.'

'I should hope so, you're being paid enough.' And with that, Gayle turned her attention towards the papers on her desk. Minutes passed before she again looked up into Des Foster's blood-shot eyes.

'Are you still here?' she snapped.

'We've finished?' Foster looked bemused.

'Do you need it in writing?'

'No.'

'Then do your job and let me do mine. Get on with it!'

He slunk towards the exit. Foster knew the bitch hated him. Big fucking deal, that was her privilege. He didn't give a shit as long as he got paid.

'And don't forget to close the door behind you.'

Gayle didn't lift her eyes again until she was sure she was alone. Then she reached into the desk drawer and retrieved a box of rainbow tissues. Delicate fingers pressed one tissue after another to her face as she cried like a baby.

What had come over her? She didn't love Mitch, she had never been in love with Mitch. In fact, she wasn't sure if she had ever even liked him. But he didn't deserve to be hounded and robbed of his moment in the sun. How had she become embroiled in this whole mess? She had tried to leave the past behind her but now it felt as if it was still exerting control and straining at the leash. A fresh clutch of sobs caught in her throat; she wasn't to blame, she told herself. She wasn't to blame.

After all, this attempt at collective character assassination was not her idea. It was on orders from above. Though why Clive Foxx should take such a personal interest was beyond her. And to use Dreary Des? Des Foster might call himself an investigative journalist but was, in reality, little more than an expert muck-raker. Clive Foxx had specifically insisted she use him. Things seemed to be spiralling out of control and it seemed as if she couldn't do a damn thing to stop it.

Cary spent Saturday night through till the late Sunday afternoon with Jayne, Jo and their two cats, Byron and Shelley. It was fast becoming a tradition. He considered their three-up-three-down in Barnes as a little piece of heaven; a haven from media machinations and the never-ending round of phone calls.

Byron curled up in Cary's lap as he reclined in a big comfy chair. Stuffed full of Jo's excellent home cooking, his eyelids were drooping, his head was nodding. Jayne and Jo cuddled up on the sofa watching the *EastEnders* omnibus. Meanwhile, Shelley was on the prowl.

Jayne aimed the remote control at the screen as the final credits rolled and looked over at Cary as the screen returned to blank. 'Wake up, granddad!' she exclaimed.

'Leave him,' Jo chided her. 'He needs his beauty sleep.'

'That's true. There can't be many people who need it more.'

Cary reached behind his head and hurled a cushion in their general direction. 'Get stuffed!' he cried but missed his target completely and only managed to startle poor Shelley who leapt behind the TV console and hissed like a viper. Byron, in contrast, merely raised his head, yawned and stretched before returning to slumber.

'See the thanks we get for doing our Good Samaritan act?' Jo turned to Jayne. 'Who else would tolerate such an anti-social bugger?'

'He just sits there, making the place look untidy. And as for the snoring?'

'Just like a foghorn.'

'You love me really.' Cary gave a sleepy smile. 'I bring a touch of drama into your dull suburban existence.'

'You should be so lucky.'

'Cue Kylie.'

'Do you still want us to keep our ears open about property in the area?'

'Sure do.'

'Good. Then you can fall asleep in front of your own TV to your heart's content without offending the likes of us,' said Jo.

'This is suburbia after all, as you so rightly pointed out. Won't you feel somewhat cut off though?' asked Jayne.

'I want to settle down. I want a place to call home.'

'Is that all? Why not buy a pad in Chelsea?'

'And a mansion in Essex?'

'I want what you've got.'

'What? Two cats, a mortgage and rising damp?'

'No. A life. Somewhere safe to hide or hibernate. Someone to come home to.'

'Are you still seeing that footballer?'

'Now and then. We're just friends really. He's got his own stuff to work through.'

'And you?'

Cary frowned. 'I'm tired of pretending to be something I'm not.'

Jayne let out a long, slow whistle. 'That's a big mouthful.'

'Are we still talking about my footballer?' Cary planted his tongue firmly in his cheek.

'Shame on you!' Jayne and Jo chorused together.

'OK, so what if it sounds dumb? It's the truth. Like I said, I want what you've got. You two? You're the perfect role models.'

'Don't you need to find the right guy first?' Jo asked pointedly.

'Maybe I have found him. Maybe he just doesn't realise it yet. At any rate, I can persevere a while longer.'

'Are you keeping some big juicy secret from us, Cary?' Jayne sat forward in her seat.

Jo leant forward to join her. 'Do tell!'

'Believe me, girls, when there's something worth telling, you'll be the first to know.'

'But not until.' Jo heaved a sigh of resignation.

'No.' Cary was adamant.

'So . . .' Jayne smiled secretly to herself.

'Yes?' Cary was now the curious one.

Jayne cast him a knowing smile before making her suggestion: 'Oh! Just go back to sleep!'

The tinted windows of the limousine shut out the heat and glare of the sun. Up front, Murat knew better than to make any comment. Even the air conditioning worked silently. Just as well, Rab was not in the mood to be disturbed. He had had enough. Enough of everything but sleep. He was dog tired; brooding, full of thoughts – and all concerning Mitch – as he and Murat headed for the only private members' club Rab was ever likely to join. Of course no fees were ever exchanged and no contract signed; membership was at the discretion of the organiser. And his criteria for membership were much more pragmatic. It had been an age since they last went in this particular direction but Murat knew his way like a homing pigeon. It was somehow instinctive.

Stutz Wagner threw these elaborate themed parties every third Friday in the month; infamous parties, men only. One had to belong to the inner circle to get an invitation and, as a close personal friend, Rab's invitation was always open. Each event promised the heaving delights of wall to wall men: well-built, well-hung muscle queens. Stutz was nothing if not superficial. If you didn't fit the narrow physical criteria you didn't have a hope of getting past the doormen.

Their host lived closer to Hove than Brighton, in what he considered the posh part, in an Edwardian house overlooking the coast, a house befitting his status in the gay world: solid and stately. Once through the gates and up the gravel drive it was like a sanctuary of serenity embraced, as it was, by a ring of trees and green foliage. The party was out the back. Rab and Murat followed the sound of chatter and laughter to be met by the sight of what looked like an authentic American Beer Bust. Bears of every variety swarmed around the lawn and patio, in sleeveless plaid shirts, cut-off jeans and the like. A gathering of intimates. So what exactly was Rab doing there?

The weather was glorious; it was an unusually hot day in early May. Stutz stood in front of a barbecue grill in a butcher's apron, denim shorts and bare feet, his naked shoulders and arms shimmering brown with oil and sweat. His shaved head and handlebar moustache made him look every inch the circus strong man. He was wielding a long fork, prodding at the sizzling sausages, burgers, chicken. The smell wafted through the dry air. Rab's mouth began to water.

Stutz caught sight of them and raised an open palm in greeting. 'Rab! Murat! You made it! Great to see you. Great to see you!' He looked up into the clear blue sky. 'How's this for holiday weather?' he asked and without waiting for an answer, 'You didn't forget how to find us?'

'How could we forget?' Rab answered with a shy smile, feeling mildly ashamed for his recent absence, he then raised his hands in a gesture of protest. 'OK, OK, so it's been a while, I admit!'

Murat was casting an appreciative eye over the crowd. Stutz caught his stare.

'You won't know many of these people? Ah, yes, the faces change but the bodies remain the same, thankfully.' He winked. 'But don't worry, they won't bite – at least, not unless that's your thing. I'm sure you'll charm the pants off them! And talking about pants –' Stutz gave a leering grin in Murat's direction '– you both look perfect.'

Rab shrugged. Murat looked down self-consciously at his wholly appropriate attire – past his very short, beige shorts, and all the way down to cream woollen socks and brown hiking boots.

Stutz continued, 'Of course, you won't be wearing them for long, I imagine?'

Murat blushed.

'Oh, isn't he charming!' Stutz exclaimed as he slapped Murat's backside.

Handing over responsibility for the grill to some swarthy Neanderthal he called Timothy, Stutz led them into the fray. Both newcomers were systematically introduced to the tribe. Rab shook so many hands he felt like the Queen Mum on a walkabout. On this evidence one would believe Stutz had a wide circle of friends – or rather, any number of small circles. Each one formed to pass around a giant-sized spliff. Murat didn't think he had ever seen so many happy smiling faces in one space before, each generously sharing their recreational drug of choice with one another.

Timothy turned out to be a medical student from the States with an accent as thick and sweet as pecan pie. His handshake was pretty impressive too. He took Rab's hand when Stutz finally made the introduction and almost squeezed the life out of it. He looked more like a butcher than a surgeon, an image accentuated by his rough handling of the blooded steaks as he slapped them on the grill.

Meaty was the only adjective to describe Timothy, solid and substantial from his compressed neck right down to his thick toes. A gothic sun was tattooed over one bulging pec and baby nipple. Rippling, tan muscles bore the jet black shadow of stubble whilst the trim moustache on his face served to accentuate white, even teeth exposed in a smile. The bulge in his tattered shorts was a joy to behold – a fulsome curve, two distinct spheres cushioned and separated by faded denim. Rab and he spoke only briefly before Stutz led Rab away by the elbow, leaving Murat to his own devices.

'Where do you know him from?' Rab asked, curious.

'Who? Godzilla? Met him on my travels – appropriately enough in the Deep South. Invited him to stay if he was ever in England. Couldn't fix up his hospital transfer quick enough. Virtually followed me home. He may look like an animal but he's more like a big puppy, really. Been here three months now!'

'Three months?'

'Yeah.'

'*Three months!* Isn't that taking advantage somewhat?' Rab wondered out loud.

'Works both ways.'

'Eh?'

He let Rab's exclamation hang in the air and guided him over towards a rough-hewn wooden bench. Stutz parked his butt and Rab sat down beside him.

'Anyone caught your eye?'

'Plenty of time yet.'

'I'll introduce you around some more in a minute. There's a few people I'd like you to meet. One in particular,' Stutz said without elaborating.

Rab unbuttoned his shirt. 'Oh, yeah? Who? Someone from the city?'

'No . . .' Stutz answered cryptically. 'Just someone I think you'll have things in common with.'

'Fine,' Rab muttered and fell silent.

When Stutz finally broke the silence there was genuine concern in his voice. 'Mitch still acting like a bastard?'

'I love him, Stutz. I just can't get past it. I love him.'

'Ah, yes, love.' Stutz shook his head. 'He's young, Rab. He's just a young man. What can you expect?'

'I don't expect anything any more. I take what I can get.'

'So forget him!' Stutz slapped Rab's thigh. 'Have some beer and party down. This is the ideal place to forget your troubles. Isn't that why you came?'

'Guess so . . . Yeah, you're right,' Rab replied but he didn't sound convinced.

Rab's head was whizzing – more from lack of sleep than the whisky-sour in his hand – by the time Stutz looked past him over his shoulder and smiled.

'Here comes the man.'

As Rab turned his jaw went slack and dropped open but whether it was shock and surprise or simply numbness he didn't really know. It felt like a dream sequence in somebody else's movie. Walking towards him, framed in a halo of light, was none other than his old nemesis.

Neither of them spoke for what seemed an age. The man looked down at Rab, an almost melancholy cast to his face. Finally, Stutz spoke up. 'I believe you two know each other?'

'Angus. Angus Stewart.' Rab looked to Stutz. 'Sure, I know him. This is the man who wrecked my marriage.'

Again silence.

Stutz shrugged. 'I'll leave you boys to get reacquainted.'

'Hello, Rab. Long time no see.' Angus chuckled self-consciously in that all too familiar way of his. A rasping noise in his throat. Rab had never forgotten it. It had been one of the things he had loved about Angus way back when. All of a sudden it was like he was back there, feeling all the feelings he had once felt. And just as quickly, the feeling was gone.

They looked at each other for one long, hard moment. Three years and neither one had changed so very much. Angus was a little thicker around the waist, a hint of silver at the temples, but still the fine figure of a man he always was. A green polo shirt and cut-offs hugged the curvatures of his muscles. Sandals revealed perfect feet.

'Looking good. You've filled out nicely, Rab.'

'I got into weight training.'

'The extra bulk suits you. And the beard, that's filled out too.'

'How's the wife and kids?' A dumb question. Dope dumb. Searching for a safe subject and getting it completely wrong.

Angus' eyebrows furrowed. 'Fine.' He looked understandably put out.

Rab softened his voice. 'Where are they?'

'Gone to the villa in Spain for a few weeks.'

'Well, this is a turn-up for the books.' Rab looked down, concentrating on the tumbler clutched between his hands.

'I came to ask your forgiveness.'

Rab took a gulp of the amber fluid. 'I forgave you a long time ago, Angus.'

'So . . .'

'So, the wife's away and you're free to sneak over here for a little recreation.'

Angus ignored the slight. 'Can I sit down?'

'It's a free country.'

Angus sat down beside Rab and leant in so close towards him that Rab could feel the warmth of his breath on his ear.

'It's good to see you.'

'Wish I could say the same.' Rab took another slug.

'I loved you back then, Rab.'

'Yeah, so you used to say.' Rab consciously chose to change the subject. 'So what are you doing here of all places?'
'Stutz.'
'Ah!'
'Bumped into him a while back.'
'Backroom or sauna?'
Angus didn't reply.
'And he invited you?'
Angus gave a nod.
'And so you're here.'
Another nod.
'Then I guess the question is why?'
'For old times' sake?' Again that throaty chuckle. 'I suppose a fuck would be out of the question?'

Rab's pulse began to race. This was no joke. It didn't feel like a request, more like a challenge. Could he fuck Angus and walk away? And if he could, wouldn't that be one helluva personal triumph. He looked Angus straight in the eye. 'Not at all,' he replied, trying his damnedest to act casual. 'I'm game if you are.'

With no more ado, Angus followed as Rab led him across the lawn, through the French doors into an oak-panelled library, festooned with books and prints, through a second set of doors into the spacious hallway, and up the winding staircase to a guest bedroom. The walls were brilliant white, mirrors hung all around, the king-size bed draped in white. Huge windows, either side of the sloping roof, flooded the room with light, making it seem more like a greenhouse baking in the warmth of the sun. French windows led to a spacious terrace.

'Impressed?' Rab asked, as he crossed the room. He grunted, manfully, as he pushed open a sash window before wiping his brow.

'And then some,' Angus replied. 'What a fabulous house.'

'Don't think this was bought with his own money either. It's old money, one of Stutz's grandfathers. Stutz got to benefit.'

Rab removed all his clothes before turning back to face Angus, bare bollock naked. Angus blushed and lowered his eyes, then flicked them furtively to Rab's groin and away again. For his part, Angus took his time undressing. He was proud of his body, proud to reveal all.

Rab's hand reached out to cup the fullness in front of Angus' pants. 'It's been a long time since that weekend.'

'Much, much too long.' Angus leant forward and kissed him tenderly on the forehead. 'So, then, let's not waste any more time, eh? Darlin' boy.'

Huge arms reached out to enfold Rab in a man-sized embrace, but at the last moment he stepped sideways.

'What? What's happening?' Angus was taken aback.

'Weather this good should be enjoyed.' Rab turned and threw open the French windows. 'How's about doing it in the open air?' He stepped through on to the emerald green carpet of astro turf. Scatter cushions lay all around. The terrace was ringed by ornate stone railings and, taking pride of place in the centre of the space, was a king-size mattress. Ever thoughtful, Stutz had provided any number of urns, brimming with condoms and lube.

The sound of the crowd below floated upwards as Angus spun Rab around and wrapped his arms round him in a vice-like grip. Lips were crushed against lips. Rab was caught off-guard by the ferocity of Angus' passion: sucking on his face, raising his hands to clasp hold of Rab's cheeks, pressing against his mouth so hard that Rab couldn't breathe. Dropping his hands and grasping Rab's buttocks in a tight grip, Angus ground his hardness against his own.

'Oh, my man. I've missed this. I've really missed this.'

Forcing Rab back on to the mattress, Angus' hand fought to yank down his own underwear. Rab's cock pulsed against his belly as Angus tugged his shorts clear of hefty, hairy thighs then he straddled Rab's face. Taking hold of Angus' erection at the base, between thumb and forefinger, Rab slapped it against his face. Finally, as it swelled to bursting, he pounced on it. His open mouth fully engulfed the length, nose pressed up against pubes. He started to gag as Angus pressed his head down.

'You always wanted it. Could never get enough. So take it,' Angus gibed him. Rab stopped wrestling and relaxed his throat. They both savoured the moment.

Rab gasped as Angus finally pulled out.

'Just give that big thing here.' So saying, Angus took hold of Rab's manhood with his fist. One brief squeeze produced a generous measure of precome. Rab relaxed back, feeling an immense surge of pleasure as Angus sank his lips over his throbbing crown.

In his mind's eye, Rab found himself transported back to their very first fuck. He had sat astride Angus' lap as Angus had performed this very same task. Rab had been in seventh heaven. Until, that is, Angus had finished with him and bid him go back to his own bed in case the chambermaid should wake them in the morning. After sharing the warmth of his body, his own bed felt twice as cold as before. And whilst Angus was soon snoring, Rab lay wide awake wondering, what next?

Nothing next. By the morning the process of Angus distancing himself had begun in earnest. He withheld even the usual measure of friendliness like he couldn't handle the dirty deed; like he was embarrassed. And Rab, like a lovesick fool, followed him around, trying to placate Angus with a surfeit of patience and understanding. Until he finally got the message. Nothing was going to be discussed. Shortly after, Linda admitted to the affair between herself and Angus and that was an end to it.

Sometime later, Rab awoke to find himself still in Angus's arms, his body still baking in the warm sun. He rubbed his eyes, still groggy. 'What happened?'

Angus cuddled him tight. 'You fell asleep!'

'While you were sucking me? I'm really sorry. I've been exhausted lately.'

'I sure hope so. Otherwise my bedside manner is in serious need of revision!'

They both laughed. Angus kissed him.

'My breath must be rank!'

'Like perfume, Sleeping Beauty.'

'You sleep too?'

'Some. Spent some time watching you snore. You sure are a beautiful sight to behold, Rab.'

'Bullshitter.'

'It's true! Let me look at you.' Angus leant back. 'We've a lot of catching up to do.'

'Three years' worth.'

'Then let's not waste this precious time we have.'

'Why? Do you plan on leaving it another three years?'

'What do you think?' Angus asked, clasping Rab's aching member against his own, within his fist.

Rab looked directly into his eyes. Oh, at least three, he thought, but didn't really care. A fuck's a fuck. He didn't have unrealistic expectations any more, did he? Mitch couldn't have been further from his mind. He looked down and watched Angus' thumb spread a sheen of mutual precome over twin purple glands. 'Less talk, more action,' Rab replied.

'Is this a private party or can anyone join in?'

Timothy filled the doorway, naked and plainly aroused. His cock, pointing skyward, twitched with all the energy of youth. Murat's grinning face appeared over his shoulder and his hand reached around to restrain Timothy's overactive cock.

Tumbling forwards, both men fell on to the mattress beside Angus and Rab. Like a Turkish wrestler, Murat flipped Timothy over and pinned him on his back. A pause, then suddenly both big men came together in one resounding clash of lips and tongues, sucking on each other's mouths as if for a last breath.

Angus' face was a picture. Poor sap, hadn't had a clue. Didn't know that they would be disturbed by such an exhibition of lust. Though now, watching the passion with which these two brutes tore at each other he wasn't going miss out on the opportunity he had been offered. He crawled backwards, out of their way. But not so far that he couldn't have a ringside view of their expert performance.

A pulsating mass of hairy flesh and naked muscle now grappled in a heap before their very eyes. Lost in loving one another. Oblivious, for the moment, to Rab and Angus. Having wrestled him on to his back, Murat now hoisted Timothy's legs into the air. Rab leapt to bury his face deep in the crack of Timothy's furry arse, slobbering and sucking. Tim, in turn, was yanking on his power tool for all he was worth.

'Yes, you fucker, eat my fucking hole. Show me you how much you want me. Fucking eat it!'

Rab was mumbling into the cavernous cleft, 'I want you, Timothy. I fucking want you,' and continued to gorge his appetite.

'Eat my fucking shithole!' Timothy demanded. 'Say you'll never leave it lonely again!'

'Never,' gulped Rab. 'Never, sweet little shithole. Never again!'

Like a little terrier sniffing out a rabbit hole, Rab's nose was pressed up against Timothy's entrance, snuffling frantically. Timothy reclined like a lion being groomed, a big cat being serviced by its mate.

Murat couldn't hold back from the action any longer and in seconds he was down and dirty, his quivering tongue stuck firmly in Timothy's navel. Drawing a trail of saliva to erect nipples, he tweaked one with thumb and forefinger, holding the other between gritted teeth.

Rab sat back and looked over to Angus who was shaking with excitement. He could almost see Angus' heart hammering at the ribcage beneath his muscular chest.

'Come on over, Angus,' Rab gasped, indicating Tim's mighty cock.

Angus hesitated but only for a moment. He dropped on to all fours and crawled over for a closer inspection. His eyes grew wide, spellbound. Then he looked to his own, comparing and contrasting. 'A wee bit bigger . . .' he mumbled. Hesitantly, he lowered his face for an intimate examination. The smell, the taste. Tentatively, the glistening tip of his tongue poked out to probe the scarlet helmet. He grew in confidence as Timothy's big dick strained and twitched at the stimulus. A greater expanse of tongue flicked over hairy bollocks, then lapped the underside of shaft from base to tip. Emboldened, Angus' mouth swooped to consume Tim's prick clear up to the plums.

Timothy was plainly ecstatic at this turn of events. He yanked Rab up and buried his mouth on his knob, rabid lips pumping double time. Murat knelt tall alongside Timothy's open thighs, his cock held aloft over Angus' bobbing head. His thumb and forefinger continued to nip tit, the other hand reaching over to grip Angus' rock solid shaft and begin to pull. Angus moaned in gratitude and his balls responded by rising high in his low-slung pouch.

Angus was begging Timothy to come, drooling from the corners of his mouth. 'Come on, Tim, give it to me. Give me your spunk, all your creamy spunk, Tim.' Angus' fist encircled the neck of Timothy's ball sack, forcing the swollen orbs to strain against taut skin. Tim let go of Rab's cock, looked down like a teenage Goliath, and began grunting. 'Timothy's going to give you his full load, mister. Tim's going to give it to you!'

Angus' mouth enveloped both bollocks, his cheeks straining to accommodate. He sucked hard, sucked harder and with a groan that threatened to bring the other guests running, Tim's entire body went rigid. Pointing his toes, Timothy fired a stream of thick, white jism. He collapsed back, squirming as Angus blew the last vestige of sperm from his heavy bollocks.

Immediately, Murat began to moan fit to burst as his hand hammered down on his rod. 'I'm going to come.'

Angus let go of Tim's balls as he reached out a hand to cup and squelch Murat's knob sack, hastening his explosive climax. And, boy, did he shoot. Wads and globs of aromatic ball-juice spurted from his swollen knobhead and splattered over Timothy's heaving pecs.

Now it was Rab's turn. 'Angus? How's about going for gold?'

Angus fell forward, pleading for Rab's dose, soliciting with his wanton mouth, but not for long. Rab's balls were only too happy to oblige. He gripped Angus by his ears and filled his throat with his bollocks as the first wave hit, forcing Rab to shoot up and over his head and shoot and shoot and shoot. Without anyone lifting so much as a finger, Angus did his party piece: squirting his spunk in an arc, spurt upon reflexive spurt, matting Tim's pubic hair with his copious dose.

The four of them relaxed back on the green baize. The sun shone down on four bodies glistening with sweat and come.

'Look here.' Rab was suddenly animated. 'Stutz must've been a boy scout. He's always prepared for every eventuality.' And with that he passed around the kitchen roll and wet wipes that had been discreetly stacked behind the cushion his head was resting on.

They cleaned up thoroughly, then relaxed back once more. Feeling the sun on their skin, listening to the music and laughter drift up from below, swatting away the occasional fly, getting their breath back. Ten minutes, no more.

Tim retrieved an ampule of lube from the nearest urn and, snapping the teat, used it to lubricate and restore his magnificent erection.

'This guy is unbelievable,' said Rab.

'An animal,' said Murat, smiling.

It didn't take long before Timothy was fully stiff and all the while Murat's eyes never blinked. He was transfixed. 'Sit on it, mister,' Tim bid him and, without any trepidation, Murat straddled Timothy's powerful loins. Angus rolled a condom over Timothy's mighty erection. Then, whilst Rab held Murat's buttocks wide apart, Tim positioned the fat phallus up against Murat's hole, drawing a glistening trail of lubricant around the tender ring. Purposefully, Murat began to press down, inch by straining inch, until he was fully impaled. Rab cradled Murat's rump as he began to bounce slowly up and down. Angus set to work licking Murat's balls, his eyes straining to see the exposed point of contact – puffy anus and slick dick.

Murat's humping became more determined. Timothy urged him on. 'Yes, mister, love Timothy. Timothy loves you. He loves you, mister. He's going to prove it. He's going to give you his cream, all the cream in his big, big bollocks.' Murat's erection was renewed full force and he began jacking his fat organ, tossing it way beyond Timothy's belly button, tightening and releasing his arse muscles as he sucked him ever deeper.

'That's good, mister. Timothy's nearly there. Timothy's going to shoot you full to the brim. He's going to love you, love you, *love you!*' Gripping tight hold on Murat's peach of an arse, Tim lunged to the core of Murat's wholesome guts and cried out in agony, in ecstasy. Mere seconds later Murat threw his head back and ejaculated. An elongated streak of semen flew through the air and narrowly missed Timothy's open, gasping mouth. Time and again he hit Timothy's neck and chest.

Tim and Murat's exertions ground slowly to a halt, a matching pair of satisfied smiles. Rab and Angus were far from relaxed, both up and hard. Tugging on each other's raw meat, their deep soul kissing forming a bridge over the crumpled bodies. Reluctantly, Murat climbed off Timothy's softening dick. Angus went for sloppy seconds; bending Murat over on all fours he positioned his gloved manhood and slipped in easily, Timothy's exertions providing the perfect lubricant to the ideal receptacle for a double dose.

As his hips thrust in rabbit-like stabs, Murat drove into reverse, speeding up to the inevitable. A handful more resounding slaps as tail-end smashed into tail-end before Angus' mouth opened in a silent scream. Then the juddering groan began. Desperately whacking his chopper deep into the silky fissure, he delivered the final thwack, planting at the root his full, ripe seed. Murat clenched his arse cheeks rapidly. Tightening and relaxing, tightening and relaxing, he drained all the goodness out of Angus' big dick.

As Angus collapsed down, pinning Murat beneath him, Rab knelt over them both and let fly, spraying Angus' back and buttocks with a vast load of jism. Jerking it out, Rab felt euphoric. Laughter bubbled up in his throat; he threw back his head and let rip. Finally it was over.

Who was he fooling. Within the hour Rab would lament that the relief of orgasm was, at best, a temporary solution. Mitch had inevitably returned and would continue to haunt Rab's every waking moment.

Twelve

In the same week that the band announced their first world tour came news of the Whammy nominations – the musical equivalent of the Oscars. The band were in the running for Best New Artists of the Year and Cary's 'With All My Heart' was a strong contender in both Record (single) and Song (ballad) categories. A wave of euphoria swept through the Bigfun camp like a bush fire. Simply being nominated meant that ticket and album sales would go through the roof and, as if the band needed it, it offered clear confirmation that they had cracked the American market.

It wasn't the only award to be forthcoming. The same week, Bigfun made the cover of *Gayz*, the premier British gayzine. Four smiling faces under the heading: 'Bigfuk – Which One Would You Like To Wake Up Next To?' Inside the cover, a nationwide poll offered an answer. A survey of the top gay fantasy lovers placed the boys from Bigfun in positions one to four. When Cary met Jayne for lunch at Il Boccacio in Covent Garden that same week it formed the hub of the conversation.

'Mitch only came third?' Jayne couldn't help but smirk, a forkful of pasta poised before her lips. 'Bet that put his cute little nose out of joint.'

'It's that kind of readership, Jayne. Disco bunnies are more likely to vote for blonds.'

'Don't devalue yourself like that. Accept the compliment for once.'

'I'm not. I'm just being realistic.'

Their waiter appeared. 'Everything OK?'

'Delicious, as always. Thanks, Mario,' Cary said.

Mario flashed the kind of smile that could melt chocolate. Cary's eyes fixed yet again on his beautiful, firm buttocks as he walked away. It was one of the fringe benefits of dining here, a place where Cary could be considered a regular patron.

Jayne caught the exchange. 'I wouldn't be surprised if he hadn't voted for you.'

'I wish!'

'You know, I do believe you underestimate just how attractive you are.'

'Well, you would say that wouldn't you – what with you being my *fiancée* and all?'

'Don't believe everything you read in the tabloids, Cary.'

'We made page five again this Sunday. "Biglove," it said. You and me at the Terrence Higgins Trust benefit, with Jo conveniently trimmed out of the picture. The thing I don't get is that your relationship with Jo is an open secret. How can they print such an obvious lie?'

'Since when did the truth have any place in the tabloids? Get real, Cary. You're a much more valuable commodity as a heterosexual and they are, first and foremost, in the business of selling in quantity.'

'*Gayz* asked for an interview, you know?'

'And?'

'Rab turned them down, claimed we were too busy in the studio.'

'He's getting very protective all of a sudden. Has he suddenly forgotten that it was the gay audience that got your career off to a flying start?'

'He remembers well enough, but he also knows that I'm getting tired of playing the Sphinx.'

'You're going to come out?'

'I don't honestly know. I haven't really decided. On the one hand, I want to keep my private life private.' He paused, frowned. 'On the other hand, I'm fed up with skirting the issue.'

'You've never denied your sexuality outright have you?'

'No, but I've lied by omission. Or else, I've answered a direct question with some clever quip. Like, they'll say: "What about the persistent rumours that you're gay? What do you think about that?" And I'll say: "I take it as a sincere compliment" or "It's a new millennium. So what? Big deal. Get a life!"'

'Sounds like a great strategy to me. And more than they deserve.'

'And what about you?'

'Me?'

'Yes, you. You must have had to think about the career consequences of coming out?'

'You forget that MNS were never as big as you boys, plus I was technically straight back then. The band split because Leon and I split, after five l-o-n-g years together. I didn't meet Jo till a year after that. Besides, I'd already decided to write and produce. I'd had enough press attention to last me a lifetime. Now, I'm in the enviable position of being in the business without being a face. In or out isn't an issue.'

'Except when you're out with me.'

'We both know I'm not your beard, Cary. If the press wants to put two and two together and make five, that's their lookout. They aren't going to stop us being friends. I won't let them.'

'So you think I should stay stumm?'

'I'm not going to advise you one way or the other. You're big and ugly enough to make your own decisions. At the end of the day you're the one that has to live with it.'

'Whatever I decide, I'll still be welcome at your place?'

'Naturally!'

'And what exactly do you mean "big and *ugly* enough". I'll have you know I'm the Number One Fuck in the gay UK!'

'Just don't let it go to your head. I've seen you first thing in the morning, remember?'

★

The demands of the world tour took their toll on the band and only added to the stresses and strains that had accompanied the making of the movie. After the fourth week the lads were spending as little time together as they could. What little free time they had was spent in separate pursuits, going their separate ways. Damon would disappear with Cassie to visit all the legendary department stores and shop to drop; Kenny played the consummate tourist and took himself off sightseeing; Cary would immerse himself in his fitness routine; and Mitch would be off with his cronies attending A-list parties.

Rab knew that Mitch was becoming a problem. Almost since the first day they arrived in the States he had been the centre of a clique. The clique was made up of members of the road crew, technicians and musicians. Their main object, it seemed, was to party, and party hard. Mitch was putting on weight but, more than this, it was the change in his attitude that was most disconcerting. His time-keeping was the first thing to slide. Then came the hangovers; the disturbing displays of arrogance, petulance even. He was acting the big star all of a sudden – believing his own publicity. What was worse, Rab couldn't seem to make him listen to reason.

The Whammy Award ceremony was beyond anyone's expectations. The glitz, the glamour, were pure Hollywood. The build-up alone had been as exciting as the event itself promised to be. Two weeks and a countless round of interviews and personal appearances paved the way to the big night. Rab was determined to maximise their chances. Doing the rounds was good PR and it won Bigfun a lot of new friends and allies.

Cary lay naked on the king-size bed in his hotel room. He was about to indulge in a long, leisurely wank after training, before bathing and final preparations for the evening's event when Mitch burst into his room without warning. Reflexively, Cary yanked the sheets across himself.

'Ever heard of knocking?' Cary asked annoyed.

'Why be so shy? You haven't got anything I haven't seen before.'

'That's as maybe but this is getting to be a habit, a bad habit. You can't just burst in when you want to like this.'

'What's the matter? 'Fraid I'll see something I shouldn't?'

Cary ignored the implication. 'You're here now, what do you want?'

'I just wanted a private word.'

'And that's the reason for barging in uninvited?'

'Thought you might be lonely,' Mitch said with a leer.

It was only then that Cary realised something was decidedly wrong. He couldn't yet put his finger on it but something was definitely out of sync. Cary lay back, immobile, as Mitch crossed to the bed.

'Mind if I sit down?'

Mitch didn't wait for a reply but, instead, sat down on the bed beside Cary, his weight pressing down heavily on the sprung mattress. He paused, leered at Cary once again. 'Been working out in the gym downstairs? All that weight training seems to be paying off big time.'

Cary didn't reply. Mitch reached into his trouser pocket, took out a packet of cigarettes and lit two. Handing Cary one, Mitch exhaled in one long stream of smoke.

Cary raised himself up on one elbow. 'What are you on?'

'Eh?'

'What have you taken?'

'I don't know what you're on about.'

But Cary wasn't fooled. Mitch's eyes were glittering with a thousand stars. There was a thin film of sweat on his cheekbones and across his forehead.

'You're on something. I don't believe this! Our big night and you're off your face. How fucking irresponsible can you get?'

'I don't know what you're on about.'

'Oh, yeah? Why would you come in here, sit on my bed and flirt? No reason. Unless, of course, you were on something. And you are on something, aren't you, Mitch?'

Mitch shook his head, toyed with his goatee, then looked

down at his hands. 'Got me all sussed, have you? Don't think so. Thought maybe you could benefit from the ache in my balls. Thought you might like the real thing instead of that puffball soccer player you've been seeing.'

'Get to the point. Are you offering? 'Cause if you are . . .'

'Yeah?'

'I'm not interested.'

'Go fuck yourself!' Mitch leapt to his feet and headed for the door.

'You too, mate. You too. Take your false courage and shove it where the sun don't shine. And if you're not sober by the time we get to the ceremony, you can accept the award yourself 'cause I won't be standing next to you!'

Mitch slammed the door behind him.

When the stretch limousine pulled up outside Media City Music Hall and the boys stepped out, the waiting hordes went wild. The four of them took their own sweet time treading the red carpet that led them to the entrance, accompanied by the relentless flashing of cameras and heightened by the buzz of adrenalin. This was their moment of glory and all four managed to put their grievances aside for the moment, and savoured the adulation.

The auditorium itself was like nothing the boys had ever experienced first-hand before. Kenny compared it to an aircraft hangar crossed with Santa's Grotto. Everywhere you looked was silver and gold. Endless rows of raked seating swept up to the skies. The stage was as big as football pitch. Every spare inch of wall was banked with video screens of various shapes and sizes. Television cameras were perched on the sidelines, on platforms and even on the end of a crane which swung out over the heads of the audience.

The usherette who led them to their appointed seats front central was called Raven — or so her name badge said. She looked like she belonged on prime-time TV. Probably an actress/singer/dancer/model wannabee, thought Cary. It seemed like everyone in this town was 'in waiting' for the big time. It was one of the things about LA that depressed Cary no end.

As they took their seats, Damon turned to Kenny.

'Is that Janet Jackson over there?'

'Janet who?'

Damon was incredulous. 'You don't know who Janet Jackson is?'

'Yes, Damon. I do know who Janet Jackson is. I just didn't hear you say her second name the first time around. What do you take me for, a complete ignoramus?'

Damon's face said it all.

Kenny was oblivious. He took another look. 'And no, I don't think it's her. It looks more like Michael to me. Though I don't know how anyone can be expected to tell the difference.'

When Alec Brewster came out on stage to announce the winner of the best newcomer award, the boys knew the result was a foregone conclusion. A wave of euphoria began in Mitch's toes and flooded through his entire body, filling his head, blocking his ears to the point where 'and the winner is . . .' sounded like he was listening underwater. 'Bigfun!' broke through the surface.

The hall erupted in a torrent of sound. Foot stomping, hand clapping, a whooping success. Clearly they were the popular choice. The underdogs had triumphed once again.

The long walk to the podium was a nightmare for Cary. Mitch was stumbling behind him, whilst Damon and Kenny brought up the rear guard. They arrived on stage to a tumultuous cheer. As agreed, Cary stepped forward to accept the award but Mitch pushed past him. Grabbing the award from Alec's hand, Mitch threw his arms around him, planting a big wet kiss on the action-hero's cheek. Alec laughed it off with good grace but Cary was livid; he felt totally humiliated. Kenny threw an arm around Cary's shoulder and manhandled him towards the microphone with as much subtlety as he could muster.

Cary was dumbstruck, his prepared speech forgotten. Rab and Murat, looking on from the audience, squirmed in their seats. Damon saved the day.

'As you can see, Cary is lost for words and Mitch is having a funny turn, so on behalf of both of them I'd just like to say we're delighted. Thanks to everyone. To our manager Rab Mackay –' Kenny plucked the award from Mitch's hand and passed it to Damon who held it aloft '– this is for you.'

Kenny took over. 'But mostly we'd like to thank the fans. Without whom we'd all be down the job centre.'

Mitch lurched towards the microphone but Damon caught him by the elbow and swung him towards the stage exit.

Kenny had the final word. 'Thank you. Thank you all.' And he guided Cary off stage.

When the news reports finally appeared there was no mention of the debacle, save for some throwaway line about the 'wacky britboys' and their 'carefully rehearsed unrehearsed performance'. No one, it seemed, had noticed that Cary walked out of the hall into a taxi and made straight for the airport and home.

Despite a concerted effort, Rab could not trace Cary throughout the coming week. In fact, Cary was determined that there was no way he would be found until he himself chose to reveal his whereabouts. He had, in fact, sought sanctuary with Jayne and Jo. He desperately needed to sort his head out first; that was the argument he had used to assure himself of Jayne and Jo's complicity. So when Rab had called they played dumb.

'What are we going to do with you, Cary?' It was the fifth day he had been in hiding and yet another sleepless night. Jayne found him in the kitchen at three in the morning.

'Sorry, did I wake you?'

She ran a hand through tousled hair and yawned. 'No. I'm just sleepwalking. Don't mind me. I'll just sit here till I wake up.' Byron crossed the linoleum and brushed his body against Jayne's leg. She, in turn, reached down to stroke the more affectionate of her two cats. 'Yes, of course you woke me up! But it's not the point. We're concerned about you.'

'If it's a problem me staying . . .'

'Did I say that? Get a grip, Cary. We're your friends.'

'I know.'

'So. How about a dialogue?'

'I've had enough, I'm worn out and, despite thinking about it endlessly, I still don't know what I ought to do.'

'And all because of Mitch?'

'No.'

'But he was the catalyst?'

'The last straw that broke the camel's back. I'm sick and tired of his shenanigans. He is so egotistical, arrogant, irresponsible, totally self-focused . . .'

'And you adore him.'

'Something like that. How did you guess?'

'Please! You are talking to the world's leading expert in affairs of the heart. Had I not been a pop whizz-kid I could have given Claire Rayner, queen of the agony aunts, a run for her money, I can tell you.'

'So, Claire, what do you advise? I thought love was supposed to make you happy as the day is long, not miserable as sin.'

'Speaking from experience . . .'

'Yes?'

'Never did tell you about my ex, did I?'

'You mean your dark, heterosexual past?'

'One and the very same. Leon, my ex, had a lot going for him – *me*, for example. Unfortunately, he was also a man with big problems – attitude problems, drink problems. I believed I was good for him. It took five years before it occurred to me to ask myself if he was good for me. I could have saved myself a lot of pain.'

'And the moral of the story is that I should steer clear?'

'No. The moral is, what do you really want and need? Listen to your own voice.'

'But that voice frightens me.'

'Why?'

'It's telling me to get the hell away from him; just quit the band and get the hell away.'

'In the words of that famous pop-psychologist, maybe you should face the fear –'

'– and then it won't be a fear any longer.'
'You got it in one.'

Once the dust had settled, the decision was made. Cary and Rab met together on neutral territory, a walk in Hyde Park, early on Sunday morning. It was a tearful discussion. Cary's distress was evident and Rab had a tough job just trying to talk him out of burning his bridges entirely. As Cary fed scraps of bread to the hungry pigeons, a form of compromise was reached and a bargain of sorts was struck. Officially, Cary would be taking time out to work on demos for a solo project. Unofficially, it was far from certain if he would ever be part of the band again.

When Rab called the remaining three band members together at the London office in order to tell them the bad news the sky was suitably overcast. Electric light lit up the boardroom, whilst outside the incoming dark rain clouds slowly turned the early afternoon to evening. Murat sat on the window seat, ever the silent observer. He leant forward with his elbows on his knees, his chin resting on his hands, watching the boys intently.

Damon was the first to react. 'How could he do this without talking to us first about it?' He was almost on the brink of tears.

'To be fair to Cary, I don't think he's up to talking to or with anyone at the moment.'

'But we're a team!' Kenny complained. 'He can't just refuse to play when he feels like it.'

Rab shook his head sadly. 'Yes, I'm afraid he can.'

'Sod him!' Mitch grunted. 'He always was a prima donna.' He turned to Damon and Kenny. 'We don't need him.' And to Rab, 'I could take over lead. We could carry on as a three-piece.'

'Shut up!' Damon lost his temper. 'Shut up for once! If it wasn't for you, we wouldn't be in this mess.'

'You what? You looking for a punch in the mouth?'

'When you're big enough.'

'Calm down, Damon. Cool it, Mitch.' Kenny took control. 'Look, this is a mess any way you look at it. There's no point in doing anything hasty. And there's no point in us falling out over it.'

'You're right there, Ken.' Mitch stood to leave. 'Because if we do fall out that'll leave you two girls like Bananarama. I'm sure Damon can tell you how many hits they had once they were down to a twosome. But I'll save him the trouble. The answer is: zero.' And with that he was out of the door.

Rab simply threw up his hands.

Murat stood up quickly. 'I go talk to him.' And he hurried out of the door in Mitch's wake.

'So what happens now, Rab?' Kenny asked balefully.

'We keep our heads. Everything will work out for the best, you'll see.' Rab only wished he was as confident as he sounded.

Murat caught up with Mitch at the lift. The doors were just closing as he pressed the call button. The doors reopened and Murat jammed his foot in the door. Mitch's face was a picture, screwed up with a level of rage that seemed completely unwarranted.

'Let me go, Murat.'
'Stay and talk things through.'
'Let me go, Murat.'
'You are only making things worse.'

Mitch lurched forward and pushed Murat out of his way. Immediately the doors began to close. 'You're not my keeper, Murat. Nobody tells me what to do any more. Not Rab, not you, not anyone. Just back off!'

And with that the doors slammed shut.

Remi, the band's trusted recording engineer, accompanied Cary to the secluded recording studio that had been booked on an island in the Bahamas. Rab had been insistent that Murat should be part of the team too; he would have gone himself but for the problems at home. Sending Murat along was the compromise. Rab was more than a little concerned about Cary; he had never seen him so down.

Rab's concern was not unwarranted. Despite the change of

scenery, with its clear blue skies and permanent sunshine, Cary had never felt so low in all his life. Remi was terrific, cracking jokes and always full of encouragement, but the recording sessions weren't going at all well and they both knew it. It seemed as if the only songs Cary could write these days were miserable ones about lost love and longing. Thankfully, Jayne had agreed to fly out in a week or so to try to iron out the personal and professional problems. In the meantime, Murat had been his usual tower of strength.

Cary had asked Remi if they could share a room; once again he didn't want to sleep alone. Sleep was becoming a problem but the sounds of Remi gently snoring seemed to tip the scales and enable him to get a decent night's sleep.

But not this night, a night that was unusually chill. A full moon flooded the room with cold light. Once again, Cary lay awake, but this time waiting for the footsteps on the stair. Remi, Murat and some of the band members had gone out to dine whilst Cary opted for an early night. A pointless exercise as it turned out since sleep seemed to be even more elusive than usual. He had tried to talk himself into a relaxed state, even tried counting sheep, but sleep refused to come. Now he found his thoughts drifting inevitably towards his new roommate .

Remi was an enigma, Cary had once concluded. They had always had a good working relationship; had always been friendly, yet without ever really being friends. Remi kept work and play in separate compartments, had kept his private life private. But their close proximity over the past couple of weeks had seen a crack appear in his armour and facts began to filter through.

Remi's parents were from Jamaica and he was the youngest of six children. All the others had been steered towards higher education and were now both successful and reasonably affluent. As the youngest, he himself had been somewhat indulged and allowed to pursue a career in music. Luckily, with success of his own. Yes, he had a girlfriend. In fact he had several, none of them serious. He liked to keep his options open, he said with a flash of his crooked smile.

From afar Cary could hear footsteps on the gravel drive signalling that the others were returning. How much time had passed just lying there wishing for sleep to come? Next came the footsteps tiptoeing down the hallway, and then the sound of the door handle being gently turned. Cary pretended to be asleep as Remi crept carefully into the room. Then, turning his back towards Cary, he began to strip naked. Heart in his mouth, Cary watched him carefully remove and fold each article of clothing until finally his underpants were gliding to the floor. His buttocks sat high on his body, round and firm. Remi strode to the window and, resting both hands on the sill, gazed out into the night sky. Moonlit in profile, Cary saw the arch of Remi's monumental cock sprouting from the mat of pubic hair as it rested on his fulsome sack.

Suddenly turning in Cary's direction, Remi asked softly, but pointedly, 'You still awake?'

Cary's voice sounded small and far away. 'Yes, Remi. I haven't been able to sleep. I've just been lying here for hours.'

'And so you've been watching me ever since I came in?'

'Yes, Remi. Sorry, Remi.'

'Why didn't you say something, Cary?'

'I don't know. I . . . It was so quiet, and all. And I just ended up watching you.'

'Watching me?'

'Yes, Remi. I like looking at you.'

Flattered, Remi let out a little laugh and sat on the edge of his twin bed. Moments dragged past in silence. 'It's a cold night outside. Are you cold, Cary? Is that why you can't sleep?'

'Yes, Remi.'

'Then maybe I should climb in there beside you and warm you.' Without waiting for a reply he walked over and slipped in beside him. He was indeed warm as toast. 'Better?' he asked.

Cary's response was half swallowed. 'Still a little cold, Remi.'

'Then maybe you should wrap yourself around me.' His powerful arms drew Cary to rest his head upon his chest, their legs intertwining. The heavy aroma of Remi's body musk swept over Cary as he nuzzled into the twin pillows of Remi's smooth, hairless pecs.

All was silent, save for the comfort of two beating hearts and the soft sound of Remi's hand as it stroked the back of Cary's neck. They lay there for what seemed like an age, their breathing synchronised and their bodies relaxed into one another.

Remi suddenly laughed in mock alarm. 'What's this big thing poking into my leg!'

Cary gulped. 'Sorry, Remi. It just feels so . . . so nice and peaceful lying here together with you.'

'Don't feel sorry, Cary. I'm glad that I can make you feel happier. And I am truly flattered.' A pause. 'How about me releasing the tension in that big muscle of yours? I sure would like to release the tension in mine.'

Another pause. Then, 'Please . . .' Cary's reply was short, but the intention was clear. The nascent lust was more than evident.

Remi's body seemed to tense slightly, as he tightened his grip on Cary and angled his body so that their faces were opposite each other. Even in the darkness of the room, Cary could see the whites of Remi's eyes. Seconds later Remi's mouth was upon his, sucking on his lips, smothering him with big beefy kisses. Cary's head swam like a dam had burst, wave upon wave of intensity gushing through his young veins, filling him up, from the tips of his toes to the top of his head, Remi's mouth, his wet and hungry mouth, feasting on his own.

'Oh, fuck!' Cary gasped. 'Oh, fuck!' Remi's kisses were everywhere. His lips and tongue traversed Cary's face, his cheeks, his mouth, his forehead, his neck. A deluge of wet, sloppy, warm kisses urging Cary on, feeding his desire and freeing him to let go, to cast himself upon Remi's lust and to let it carry him away. Cary wanted two to become one; he wanted to give himself over, body and soul; to abdicate all responsibility and simply belong to another, if only for one night.

Their bodies were locked together in a writhing morass of mutual lust. Hot animal passion mingled with tenderness and restraint. Remi rolled on top of him and, looking into his eyes, whispered, 'I am going to enjoy you, Cary. Enjoy your body, enjoy giving you pleasure. And you? You are going to enjoy me.'

'Yes, Remi. Please.' Cary's voice was like a low gurgle at the back of his throat.

Gripping Cary's hands tightly, Remi pinned him on his back, sticking his tongue so far down his throat that Cary thought he'd choke. Then tender kisses rained down a trail from his chin, past his throat, to his nipples, where Remi sucked for milk like a starving animal. Cary squirmed with pleasure.

'Ticklish, are we,' Remi teased, chewing on the flesh above Cary's hip, forcing Cary to double up with laughter. His cock sprang up to hit Remi's face.

'Whoa, you'll poke out my eye with that big thing!'

And suddenly Remi's mouth sank on Cary's full length.

Gagging, he withdrew, just long enough to gasp, 'You are so tasty, Cary. So tasty!' Then he began nibbling and nipping and washing Cary's cock with his coarse tongue. Cary's fingers ran over his shaven head. Grasping hold he found himself bucking and jerking into Remi's open throat. Cary felt the itch in his groin but it was too soon.

'Stop! Remi, stop!' Cary moaned, pulling Remi's head back to be met with his puzzled gaze.

'What is the matter, Cary? Too rough for you?'

'No, Remi,' Cary stuttered. 'I was . . . I just want this to last a little longer.'

Remi smiled his broad, good-natured, smile. 'No problem, Cary. We've got all night! Let's take a little break.'

Cary lay wrapped in Remi's arms and, to his surprise and delight, Remi began to sing. At first it was just a low hum, but then Cary could make out words. An old lullaby filling the silence of the room. Remi's voice, rich and low and sweet.

In the quiet that followed Remi asked, 'What now, Cary? Do you just want to fall asleep in my arms, or' – his fingers brushed Cary's nipples – 'do you want me to relax you some more?'

The low groan from Cary and the arching of his chest to meet the fingers, now tweaking his nipples erect, was all the answer Remi required. Once more his lips found Cary's, slipping his tongue deep into the wet warm embrace. Cary's body continued to writhe and the tit play became more intense, the nipples now fully erect. Remi's strong hands massaged his chest, his belly and, reaching down every few moments, jacked his cock, keeping it primed, ready, fit to burst. Cary's body felt electric, like there was a low level current being generated somewhere deep inside and spreading over his skin, following the trace of Remi's hands. The rage of pleasure was becoming unbearable.

'I can't ... Remi, I can't take much more of this,' Cary choked hoarsely.

'Much more of what?' Remi replied, while at the same time twisting Cary's nipples sharply.

'Oh fuck, Remi. I – Can we do something else?'

More tit squeezing. 'Like what, Cary?'

'Can I kiss your backside?'

Remi let out a chuckle. 'Would that make you happy, Cary?'

'Very.'

'Then sure you can kiss my backside.'

And so saying he released his grip and turned around to lie on his stomach.

Moonlight bathed on Remi's buttocks, the silky sheen of his skin highlighting the delicious curves of his peach of an arse and a shadowed cleft. A cleft in which Cary longed to sink his face and drown. Hard as marble, black as onyx. This man had all the attributes of an heroic statue – and much more. Fortunately for Cary, he was flesh and blood.

Cary's hands reached out to cup both beautiful gleaming cheeks, kneading them with his fingers, parting them to reveal the soft dark centre. Running his nostrils along the cusp, Cary inhaled fully, savouring the fresh, sweet and sour scent of intimacy. His mouth watering.

'Good enough to eat?' Remi asked, looking over his shoulder, treating Cary to his dazzling grin. 'Go on, eat it, Cary.'

Without a second thought Cary buried his face between both orbs, feasting on Remi's hole, his tongue foraging for the entrance. Then in, right on in there, sniffing, gnawing, swallowing. Remi ground his belly against the mattress, groaning and squirming like a man possessed.

'*Fuckohfuckohfuckohfuck . . .*'

Parting Remi's legs, Cary's tongue found its way down to Remi's succulent bollocks whilst Cary's index finger continued to tease Remi's ring piece. Each hard-boiled egg in turn popped into Cary's hungry mouth. Then both got stuffed and crammed in there, bloating his cheeks like a baby hamster.

'*Enoughenoughenough!*'

Remi spun around, pointing his blistering manhood over Cary's head and shot a load, so thick, so pungent, so copious, Cary thought he would be covered from head to foot. Spurting on and on and on. Spunk like a waterfall, crashing down on the rocks below. Cary suckled on his balls till Remi grew soft, draining every drop of tension whilst Remi's body juddered and shook; then melted back into the pillow, exhausted.

Cary cleaned up the both of them with a handful of tissues then clambered up the bed to lie alongside Remi, his head on his chest. Eyes closed, a satisfied smile curled the corners of Remi's mouth. Beads of sweat covered his brow and, with the full width of his tongue, Cary wiped Remi's forehead.

'You sure are one thirsty pup!' Remi whispered, locking his fingers behind his head.

Cary was struck by the heavy scent of Remi's armpits. His mouth fell upon them, sucking and licking each mound in turn.

'Oh, but I want to eat you, Remi. I want to eat you up. All of you, all of you in my mouth, in my belly. I want you to love me, just for tonight. I don't ask for anything more.'

Remi slipped a powerful arm around Cary's shoulder and drew him to rest his head once more upon his chest. 'Tonight, I can give you, Cary. I'm loving you now.'

They fell into an effortless sleep. Cary awoke as dawn crept through the windows. Remi, resting his head in one hand, looked down at him and smiled.

'Look at what you have done to me, Cary.'

Cary looked down to see Remi's fingers position his stiff, juicy dong so it pointed to the ceiling.

'Yes, you did that,' Remi said with a nod.

Cary's voice was thick with sleep and lust. 'I want you to put that inside me, Remi. I want you to force all of it inside me. I want to give you my hole.'

Remi's eyes narrowed. 'You think you can take it all?'

'I can take it. Believe me, I can take it. Fuck my hole. Please, Remi. Please.'

'OK, but let's take it slow.'

Cary's arm reached out and pulled a tube of lubricant and rubbers from the top drawer in the bedside table.

'Straddle me,' Remi insisted. 'I want you to have some control.'

Cary climbed astride him, watching Remi stretch the translucent rubber over his engorged tool. Then he parted his cheeks to let Remi slide a couple of fingers up there. He ground his hips, begging for Remi to stretch his tight, itchy hole. 'I want this so badly. So badly.'

'Sit on it!' Remi ordered him, suddenly taking firm control. 'Sit on it, Cary!' Positioning himself, Remi rolled the mushroom head up against Cary's steaming entrance, prising it open. 'Now sit!'

First pain, then pleasure. One long 'Oooohhhh . . .' and Cary slid down the full length like a professional. 'It's so big, Remi. So big. You fill me up.'

Remi hadn't a clue how many big things had been up Cary's arse in preparation for such a moment; stretching himself wide and deep seemed to have paid off.

'Now bounce on it.' Remi held him firmly by the hips and began to guide him up and down, up and down. 'Yes, that is it. Just as I like it.'

Cary had no more reservations. In a dreamlike state of ecstasy, he humped and bumped, his tight arsehole chewing on Remi's cock, sucking him ever deeper in. Cary could have sworn he could feel the head pressing into his guts. And he was gone, sat on a rocket, shot over the moon.

Remi spat on his hand and rubbed it over Cary's stiff prick.

Shock waves ran through Cary's body. Yanking and tugging on Cary's meat, Remi urged him on.

'Deeper, Cary. Oh, yes. Come for me, honey.'

Cary slammed down as Remi thrust up into him.

'Take it, Cary. Take it all. Give yourself to me, give your whole self to me.'

And with one more gut-wrenching shock wave Cary shot his load. On and on and on and on.

'Fuck, where's it all coming from? Fuck!' Splattering the pillow, Remi's face, his pecs. Then Remi began to growl, low at first, then on up the scale to a crescendo.

'*Ohfuckohfuckohfuckohfuck!Iloveyou!loveyou!loveyou!*'

Thirteen

A celebrity death is always good news to the tabloids – at least to their sales figures. And especially when it concerns someone so young, so handsome and so *alive*. 'Cut down in his prime,' the scandalmongers chorus. 'His whole life was ahead of him.' 'A tragic loss.' But that doesn't stop them from playing up the uglier aspects of the tragedy – usually a drug-and drink-binge with deadly consequences.

Rab had been trying to get hold of Mitch all weekend but the phone seemed to be off the hook. By Sunday, he was nearly frantic. So frantic that he jumped in his car, determined to drive up to London and check things out personally. Locked in traffic on the M25, he rang one last time from his car phone. But this time, much to his surprise, the phone rang. And rang and rang.

Finally, someone picked it up and a timid voice spoke as if from somewhere far away. 'Hello?'

Thank God, thought Rab. 'Mitch? Mitch? Is that you, Mitch?'

There was an interminable pause. Then came simply an equally timid, 'Yes.'

'Are you alright?'

'No. No, I'm not alright. Nothing's alright. Everything's all wrong.'

Rab was more than worried now. He could hear the tears in

Mitch's voice, however faint. 'I'll be with you in thirty minutes. Hold on, Mitch.'

'But . . .'

Rab's voice grew bolder. 'I said, I'll be with you in thirty minutes!'

A little over half an hour later, Rab found Mitch curled up alone on the floor in the sitting room of his luxury apartment. The telephone was still beside him; one hand clutched a bottle over two-thirds empty; newspapers blanketed the floor. He was deathly pale. The tracks of tears streaked his face, dirtied by newsprint. For one awful moment, Rab thought Mitch was dead. Then he saw his chest rise and fall in silent breathing.

He wanted to scream and bawl. He wanted to knock some sense into the dumb fucker. But he did neither. Instead he dropped to his knees and began to gently stroke Mitch's head. They had had next to no contact since Mitch had stormed out of the meeting. If Mitch was intent on a downward spiral, what good was Rab's disapproval? None. Mitch had to hit rock bottom and then some. 'Tough love', the pop-psychologists call it. Loving someone enough to let them make their own mistakes. But Rab was going to hang around to help pick up the pieces.

Mitch opened his eyes. 'Alec's dead.'

'I know. I heard on Friday. I'm so sorry, Mitch.'

'I can't believe it.'

Rab was silent.

'But I have to believe it.'

Rab nodded, stroked Mitch's head again. 'I've been trying to get hold of you all weekend.'

'I made myself . . . unavailable for comment.'

'You got wasted?'

'Something like.'

'When was the last time you had anything to eat?'

'Don't know. Friday, maybe.'

'Come on. Let's get you to bed. I'll rustle up something.'

'Don't leave me.'

'I won't leave you.'

'It could have been me.' Mitch gripped Rab's hand. 'I don't want to end up like Alec.'

'You won't.'

'Help me.'

'You ready to help yourself? Are you ready to make some changes?'

'I . . . I think so.'

'Think so, or know so?'

'Know so.'

'Then I think I know just the place.'

Next morning, Mitch checked into the rehab clinic. It was kill or cure. Rab hoped to God that Mitch could learn from someone else's mistake.

'Mind if I smoke?'

'Yes, actually, I do.' Gayle pointed to the 'Thank you for not smoking' sign on her desk. To be honest she really didn't care if Des Foster smoked. In fact, at that precise moment, she couldn't have cared less if he had burst into flames and turned into a pile of ash. She would have been only too happy to let him burn and then to have swept the debris under the carpet.

Foster reluctantly replaced the packet of cigarettes into the pocket of his crumpled overcoat and attempted to relax back into the stiff leather upholstery of the office sofa. 'Makes for interesting reading, doesn't it?'

Gayle's fingers trembled as she read the file. This stuff was dynamite, she knew that. She only hoped she wouldn't be around for the explosion.

'And that's just the start,' Des added with a smarmy grin.

After a further ten minutes' silence, Gayle closed the cover and placed the file on the desk in front of her. She shuddered, she felt dirty, but she knew, once again, that she had to maintain a controlled exterior. She brought the tips of her fingers together in a prayerful pyramid and stared into space.

'So, to summarise,' Gayle began, 'Linda Mackay left Rab because of his infidelity with another man, a man who just happened to be his best friend and the man she then chose to seduce.'

'Yes, that's about it. She'll swear to it all of course and can provide photographs of the parties involved and letters, that kind of thing, though I agreed not to reveal her as our primary source of info – something to do with a button-lip clause in her divorce settlement. No, the information can be attributed to a 'close personal friend'. That notwithstanding, she is demanding a considerable fee.'

'No wonder he left the bitch,' Gayle muttered under her breath. 'Then we come to Mitch Mitchell.'

'Indeed we do. Who'd have guessed the heart-throb of millions could once have been had for a hundred quid a pop.'

'Are you absolutely certain of your information? You do realise that this is going to ruin his career.'

'Should've thought about that before, shouldn't he?' When Gayle failed to respond Foster continued, 'Yes, I've got the documentation. Hotel registers, sworn statements, the lot. You'll also note the copy tapes of all the relevant conversations? Of course, those involved didn't know they were being taped but I like to have some insurance should they suddenly change their story.'

'How resourceful of you.'

'You don't have to tell me my job, Gayle. I'm always thorough. A man has to cover his back in this business, if you'll excuse the pun.'

Gayle shot him an acid glance. The arrogance of the man! 'I doubt very much that you have any reason to worry about anyone sneaking up behind you, Mr Foster.' Except, perhaps, with a carving knife, she thought to herself. Nevertheless, it was a pity the boys hadn't been of the same persuasion. They would have saved themselves untold grief.

The folder now lay before her on the desk. She pressed her hands down on the front cover as if trying to keep the secrets trapped inside. 'You said this is just the start?'

'Tip of the iceberg, darlin'. That Cary? Goodie-goodie two shoes? Well, there's more to him than meets the eye.'

'Meaning?'

'Meaning: watch this space. I never spill the beans unless I'm a hundred per cent certain.' Foster took a cigarette pack and matchbook from his pocket. 'Just keep signing the cheques, Gayle, darlin'.' He lit up before he reached the door, turned and blew a stream of smoke in her direction. 'I'll be in touch.'

As the helicopter landed on the island helipad, Cary was reclining on the back seat of their rented car. It had an open top and the blades of the copter sent waves of hot air across the tarmac to ruffle Cary's hair. A moment later he sat bolt upright; it was something of a surprise to see Rab follow Jayne from the cockpit.

Rab was the first to throw his arms around Cary as Jayne hugged Murat. 'Just thought I'd tag along for the ride,' Rab said, but of course he was lying. Murat had been keeping him up to date with Cary's progress, or rather lack of it, and so here he was, determined to take care of business.

Cary turned to hug Jayne. 'Boy, am I glad to see you,' he said with utter sincerity. 'This album is in desperate need of a miracle. Hope you packed one in that bag of yours.'

'I know he looks a little worn around the edges but that really is no way to talk about Rab,' Jayne replied.

It was the first laugh Cary had had in an age.

Seated at the mixing desk in an unfamiliar recording studio, Jayne listened intently as Remi played the latest song Cary had been working on. When it was over, she didn't speak for what felt like an age. She seemed to be on the verge of tears. And when she finally spoke, her voice was full of emotion. 'That is totally beautiful, Cary. I mean it. Heart-rending, heartbreaking, perfect.' She paused, shivered. 'But what about the lyrics?'

'There are no lyrics. Not yet. I've tried and tried to come up with something but still come up with nothing.'

'Nothing at all? Not even a title?'

'No, zip. All my words seem to have left me.'

'Now that's not true, Cary,' Remi interjected.

'Not quite, Remi, you're right.' He swivelled his chair back towards Jayne. 'The fact is, I don't want to write any more sad songs. They make me miserable. God knows, I don't want to do the same to my audience.'

'Sadness is part of life, Cary. We can't escape that fact. And sad songs can be part of getting better. When they strike a chord in people, they can help the listener to cry at a time when they need to cry. That's an OK thing to do.'

'I take your point, sure, that's fine in small doses, but twelve songs on one album? Give the poor audience a break!'

Jayne pursed her lips in mock reproof. 'We'll just have to buy you some happy tablets, won't we?'

Cary's face clouded over. 'Don't bother, I think Mitch has already cornered that particular market.'

Rab stood gazing out at the bay. Fishing boats were moored close to the harbour and the sun was setting on the aquamarine horizon. He had his back to Cary, his words carrying over his shoulder on the salt-sea breeze.

'Come home for Christmas, Cary.'

'I don't think that's such a good idea.'

'Why not? Spending the holidays here is preferable?'

'Not particularly. I think I've had enough sun, sand and sea to last me a lifetime.'

'Then why?' Rab turned round to face Cary. 'And will you take off those sunglasses! You don't need them now, and I'd quite like to see your eyes while I'm talking to you.'

Cary did as he was asked, slipping his Ray Bans into the top pocket of his short-sleeved shirt. 'It's not a good idea because I don't have a home to go to.'

'You'll always have a home with me, you know that.'

Cary didn't look at all convinced.

'I'm organising a Christmas get-together. Just the party faithful. It won't be the same if you're not there.'

'It won't be the same full stop.'

'That's as maybe, but time doesn't stand still. Look, Cary. The album isn't working; the band isn't working; everyone is miserable. Mitch knows that he lost the plot back there and he's suffering for it, just like you are.' Rab paused for emphasis. 'He's gone into rehab.'

'What?'

'He's trying to get himself sorted. The prognosis is good. His counsellor seems to feel he's sufficiently motivated. He may be home for Christmas too.' Rab turned back towards the sea view. 'Believe me, I have no intention of trying to justify what he said and did or didn't do. The point is, the combination of the four of you together is what made the band. Let's try one more time, OK? Damon and Kenny want to meet with you, want to talk things through. Me? I'm just the messenger. What do you say? What will I tell them?'

The fifth of December saw the release of Bigfun's double A-sided Christmas single: 'Christmas Kisses/Happy New Year (Back together again)'. Ironically, it had been recorded on a hot summer's day the previous August. Ever the forward planner, Rab had arranged some space in the band's schedule to accomplish the task well in advance. A Christmas single had been his suggestion and Cary and Mitch each took up the challenge. Both tracks were recorded in the space of two days. As a bonus it meant they got the rest of the week free.

It had surely turned out to have been a fortuitous suggestion indeed. Nothing by the band had been released since the film soundtrack album and accompanying singles, the last of which had slipped out of the charts in late July. The release of the single was treated as a major event and helped, somewhat, to stem rumours of a split.

Then again, the lack of band product in the preceding months actually worked to their advantage and actively helped to propel the single to Number One on its first day of release. There it would remain throughout the entire Christmas period.

Out of necessity, the accompanying video had to be animation – the band in cartoon form with cartoon snow and cartoon kisses. There was simply no other way around it. When the video went into production there was no band to speak of.

★

It was a week before Christmas when the train pulled into the familiar village station to find Kenny and Damon waiting on the cold and frosty platform. What had promised to be an awkward reunion proved to be just the opposite. No sooner had Cary stepped down from the train than Damon's arms were round his neck and a big, wet kiss was hastily plonked on his cheek.

'Damon!' Cary exclaimed. 'Your nose is as cold as ice!'

'So? Suffer it! Yours would be too if you'd been stood out here freezing your nuts off for the past half hour.'

'I did tell him to wait in the car,' Kenny said.

Damon dismissed Kenny's comment with a wave of his hand. 'Well, I was too excited. Come here.' And with that Damon hugged Cary again.

Kenny joined in. 'Don't leave me out!'

And the three lads formed a scrum.

As they left the station Cary looked around the almost empty car park, somewhat confused. There was no sign of the limo.

'Where's our transport?' Cary asked, nonplussed.

'Over there,' said Kenny, pointing.

Cary could hardly believe it. Glistening in the crisp, clear afternoon sunlight was Damon's old scrap heap of a Mini. But a scrap heap no longer, it had been completely transformed. The chrome shone, the paint work was immaculate, the inside looked to be expertly reupholstered.

'That can't be what I think it is.' Cary was amazed.

'Oh yes it can!' Damon was as pleased as punch.

'But how?'

'Kenny,' Damon replied, throwing an arm around Kenny's shoulder.

'Kenny? You did that?'

'Well, I had plenty of time on my hands what with you off gallivanting.'

Cary walked full circle around the vehicle. He was seriously impressed. 'You are in the wrong line of work, my friend.'

'Think so?'

'He's such a man!' said Damon. 'Too butch to take a compliment.'

The journey back was unhurried. All three were talking ten to the dozen, making up for lost time. Kenny had to keep insisting Damon should stop turning his head towards Cary in the back seat and instead watch the road. Damon told Kenny to stop clucking like an old mother hen. Cary couldn't help smiling. Some things never change, he thought to himself, yet found himself secretly pleased.

As the Mini glided down the final stretch of road the three lads had settled into a comfortable silence. Cary chose his moment to ask the one question he had been avoiding.

'So, where's Mitch?'

'He was in the studio with Remi when we left him,' Damon said quickly.

'Said he had something important he wanted to finish off.'

'Bloody typical,' said Cary, 'I suppose it was too much to expect any drastic change.'

'Oh, but he has changed.' Damon turned off the country road, passed through the wrought-iron gates, and headed up the driveway.

'It has to be seen to be believed.' Kenny added.

Having dumped his bags in the entrance hall, Cary made straight for the studio; he reasoned that his best line of defence was a good offence. But as he approached he heard the closing strains of a familiar tune through a crack in the door. His tune, the one from the Bahamas, the one Jayne had loved so much.

He pushed the door wide open to find Remi and Mitch both grinning from ear to ear.

'Am I interrupting something?' Cary asked.

Remi looked like he had been caught with his hand in the cookie jar. 'Uh – I'll just leave you too guys alone for a minute. Let you get reacquainted.'

'Sounds like a wise move to me,' Cary said as Remi shot past him. He turned to Mitch. 'Were my ears deceiving me or was that my song I was just listening to?'

'Our song, I hope,' said Mitch.

'Am I missing something?'

'Jayne brought a tape back with her, said you were having problems with the lyric, thought maybe I could give you a hand.'

'Nice of her to tell me.'

'I'm not sure she thought it would be such a good idea at the time.'

'Probably a very wise move.'

'But I did come up with something. If you'll allow me, I'll play you the finished version.'

Cary sat down in the swivel chair that Remi had only recently vacated. 'Please,' said Cary, 'I'm all ears.'

Mitch reached across the desk for the play button. 'One last thing, the title –'

'Yes?'

'It's called "Please Forgive Me".'

That shut Cary up. By the time the song faded he could barely hold back the tears.

'So? What do you think?' Mitch waited expectantly.

Cary stood and silently walked towards the door. He turned his head as he reached for the door handle.

'You're forgiven.' Cary's voice was thick with emotion. 'And the song –' He swallowed hard. 'The song is perfect. Just perfect.'

Mitch thought better than to say anything as Cary turned and made his exit. He had nothing to add.

By the following day Murat was relieved to be able to report back to Rab that things seemed to be rapidly returning to normal. In fact, if anything, the atmosphere was better than it had been in the longest time. The tension of the preceding months had all but evaporated, though Mitch and Cary did seem a little more subdued than usual. Rab was not too concerned. These things take time, he reasoned.

For his part, Rab had decided to keep a low profile and remain in the city for the next couple of days. He did have pressing business to attend to but more than this he felt he should step back and let the boys sort through their own issues without his interference.

★

It was late afternoon and Cassie and Damon had taken it upon themselves to trim the Christmas tree in the drawing room. A task for which Kenny's help proved indispensable. Damon had been humming 'Silent Night' interminably and Kenny's nerves were beginning to fray.

'Will you shut it!'

'What's your problem, Ebenezer? Don't you know it's the season of goodwill to all mankind?'

Kenny looked at Cassie then rolled his eyes in exasperation.

Thankfully, the decorations were all but in place and Damon fell silent as he unwrapped the pièce de résistance – the star to sit atop the tree. He held it out in both hands.

'I've been waiting all year for this moment,' Damon cooed.

'Just goes to prove what a sad bastard you are!' Kenny replied.

'You shut it, bonehead,' Damon retorted. 'I'll have you know I got this in the January Sale at Harrods and it still cost an arm and a leg.'

'You mean to tell me there's a one-armed, one-legged man wandering around because you wanted that piece of tat? You were done! And as for the other bloke –'

Damon turned to Cassie. 'He thinks he's funny!' Then he turned back to face the tree and stood on tiptoe but, despite his best efforts, he simply couldn't reach high enough.

'Give it here, squirt,' Kenny said helpfully as he plucked it from Damon's grasp and stuck it unceremoniously in place.

'What do you think?' Damon asked Cassie.

Kenny volunteered his opinion before Cassie had drawn breath. 'I think it would look better with a Christmas Fairy.'

'So jump up there yourself!' Again Damon turned to Cassie. 'Now do you see what I'm up against? I try to educate him about the finer things in life but he is content to remain a Philistine!'

Cassie was toasting bread by the open fire. 'All this reminds me of Christmas at home when I was little.' She smiled at the memory.

'You mean the tree and the tinsel and the' – Damon planted a kiss on the top of her head – 'the mistletoe!'

'No. I was thinking more about my brothers fighting like cats and dogs. Fortunately, Daddy was always there to sort them out.' A pained expression clouded her flawless face. 'I miss Daddy, Christmas isn't the same without him.' Then she seemed to deliberately shake off the memory. 'My brothers still fight, of course, but the bottom line is that they have that privilege – the bottom line is love. So shut up, the pair of you, and come and sit by the fire.'

'*I* will' – Kenny took a step towards her – 'just so long as he doesn't expect us to sit around roasting our nuts and joining in with his Christmas carols.'

'I'd never expect you to do anything of the kind, Kenny.'

'Good!'

'No, because we'd have to wait another ten years until you'd learned how to sing!'

Letting himself in at the back door, as had become the habit, Cary walked into the kitchen and straight into a half-naked Mitch, a bath towel wrapped around his sturdy waist. All muscles, tattoos and sunbed tan. One sturdy hand rubbed a hand towel over his head, the other tipped the contents of a steaming kettle into a mug of instant coffee.

'All right there, Cary?' Mitch winked, flashing that toothpaste smile.

Cary was taken aback. He was actually lost for words. He just couldn't get used to Mitch being so agreeable.

'Where've you been?' Mitch continued.

'Jogging.'

'You should've said. I'd have come with you.'

Cary passed by him. 'I need a shower.'

'Plenty of hot water.'

'Good. I'll go do that then.' Cary paused as he made to exit. 'Why don't you pop into my room like you used to do? Say in fifteen minutes? I miss our little chats.'

'Sure thing.' Mitch smiled as Cary passed quickly through the door and disappeared up the stairs towards his room. Damon was waiting for him on the landing.

'Got a minute, Cary? Come through to my room.'

'Sure. If you can live with the smell.'

Damon closed the door behind them. 'It's about Cassie.'

'Why are you whispering?'

'Because this is top secret.'

'But there's no one in the room except you and me.'

Damon looked around him. 'The walls . . . they have ears you know!'

'Get on with it, you idiot.'

'It's Cassie. She's –'

'– really a man?'

'No.'

'Joined the Moonies?'

'No!'

'Won the lottery?'

'No! Will you shut up!'

'Just trying to be helpful.'

'Well, don't! Cassie is –' Damon was severely tempting fate but could not help but milk the moment for every last drop of drama '– three months pregnant.'

'Damon!' Cary grabbed him and hugged him. 'Congratulations! I never knew you had it in you.' Then he pulled back sharply, holding Damon at arm's length. 'Congratulations are in order, aren't they? I mean you are happy, aren't you?'

'We're delighted.' Damon beamed. 'We're planning a quiet wedding ceremony. Murat's giving her away, Kenny is best man, but Cassie wants you as maid of honour. What do you say?'

'As long as I don't have to wear a three-quarter-length Kelly-green bridesmaid's dress, you're on.'

When Mitch entered Cary's bedroom there was no sign of him.

'Cary?' Mitch called out.

Then Cary's voice echoed from the cavernous bathroom. 'I'm in here. I decided to have a bath not a shower.'

'Should I come back later?'

A beat. 'Since when have you been shy? Just come through.'

Mitch crossed to the bathroom door. 'What exactly was the reason behind this invite?'

'I believe we have some catching up to do.'

As the hot water sloshed out of the tap, Cary sat on the rim of the marble bath and tugged off his socks. Had he stripped simply for Mitch's pleasure, Mitch couldn't have been happier. He sat on the lid of the lavatory seat and watched Cary stand and slide his jogging bottoms and underwear over the smooth, firm contours of his arse cheeks and down over muscular thighs and calves before shuffling them over his feet and kicking them aside. He yanked the sweat-shirt over his head and stood naked and proud before Mitch.

His cock, like a thick length of pipe, arched out of a blond thatch of pubic hair. His balls hung low, filled with promise. He grinned, one of his glorious grins.

'I was just wondering . . .'

Mitch cast his eyes up to the ceiling. 'Yeah?'

'The lyrics you wrote, they were something else.' He climbed into the tub. 'I mean, I always thought your lyrics were clever but I never saw them as . . .'

'Meaningful?' Mitch suggested.

'I guess so.'

'Yeah? Put it down to counselling. I'm a changed man.'

'It's fazed me a bit, you being nice all of a sudden.'

Mitch smiled. 'Why?'

'I don't quite know.' Cary sank back under water and, with a whoosh, resurfaced, his hair slicked back. Mitch looked directly at him. Droplets of water were glistening on Cary's tanned skin. 'You're just full of surprises.'

'Isn't that the spice of life?'

'No.' Cary squeezed water from the end of his nose. '*Variety* is. But those lyrics . . .' He paused. 'There was a lot of love there.'

'I guess.'

Cary's eyes took on a new intensity. 'I mean, don't tell me that the words weren't written for me.'

A moment caught in time. Mitch's heart began pounding like

a hammer. For a second he was tempted to make some flip comment like the Mitch of old. The bath towel, still wrapped around his waist, cushioned his cock and balls as they gradually began to swell, and added an extra special friction. It made him think twice. Then he spoke again.

'Could be. But don't worry. I'm not about to leap on you. You made it clear you're not interested.'

'Maybe you give up too easily.'

'No. I just know the boundaries.'

'Well, you can do one thing for me if you're not altogether frightened of testing the boundaries.' And again Cary grinned. 'Wash my hair?'

'Is this a dare?'

'No. A simple request. Are you up for it?'

'Sure. Why not?'

'Come over here then.'

Naked from the waist up, Mitch knelt beside the tub as Cary submerged once again, throwing his powerful legs and feet out of the water. Mitch watched and waited. Eyes closed tight, Cary lay beneath the surface. Now and then, little air bubbles would escape his mouth and rise quickly. His thick, tubular cock floated, like a submarine adrift, casually grazing the smooth surface of two large boulders. Beneath the cloak of heavy foreskin, his fat mushroom of a cockhead was clearly defined. Shielded but still visible. Cary exposed to prying eyes. Mitch's privilege.

Then, slowly, he re-emerged to meet Mitch's hands as he spread a palm full of shampoo over Cary's slick, blond hair. Mitch's fingertips folded through his locks, pressed down against his scalp, and began to deeply massage the pliant skin.

'Feels good . . .' Cary sighed, contentedly. 'You'll have to give me the address of that counsellor of yours. I'm going to thank him for a job well done. You never would have done this six months ago. What has happened to you?'

When Mitch spoke his voice was small. 'I was scared of intimacy.'

'And now?'

'I like myself now.'

'You didn't like yourself before?'

'I thought I did, but I never let anyone come close enough to see me for who I really am. But now I've learnt that it doesn't matter. It doesn't matter if people don't love me for who I really am.'

'Because now you really do love yourself?'

'No.' Mitch adopted a deadpan expression. 'Because I'm a fuckin' *millionaire*.' He threw back his head in a full-throated laugh. 'People can think what they damn well like!'

Cary couldn't help but join in the laughter. There was still some of the old Mitch left in there; still some of the old laddish charm. He was glad, it was a part of Mitch he loved a lot.

Mitch stopped lathering. 'Rinse that off.'

Another whoosh and Cary submerged once more below the water, his hands working through his hair to rid himself of the foam. As he came up for air he found his gasp smothered by Mitch's hungry lips. In the moment, Cary experienced the unmistakable rush of déjà vu; a sense memory. Hard, wet, minty kisses, surely he had tasted them before. But where? The thought didn't have time to linger. Cary gave himself up to Mitch's yawning mouth.

Cary's passionate response made Mitch grow even bolder. His words tumbled out in a rush of kisses. 'I love you, Cary. I've loved you since I first laid eyes on you but I didn't know what to do with those feelings.'

'It's OK, Mitch. It's OK.'

'No, it isn't OK, Cary. It's lousy having to settle for fantasy when you'd rather have the real thing.'

Cary clamped his eyes tight shut. 'This is the real thing.'

'I want to give you something special.'

Cary opened his eyes wide as Mitch let his towel drop to the floor.

Mitch swung around, cupped his arse cheeks in his hands and parted them. 'Don't know if you would prefer it gift-wrapped? Hopefully, you're the kind of guy who'll take it as it comes.'

'I must have done something good this year. Looks like I'm

going to get what I always wanted,' Cary replied, in awe of Mitch's beautiful backside. 'Open wide,' he instructed as he climbed out of the bath. 'Here I come!'

Mitch leapt to his feet and ran through the bathroom door, hurling himself on to the double bed which groaned under the strain of his landing. Moments later, dripping wet, Cary leapt on top of him, then roughly flipped Mitch on to his back.

'Look what you've done to me.' Cary nodded in the direction of his groin. His erection overwhelmed Mitch. He shuffled down the bed for a closer look. Up close one could see heavy veins pulsing with life blood; a sprinkling of golden hair along the thick undershaft and his balls, big, big balls resting in a smooth, relaxed sack. Dripping wet but for another reason, precome glistened on the wrinkled spout of his foreskin. Cary eased back the tight, sticky foreskin and revealed his giant helmet. Spitting on his hand, he began to caress the chunky head.

Reflexively, Mitch reached out a hand to cradle and scrunch Cary's bollocks but a hoarse whisper put a swift end to that idea. 'Don't touch me. Not yet. Just watch.'

So Mitch did as he was told, letting Cary do his thing. He positioned a pillow under his chest, his own stiff prick pressed against the bed cover and slowly, almost imperceptibly at first, he began to grind it into the mattress in sure and certain knowledge that tonight he would come a monstrous load. Cary's eyes were closed, intent and focused on one aim.

Cary began to tease him. 'Look at it, Mitch. It's a beautiful cock, isn't it; a big man's cock, and big balls. Big balls full of come. I'm going to give you my come, Mitch. So much come you'll be able to bathe in it. Imagine it, Mitch, this cock up your arse. It's going to happen. Believe it, it's going to happen.' His shaft was glistening now, glistening with spit and precome as he slid his fist backwards and forwards, occasionally slapping the iron cosh against his belly

Mitch snuck forward; first his tongue, then his lips, found Cary's ball-sack and began to gnaw and nibble. He opened his mouth wide, consuming first one, then both, weighty bollocks.

'It's OK, Mitch. You don't always have to be top dog. You don't have to be top dog with me. You can relax and play bottom. You'd like that, wouldn't you, baby. You'd like to be able to let go of all responsibility and play bottom.'

Mitch mumbled his agreement, his mouth too full to articulate his gratitude.

'Oh, yeah, you want it, don't you, Mitch? Dying for it, aren't you? My hot fucking spunk squirting over your beautiful buttocks. You want it? Beg me for it, Mitch. Beg me for it, baby.'

Mitch groaned as he released Cary's swollen orbs. 'I want it, Cary. Give it to me. Have mercy.'

'You'll have to do better than that,' Cary tormented him.

'Fuck me, Cary. Don't make me wait. It's what I want. Give it to me. Do it. Fuckin' do it!'

Cary suppressed the powerful urge to come right then and there and held still. 'Why do you want it so bad, Mitch? Why should I fuck you?'

Cary's cock shimmered only inches from Mitch's face. Cary's fist tightened its grip and his erection bloomed anew.

'You see this big dick, Mitch? This big dick could win prizes. It could earn me my living, Mitch. But you want it for free, don't you? And you know why? 'Cause you love me, don't you? Don't you? What do you do?'

'Love you,' Mitch gulped.

Cary grinned. 'Say it again.'

'Yeah, yeah, I love you. I fucking love you!'

'On your knees.'

Wordlessly, Mitch complied. Spreading his buttocks wide, each hand cupping a solid curve, he held firm. With expert fingers, Cary lubricated Mitch's unusually tight, little hole. Lovingly but deliberately, he worked the tender circle of flesh until it began to relax and welcome him inside.

Mitch closed his eyes and buried his head in the pillow as Cary positioned his dick. He felt Mitch tighten at his touch.

'Relax and breathe, baby. Remember, big deep breaths and r-e-l-a-x . . .'

As Mitch exhaled, Cary's cockhead slipped slowly through the greased-up porthole and, with gentle pressure, he eased his length inside with no further resistance. Mitch moaned with pleasure as the delicious sensation of fullness swept through his body. Cary's phallus filled him to capacity and seemed to radiate a heat that warmed him from the inside out; it pressed up against his prostate and stimulated his own erection, which now twitched reflexively as Mitch tightened his grip on the base of Cary's dick.

Mitch raised his head from the pillow. 'Fuck me, Cary. C'mon, fuck me.'

Slowly, very slowly, Cary began to pull his penis out. 'I don't want to fuck you,' Cary replied.

'Ah, Cary, don't mess with my head. Just do it! Fuck me!' Mitch was pleading now.

'I'm not going to fuck you, Mitch. I'm going to make love to you.' Cary's cock was already halfway out. He swallowed hard. 'Because I do love you.' He thrust his hips, plunging his cock up to the hilt.

Mitch gasped. Again Cary began to ease his shaft free. 'I'm going to give you my love. Every thick, long inch.' And again he thrust.

And again Mitch gasped. 'Then love me, Cary. Just love me.'

Cary pulled all the way out, fascinated by the sight of Mitch's pink, gaping hole as it reluctantly let go its grip but remained open to receive him as he plunged back in. This time he pushed forward, grinding his still damp groin into Mitch's arse, letting his balls swing and slap against the top of Mitch's thighs. He reached forward to grip Mitch by his shoulders, pulling himself into an even tighter lock. Mitch growled in pleasure.

'Yeah, Cary, fill me up. All the way up.'

Cary was happy to oblige. He pumped his hips forward and back, forward and back, and the rhythm of his thrusts took on an hypnotic quality. His eyes closed, his let his mind drift where it would. Filled with thoughts: thoughts of first meeting Mitch; the audition; the first sight of him all those years ago. The first days at Rab's country retreat, the concerts, the recording studios.

All these images and more came flooding back, flashing before his eyelids like a Hollywood bio-pic. Like everyone else, he had heard how your life was supposed to flash by just before dying in an accident, but he had never heard of it happening when you were feeling the most alive you had ever felt in your life.

Fuck that, thought Cary, pulling his cock right out, and thus jolting himself back into the present. I can't believe this is fucking happening; that this is really, finally happening.

His body was flooded with an energy he had never known before. His skin was tingling, and it felt as if his whole body was on fire – fully alive for the first time. His mind was racing, his thoughts were all a jumble. And then he began to laugh.

Mitch had been looking behind him from the moment Cary pulled out, watching the play of Cary's facial muscles, and trying to read what was going on. He was as surprised as Cary by the laughter. But it was infectious. Mitch began to laugh too. And next thing they were rolling on the bed together, hugging and laughing as if their hearts would bust. It went on and on. Their laughter resounded through the bedroom and exploded out, threatening to fill the entire house with their joy and happiness.

'I can't believe this is happening,' said Cary.

'Fuck. Me neither,' said Mitch.

'It all seems like so long ago, that first meeting. And all that has happened to both of us. And now this!'

'Well, I guess it was fated in some ways from the very beginning. I mean, being thrown together in the same session, one after the other. And I thought you were shit-hot even back then.'

'Honestly?'

'Honestly. I remember looking at you –'

'– I remember you staring.'

'And you blushed!'

'I bloody well did not!'

'Yeah! Yeah, you did! And later I asked you to go for a drink but you blew me out.'

'Too right I did.'

'And you've been blowing me out ever since.'

'Until tonight. Let's just say I've had a change of heart.'

'And a change of cock by the looks of it. Just look at it! That thing knows what it wants.'

'Yep,' Cary said as he curled his fingers around his stiffness. 'I believe it wants to go home.'

Mitch grinned one of his inimitable grins, and rolled over. In seconds, with a fresh condom in place, Cary was pressing the head of his swollen cock against Mitch's hole, slowly opening it up. As it slipped inside he paused, and then pulled it out again. Mitch groaned and pushed backwards, willing Cary's prick back inside. Cary obliged once again, but only momentarily, then pulled out again.

Mitch was fit to bust. 'For fuck's sake, Cary, have some pity. Just ram that fucker right into me.'

All eight inches of Cary's thick link slipped effortlessly now inside Mitch's hot and welcoming hole. This time there was no turning back. Cary began to pump. In and out. In and out. With each stroke he pulled right back, taking his cock almost all of the way out, leaving just the head in place. Then he slammed back in, his cock filling up the empty space. It was a tight fit, a snug fit, the sphincter gripping tight, reluctant to let him go. Going home. Mitch responded in kind. Pushing backwards to receive Cary's thrusts, contracting his arse muscles to keep Cary in place. As the pace accelerated, sweat poured from both of their bodies.

Cary reached forward to play with Mitch's tits. Mitch arched his body backwards to allow Cary more access. They were kneeling upright now. Mitch was grinding back on Cary's stiff rod, his sweaty back rubbing against Cary, his moans growing louder as his nipples were worked over.

Falling forward, the pump action resumed once more. But this time there was a finality to the rush. The feeling of flesh on flesh; the warmth emanating from each other's bodies; Mitch's loud groans of pleasure.

Mitch's arse was full of cock, whilst his hand was filled with his own – pumping hard. Which cock was which was impossible to work out. The cock inside him felt like his own flesh; like a part of him, as much a part of him as the cock in his fist. It was like having two cocks, each belonging to Mitch alone, and each having pleasure as their aim. He had given himself over to the sheer sensual delights of the moment; a transcendent feeling brought on by this total body experience, he was lost inside his own head. Cary's voice brought him back to awareness.

'Now, Mitch. Now I'm ready. Oh, Mitch, you're going to get it now. You're going to get all you deserve – big dick and big balls just aching to wash you clean.'

Cary pulled out and tore off the condom. Flinging it aside, he stuffed three fingers of his free hand back into Mitch's juiced-up arsehole as the other hand jerked himself to climax. As the first tortured groan escaped his lips, Cary's chin fell on to his chest and the first bolt of jism was propelled across Mitch's heaving buttocks. Cary's eyes opened wide as he continued to pour forth, quaking and trembling, gushing and dumping load upon load upon load, each one a direct hit.

The veins on Mitch's tube were engorged to bursting point as he yanked on it with full force and, in the instant, he came too. Erupting wildly, come flying high and wide. Each squirt was profoundly felt as his ring piece tensed and relaxed against Cary's supple fingers. Jism splattered the bed cover in creamy pools and his head was swimming.

Almost empty, Cary directed his smooth cockhead on to the soft down of one lightly haired buttock and luxuriously squeezed out the last few drops. 'Yeah, take that, my darlin'. Bathe in the milk from my big juicy bollocks, that's a good man. You like that, don't you, Mitch?'

'Yeah, Cary.' Mitch licked his dry lips. 'I fucking love it.'

Cary collapsed alongside Mitch. He reached out to the bedside table. 'Better clean you up.' He pulled a handful of tissues from the box and began to wipe the come from Mitch's back and buttocks.

A deep feeling of serenity overwhelmed Mitch and he relaxed with a sigh. Finally, to relax and feel safe.

'I need a piss,' Cary said, as he jumped up from the bed and headed for the bathroom door, suddenly businesslike. 'Maybe we could do this again sometime.'

'Only maybe?' Mitch was alarmed.

Cary's voice echoed once again against marble and chrome. 'I love you, Mitch. Don't hurt me. Don't ever hurt me again.'

Mitch waited. Silence. Mitch waited some more. Eventually, Cary re-emerged and returned to sit on the edge of the bed, his back towards Mitch.

When Mitch finally spoke his voice was subdued. 'I never gave my arse to any man before.'

Cary's head spun around and he stared at Mitch incredulously. 'What, never?'

'No, never.' He smiled sheepishly. 'OK, so it's no big surprise that I've been around –'

'That's true.'

Mitch gave him a playful punch. 'Shut up and listen! And I'm not saying I haven't played with my arse.'

'Like one does.'

'I said, shut it!' Mitch glowered in mock warning. 'But I never let anyone fuck me before.'

'I'm honoured.' There was no trace of irony in Cary's words.

'Damn right! I never let it happen 'cause I always had to be on top.'

'But not with me?'

'Not any more.' Again there was a silence, but a silence full of meaning as Mitch gazed into Cary's eyes. And then: 'Why are you sitting over there when you should be here by me?'

Cary climbed on to the bed and into Mitch's open arms.

Next morning, Rab arrived back and Mitch found himself summoned to his study.

'You wanted to see me?'

'Yes. Sit down, Mitch.'

'Will this take long? Only we're in the middle of something.'

'That depends.'

'On what?'

'On whether you've thought about my proposal.'

Mitch's face dropped. 'Your ultimatum, you mean? I told you not to put me under pressure.'

'But I love you, Mitch. I need to know where I stand.'

'In that case, Rab, my answer will have to be no. No, I don't want to move in with you. No, I don't want a monogamous relationship. No. N.O. Clear enough for you? I learnt that much from my counsellor. No means no.'

'Why do you hurt me, when all I do is love you?'

'Oh, give me a break, Rab! I can't help it if we don't want the same thing. You just won't back off, will you?'

'Is there someone else?'

'No. No one else. Why does there have to be someone else? This is between you and me.'

'I see.'

'I doubt it.' Mitch raised his eyes to the ceiling. 'Can I go now?'

'OK. But if you change your mind –'

'I'll let you know.'

Fourteen

Christmas celebrations proper were spent at Rab's country retreat. Damon and Cassie, Kenny and Murat, Cary and Mitch and Rab, Jayne and Jo. A family Christmas. Rab sliced the roast turkey, Damon carved the vegetarian alternative. Everyone wore paper hats, pulled crackers and drank too much. After dinner entertainment consisted of a group snooze through Christmas TV whilst sitting around the crackling fire in the palatial lounge. Finally roused, the evening ended with the inevitable party games.

'Here! Here! Listen to this!' Damon's voice was slurred with wine as he clutched the crumpled piece of paper in his hand and attempted to focus. ' "Kylie" met "George Michael" "by the wet wipes in 'Poundstretcher'." She said: "Ooh, I never realised you had such a long tongue." He said: "You don't sweat much for a fat lass." After that, they both "spent a year on the dole". The consequence was: "She couldn't sit down for a month and he donated his body to medical research but they refused to accept it." '

One had to be drunk or stoned to fully appreciate the joke. In the circumstances, the assembled group had no problem at all to see the funny side.

When they finally said their goodnights and went to their

separate rooms it was already two in the morning. When Mitch's mobile phone began to ring a mere six hours later he was in no mood to pick it up off the bedside table.

'Yes!' Mitch growled into the mouthpiece.

'Mitch? Is that you, Mitch?'

The voice was unmistakable and the sound of it swept over Mitch like a wave of nausea. For a moment he was about to deny all knowledge of his former client. He had been living in fear and dread of just such a moment for longer than he cared to remember. But he swallowed the fear and took a deep breath before simply replying, 'Jack?'

'Mitch! Thank God.'

'It's been a long time, Jack. What can I do for you?' In his mind's eye, Mitch had a flash memory of Jack hunched over his feet, licking his own come from Mitch's toes. He shivered reflexively.

'We need to talk.'

'Do we, Jack? Isn't it a little early in the morning for a chat?'

'I don't want a fucking chat!' Jack sounded close to snapping. 'This call isn't about me, it's about you. I think you'd do well to shut the fuck up and just listen if you give a shit about keeping a lid on your murky past.'

It was Murat who let Gayle in through the back door to the kitchen. He had no need, she still had her keys. She placed her shoulder bag on the wooden kitchen table and looked around fondly at the familiar surroundings. It was as if, just for a moment, she was transported back in time.

Murat brought her back to reality. 'Rab's expecting you.'

She looked at him. Her eyes were sparkling. 'How are you, Murat? It's been a long time.'

'Not so bad.' He gave a winsome smile. 'And you?'

'Not so good, I'm afraid.'

'I'm sorry to hear that.'

'Don't worry. Things are getting better by the minute. Is Rab coming through to meet me or shall I . . .?'

'He said to send you straight through.'

'His study?'
'As always.'
'Then I think I can find my own way.'

Jack was waiting in the service station cafeteria when Mitch arrived. He sat alone at a table for four, resting his elbows on the smooth teak-effect formica, sipping a coffee, smoking yet another cigarette. He looked rough; unshaven, dark rings under his eyes. Mitch acknowledged him with a nod and walked over to the service area and a coffee of his own.

Christmas decorations hung everywhere but the atmosphere was subdued. Bright lights inside made the dull winter's day seen through the window seem even gloomier than it should. A surprising number of customers filled the space, reluctantly making their way home after a spending the previous Christmas Day with family, Mitch imagined.

He took the seat opposite Jack and tried to conjure up a smile.

'Good to see you, Mitch.' Jack reached a hand over the table and easily covered Mitch's. As Mitch looked down, Jack's hand squeezed his, then returned to the handle of his coffee cup. 'I only wish it was in different circumstances.'

'This better be good, Jack.'

'I've missed you. Thought the world of you, d'you know that?'

'You look like shit, Jack.'

'You don't look so great yourself.' Jack gave a rasping chuckle, then cleared his throat. 'You're not the only one who's been put out.'

'Cut to the punchline. What's this all about?'

'Someone's been asking questions.'

'Which someone?'

Jack reached into the breast pocket of his checked flannel workshirt and removed a tattered business card. 'Said his name's Foster. And he seems to know an awful lot about you.' He handed Mitch the card.

'D. Foster. Private Investigator,' Mitch read aloud. 'Who the fuck is this D. Foster?'

'A real creepy bastard, that's for sure.'

'And you? How'd he find out about you?'

'Motel register, I understand.'

'But we always signed in under false names.'

'Yeah, but not false number plates. I had to give my car registration. Remember?'

Mitch had to smile. This D. Foster was certainly a resourceful bastard. 'So what's the story?'

'Says he had a tip-off from one of the receptionists – said she'd told him we were regular customers.'

'And what's he after?'

'Anything, he said. Anything I could give him.' Jack took another swig from his coffee cup. 'He's offering big money, Mitch.'

'I'm sure.'

'And work's been pretty slow of late. The bottom's fallen out of the property market. Nobody's buying . . .' Suddenly, a look of pure hatred curdled Jack's face. 'But it was the threats he made that I took offence to.'

'Threats?'

'Asked me how the wife would react if she found out about our little assignations – *assignations*, yeah, that's what he called them, clever bastard. Thing is, that's where he made his mistake. Got his facts wrong, didn't he. Jean's been gone these past eight months.'

'Shit. I'm so sorry, Jack.'

'Don't be.' He smiled ruefully. 'She ran off with her sister's husband. We're both glad to be rid of 'em. Still, there's the kids. They don't know nothing. Said he could keep it that way, keep my name out of it, but I'd have to *cooperate*.'

'And did you?'

'What do you think!'

'I wouldn't blame you, Jack. You don't owe me anything.'

Once again, Jack's hand covered his. 'You really don't know how much you gave me, do you?'

Mitch looked around at the other diners. Just as he suspected, no one was taking a blind bit of notice of this small exchange of tenderness. He had been embarrassed. Embarrassed by the words, embarrassed by the gesture, but somewhere deep inside he was secretly touched.

'So I told him I'd have to think about it. He told me to take my time, said he'd more than enough information to be going on with. It didn't sound good, Mitch.'

'Where do we take it from here then?'

'That bastard isn't going to grind me down. I'd kill him first.'

Mitch was scared, he was sure Jack meant it. 'Come on, Jack. Don't get like that. We'll sort something out.'

'Well, whatever it is, it better involve quick thinking. It's making me ill and that's no joke.'

'Leave it with me for a couple of days, Jack. I'll sort something. Trust me. And Jack . . .'

'Yeah?'

Mitch's hand attempted to cover Jack's. It looked tiny in comparison. 'Thanks, mate.'

Mitch returned to the Manor with no particular strategy in mind other than to talk with Cary. Cary would listen and care. But as he drove up to his parking space it was Murat who was waiting to talk to him.

Murat's face was full of foreboding. 'Rab wants to see you in his study straight away.'

Oh no, that's all I need right now, thought Mitch. More earache.

He entered the study all guns blazing. 'What's this all about, Rab? I don't have time for this right now . . .'

His tirade was cut short. Rab wasn't alone. Mitch had walked in on a family meeting. Murat closed the door silently behind him and took a seat. Damon and Kenny sat on one sofa, Rab stood by the open fireplace. Cary sat in an armchair and on the arm of that chair Gayle perched uncomfortably.

For a moment Mitch forgot his own agenda. 'What on earth's the matter? Has somebody died?'

No answer.

'Gayle, what are you doing here?'

No answer.

Mitch was exasperated; he was also growing increasingly scared. 'Will somebody please tell me what's going on? I'm not a bloody mind-reader!'

'You better sit down, Mitch.' Rab went to the drinks cabinet and poured Mitch a brandy. 'Here, take this. I think you'll need it.'

Mitch took the glass offered to him. 'What is Gayle doing here?'

'Gayle has just presented me with a very challenging offer.' Rab paused to light a cigar. He blew out the lighted match with the first thick puff of smoke. 'It concerns her current boss, Clive Foxx. You might remember him . . .'

Mitch nodded. 'The dirty old letch?'

'One and the same. Well, it would appear that he's been digging up dirt on all of us. He knows about Murat's marriage, for example.'

Damon looked up. 'You're married, Murat?'

Rab answered for him. 'Purely a marriage of convenience. It was the easiest way to secure citizenship. However, it is totally illegal. Then there's my own marriage difficulties which don't bear going into. After that, we come to Cary. He knows that Cary was expelled from his last boarding school and the reasons why. He also knows about a certain three-way he had with a couple of nightclub bouncers, plus his friendship with a certain professional footballer.'

Cary sank lower and lower in his seat.

Mitch snorted. 'I don't believe this. It's like some nightmare soap opera.'

Damon piped up, 'I doubt these storylines would ever appear on *Eastenders*.'

'Or *Corrie*,' Kenny added somewhat redundantly.

'Then we come to you, Mitch, and your previous *career*.'

The penny dropped. Mitch clapped his thigh. 'D. Foster!'

'How do you know that?' Gayle asked.

'What's she still doing here!' Mitch was suddenly furious.

'Calm down, Mitch.' Rab watched a smoke ring float in the

air. 'Gayle is on our team. Fortunately, Clive Foxx has yet to find out. She's our secret weapon.' Rab deferred to Gayle with a nod of his head, as in days gone by. They both smiled in recognition.

While everyone else in the house was sleeping, Kenny remained wide awake. It had been snowing all evening, but now the clouds had passed and a crescent moon half lit up the night sky, shedding its pale light in through his bedroom window. He sat on the window seat, naked, hugging his knees to his chest. Outside was looking like a proper winter landscape with the white blanket covering the ground as far as the eye could see. Kenny didn't feel at all tired but instead strangely excited, aroused even. The temptation to be out in the open air, to feel the frosty tingle on his cheeks was too great. He threw on his clothes and decided to go exploring.

Slipping out of a side door, he turned the corner towards the back of the main house and, digging his hands deep into his pockets of his overcoat, he crunched his way across the otherwise silent lawn, leaving a clear trail of footprints behind him.

This first snowfall had made the familiar landscape look as if it had been thickly dusted with icing sugar. Trees became cake decorations. The night sky was still and clear. Kenny revelled in the sensuality of the moment: the flat, dull sound of his boots compacting the snow with each step forward, the rush of blood to his cheeks and the sight of his fog-like breath. Moonlight reflected off the white surface casting a ghostly glow which made the white lattice pavilion up ahead almost invisible. Or more, it would have been invisible, if it hadn't been for the darkly dressed figure seated just inside the entrance. Moving closer, Kenny recognised the bullish frame slumped on the bench. He speeded up, his mind now racing.

'Rab? What on earth are you doing here?' The surprise and worry were evident in his voice.

Rab turned to face him, wiping his cheek with a rapid motion of his hand. 'Oh! It's you, Kenny.' Rab patted the bench beside him. 'I was just reliving a few – how would one put it? – fond memories.' He held up a flask of whisky. 'Want a wee dram? It'll warm you up.'

'No, thanks. I'm warm enough.' He sat down on the bench beside his boss.

'No? Suit yourself. But I think I need another drop.' Rab raised the flask to his lips and took a short snifter. The whisky burnt a path down his throat. 'That's just the ticket.'

'Haven't you had enough for one evening?' Kenny's voice took on an authoritative edge.

Rab couldn't help but smile. He screwed the top firmly on the container and passed it to Kenny. 'If you're so worried, maybe you should look after this for me.'

Kenny appeared flustered by this sudden turn of events, but it didn't stop him pocketing the flask. He waited for Rab to speak again.

'Nice night for reminiscing, don't you think?' Kenny looked a little puzzled, but Rab continued. 'Cold night air clears the mind. Gets rid of all of those cobwebs. Allows a man to see things the way they really are.' He turned his eyes once more upon Kenny. Kenny had grown up fast. There was little evidence of the callow youth he had been when they first met; here was a confident young man. And Rab could not help but further note that Kenny's body had also filled out nicely. His determined jaw seemed that much firmer than it had been, and the muscles he had acquired sat well on him.

Kenny fingered the flask in his pocket. 'I just don't think it a good idea to sit out here alone drinking.'

'But I'm not alone, Kenny. You're here with me. So now we could just have one together, what do you say?'

'I don't think I'm really in the mood right now, Rab.'

'Well, please yourself, Kenny my boy.'

'I'm not a boy, Rab. I'm a man.'

'Fair enough.' Rab corrected himself. 'Kenny my man. And a good one at that.' He said it almost wistfully. 'You and Mitch are the best of friends, aren't you?' His voice seemed to come from far away and was full of melancholy.

'What's that got to do with anything, Rab?'

'I'm glad,' Rab said with a weary smile. 'You're a good man and he's' – his glistening eyes refused to look at Kenny, instead gazing out over the snow-covered bushes of his rose garden – 'a bit of a tearaway. You'll look out for him, won't you, Kenny?'

'He can look after himself, Rab. He doesn't need . . .'

'But if needed,' Rab interrupted, looking him in the eye, 'you would look after him, wouldn't you?'

Kenny was somewhat confused, wondering what this was all about, but finally answered in the affirmative. 'Yeah. Of course, Rab, we all would. You know that.'

'That's just the way it should be; just the way I always hoped it would be. Look after him for me, Kenny.' This time Kenny noticed the trickle run down Rab's cheek, just before Rab buried his face in both his hands.

'Oh, Kenny, I've made such a mess of everything. Such a big fucking mess of everything.'

Kenny sat there, not sure what to do. 'Don't worry, Rab. It'll be OK. Everything will be OK.' He reached forward to touch Rab's shoulder. 'Honestly, Rab, everything will be OK. Just talk about whatever is bothering you.'

Rab turned slowly, his face still covered by his hands. 'I wish . . . I wish it were that easy, Kenny.' His voice was little more than a whisper and Kenny had to strain to catch everything he said. 'I wish life wasn't as complicated as it is. It's all such a fucking mess. And it's all my fault. All my own fucking fault. I should have known this would happen. I should have seen it coming. But I was too close.' He dropped his hands and looked Kenny straight in the eye. 'I've lost sight of everything. I need to get a new perspective.'

Rab's face was just inches away. Their frosty breath met and mingled, flowing back and forth between them. Kenny's nose caught the full impact of Rab's whisky-scent and he found himself intoxicated. Reflexively, his groin lurched into life. His mind raced, trying to sort out what Rab was going on about.

'Rab, you're not going away, are you? You can't go away. Not now.'

Rab's gaze never shifted. His breathing became heavier,

deeper. Reaching out, he placed a hand firmly on Kenny's knee. 'No, of course not. Not now. But sometime. Maybe sooner, maybe later. It all depends.'

'Depends on what, Rab?' Kenny was aware of the pressure of Rab's hand inching its way up his thigh. Aware too of his own cock stirring inside his jeans.

This time there was no reply. Rab's hand had found the swelling mound. His fingers pressed it, stroked it. His eyes looked deeply into Kenny's and the moan that escaped his lips was rich with meaning. The pulsing in Kenny's cock was matched by a hammering in his ears.

Kenny's voice cracked, 'I don't understand anything, Rab.'

Rab's thick fingers continued to massage Kenny's crotch. He sighed heavily. 'What's to understand, Kenny?'

'Please, Rab . . .'

Rab drew away. 'Maybe this is the wrong time to get into all of this.'

'Please, Rab. Let's talk about it. I think you need to talk about it. I won't tell anyone.'

Rab heaved a heavy sigh. 'You've got an old head on your shoulders, Kenny. Maybe you'll understand. But you mustn't tell anyone what I'm about to tell you now.'

'I swear, Rab. Cross my heart.'

Rab offered no further resistance but poured forth. 'I let you all down. Mitch and me . . .' His eyes began to well with tears. 'I had responsibilities . . . or maybe I was just too much of a coward to face the truth.' A fresh trail of tears rolled down his cheeks.

Kenny leapt to his defence. 'You're not a coward to me, Rab! I think you're a fucking hero!'

Rab looked at Kenny with an overwhelming tenderness in his eyes. Taking Kenny's face in his palms he whispered, 'Kenny. Why wasn't it you? Why weren't you the one?'

'Maybe if you could've lifted your eyes off of him for a moment you'd have seen me lurking in the background.'

'Was it so transparent?'

'Only to a trained eye. I knew what to look for.'

Rab looked into Kenny's eyes and held his chin between thumb and forefinger. Rab shook his head. 'How could I have been so blind?'

'You weren't blind, Rab, just preoccupied,' Kenny stuttered, almost biting his lip at having said too much.

Rab smiled a big, teary smile. 'What do you say we get out of this cold, get you back to the house. Maybe I can make this up to you in some way.'

'Whatever you want, Rab. Anything, anything at all.'

Leaving the pavilion, Rab slipped an arm around Kenny's shoulder. They strode across the blanket of snow leaving fresh footprints in their wake.

Kenny lay on his back, his head nestling between Rab's powerful thighs, mesmerised by his poker-stiff penis as it twitched upright in the glow cast by the open fire. He reached up and took it reverently in his hands. 'I know all about taking care of business, Rab. And I know how to relieve the ache in these big balls.' Kenny kissed each one in turn. 'I'm not Mitch –' he traced a line with his finger along the underside of his shaft '– but I know how to please a man.' He kissed Rab's cock head. 'And this, this beautiful big fat thing pleases me.' Kenny dipped his tongue into Rab's yawning piss-slit. 'I'm going to make you forget him, Rab.' He massaged Rab's knob-sack. 'Mitch didn't deserve you.' He began to suck. 'Don't waste it. I want it. Give it to me. Give it to me!'

Rab stuffed his manhood into Kenny's mouth, inching his way down his open throat until balls touched base with his chin. Silently, determined, with one shared purpose, Kenny relaxed into the rhythm as Rab continued to feed him his length. Flesh, burning flesh slipping and sliding and fucking his throat. Gliding rapturously into Kenny's moist, cavernous need; loving the fullness of Rab's tubular cosh. Pumping slow and easy. Unable to speak, to think. Only able to milk the object of his heartfelt desire. Kenny's nose brushing up against Rab's bushy, auburn pubes.

No further words were exchanged, none were necessary. Rab

simply rode home, taking his time, a long, lazy ride towards the inevitable destination.

When Rab finally rocked his cock free from the welcome orifice, gallons of come spasmed over Kenny's trembling belly. Kenny, in turn, dipped his fingers in the pool and used it as lubricant, bringing himself off in a matter of seconds. Squirting his own load to mingle with the first.

Rab bent down to face him, his whisky breath intermingling with deep, wet, loving kisses.

'Did I do good?' Kenny asked.

'You did better than good,' Rab said finally, tousling Kenny's hair. 'Done this kind of thing before, have you?'

Kenny simply smiled.

'Now you won't breathe a word, will you, Kenny? This has to be our little secret, right?'

Kenny's brow furrowed. 'But we'll do it again, won't we, Rab?'

Rab looked into the flames. 'We'll see, Kenny. We'll see.'

The elevator doors to the fourteenth floor opened on to the expansive reception. The secretary was not at her desk. Not so surprising, it was Sunday morning after all. No matter anyway, for behind the unoccupied desk, the door to Clive Foxx's office stood ajar.

'Anyone at home?' Gayle called out.

'Just a minute, dear,' Foxx's reptilian voice rattled, 'I'll be right with you.' Moments later he appeared in the open door way, a vision of unloveliness draped in a silk kimono. 'Gayle, my dear. What a plea –' Foxx's face dropped with a resounding clang. 'What's *he* –'

'Doing here?' Rab stepped out from behind Gayle but didn't bother to offer his hand in greeting. 'What kind of welcome is that, Clive? I thought you prided yourself on your social graces.'

'What do you –'

'Want? Gayle told me all about your kind offer. It was touching to hear that you should take such a personal interest in my boys and myself. That you should then be so generous as to let us have the opportunity in being involved in our own ruin is testament to your true strength of character.'

'Get –'

'Out? No, I don't think so, Clive. Not until you've heard the terms of the deal I'm about to lay before you.'

Rab eased his way past Foxx, leading the way for Gayle to join them in the inner sanctum.

'What's this all –'

'About?'

Foxx was red in the face and about to explode. 'Will you –'

'Stop finishing your sentences? I'm sorry about that, Clive, but I can't help it. You're just so predictable, I'm afraid.'

'For goodness sake, spit –'

'It out?' Gayle took up the mantle.

'It's like this,' Rab began. 'You aren't going to print a single word about me, my colleagues, or my boys. And in return, I won't drop you in the shit.'

'This is pre –'

'Posterous?' Gayle tagged it again.

Rab smirked. 'No, not preposterous at all. You see, thanks to the tip-off from Gayle here, I was able to enlist the services of my own private investigator. You've been a naughty, naughty boy, Clive, and on more than one occasion if the evidence in my possession is to be believed. You know, you really should be more careful about the kind of methods you employ in order to strike a deal.'

'I will not be –'

'Blackmailed?' Rab pipped him to the post.

'I wouldn't be so hasty or self-righteous if I were you.' Gayle fixed Foxx with a cold stare. 'It would seem that there are any number of people who would be only too happy to see you knocked off your pedestal. I would advise you to listen very carefully to what Rab is saying.'

'You think you've got some stuff on us? That's nothing compared to what we've learnt about your machinations. I bet you could give Lady Macbeth a run for her money. Want me to spell it out?'

By the time Rab was finished Clive Foxx was struck dumb. His thin lips were so fixedly clamped together that they all but disappeared. And if looks could kill Rab would have been six feet under.

'Do I take it that your silence is a sign of your tacit agreement?' Rab finally asked. 'Doubtless, your word would be your bond but frankly I'd actually prefer to have it in writing anyway.' He turned to Gayle in triumph. 'Could you pass me the papers, please.'

Fifteen

Mitch arranged to meet Jack at the motorway service station one more time. And this time Rab came along for the ride. As they entered, Jack was seated at his usual table and was more than a little surprised to see the red-headed Scot following closely on Mitch's heels.

Once they had reached his side, Rab stepped forward, offering Jack his hand, together with a warm smile.

'Nice to finally meet you, Jack.'

Jack looked at the proffered hand then turned his eyes to Mitch. 'And who might this be when he's at home?'

'Meet my boss, Jack. This is Rab Mackay.'

Jack raised his eyebrows, then offered his own hand. 'Never shook hands with a millionaire before.'

'Billionaire,' Rab said as a matter of fact and punctuated his handshake with a squeeze of the big man's palm. 'I believe we owe you a huge debt of thanks.'

Jack dropped his eyes and looked down at the table – an action that was both bashful and charming at the same time. 'Nah. I did it for Mitch. He's thanked me himself.'

'Nevertheless, by helping Mitch you helped us all and you deserve our thanks in return. Anyone who does a favour for my boys does a favour for me.' Rab motioned to the seat beside him. 'Mind if we sit down?'

'Please do.' Jack looked just a tad uncomfortable as Rab sat down opposite him.

Mitch remained standing. Rab looked up at him. 'Go and get us a cuppa, Mitch.'

'Sure thing.'

Rab looked directly across the table at Jack. 'Would you like anything?'

'I'll have another coffee if you're paying.'

'Coffee it is. Coming right up.' Mitch turned towards the serving counter.

'Don't look so worried, Jack. I don't bite.'

Jack shrugged. 'Do I look worried?'

'Yes, a little. But there's really no need.'

Again Jack shrugged.

'Mitch tells me you're a builder?'

Jack nodded. 'Though not that you'd notice these days. As I told Mitch, work's been pretty thin on the ground of late.'

'Yes, so I believe.' Rab looked casually around the room. 'Actually, that's why I'm here. I've been on the lookout for someone to take care of my property for some time now.'

'With the job market the way it is, it shouldn't be hard to find somebody.'

'Yes, Jack. But I don't want just anybody. I want somebody who knows what they're doing, somebody' – Rab placed his elbows on the table and leant forward – 'I can trust.'

'And why are you telling me all this?'

'Thought you might be interested.'

'You offering me a job?'

'Would you be interested?'

Jack suddenly grinned. 'What's your game?' He struggled to contain his excitement but barely managed it. 'What if I was interested?'

'Then you had better come back and take a look, see if you're up to the challenge. Though I'd better warn you, it's an old property. A listed building, in fact. It'll take some looking after –

inside and out. But you'd get a decent salary and there's a cottage on the grounds that goes along with it, rent free.'

Jack fixed his eyes on Rab's and said with some pride, 'I can turn my hand to anything in the building line.'

'I don't doubt it,' Rab replied.

The band set to work writing and recording material for a new album, but this time the procedure changed. Cary handed over his 'tunes' for Mitch to write the lyrics, whilst Jayne became co-writer with Damon and Kenny. These new dynamics worked like a dream. The set was effortlessly written and recorded within a matter of weeks and everyone agreed that this album was the best thing they had ever done.

Conformation came with the album's April release. The first single brought Bigfunmania to fever pitch. 'Please Forgive Me' was Number One throughout Europe and the Americas. Cary and Mitch's songwriting debut brought comparisons with Lennon and McCartney along with it. Kenny said he hadn't a clue who Lennon and McCartney were but it was just another ruse to wind Damon up. A ruse that worked perfectly. It took Damon an hour and forty minutes to recount the history of the Beatles. It was only when he had finished that he realised the others had long ago escaped to the local pub.

In the first week of release, both the album and single topped the charts simultaneously. Nothing released that year would come close to its success. It would go down in the *Guinness Book of Pop* as having set some kind of record; a record Damon would forever after be only too happy to recount at the drop of a hat.

It was amidst this fresh surge of popularity that the story first appeared, quietly, one Sunday morning. It would give no indication of the wave of media madness to come. By Monday morning Bigfun would make the tabloid headlines in a big way. Repackaged for mass consumption, their 'revelation' would hit the news-stands like a bomb.

The interview that Cary and Mitch had given to the serious

Sunday paper was more than a clever exercise in damage limitation. It was frank, honest and unapologetic. It was also thorough because, whilst the band knew it wouldn't be the last word on the subject, it would be their last word for now. By the time it hit the news-stands they were holed up in Rab's country retreat whilst Rab, Gayle and Cassie stayed behind at the central London office to field the thousand and one enquiries that would surely pour in.

The boys were all sitting around the breakfast table when Murat returned from the village with an armful of the Sunday morning edition. Only Damon managed to have a healthy appetite as he tucked into a cooked breakfast. Kenny nibbled on a slice of toast. Mitch and Cary settled for black coffee.

Murat pulled up a chair. 'I took every copy from the newsagent's. I don't believe the locals will be very happy.'

The next ten minutes were spent in a fevered silence save for the rustling of pages.

'You didn't pull any punches did you?' Kenny thought aloud.

'A few.' Mitch grinned. 'But there's more than enough here to keep the media hyenas happily chewing and off our backs.'

'There's barely a mention of me,' Kenny noted.

'Think yourself lucky,' Damon retorted. 'Maybe when you've made your mind up . . .'

'Up yours!' Kenny replied.

'In your dreams, Kenny,' Damon replied with a grin.

'You come out of it quite well, Damon,' Murat remarked.

Damon stood, taking his empty plate to the dishwasher. 'Yes, I know. Ever the faithful friend. Proud to stand alongside my gay brothers . . .'

'And what about this bit?' Kenny interjected. '"It will come as a surprise to many that Damon is straight when most of the gay rumours had previously focused on him".'

'Serves them right. Who gives a shit what *they* think. Who are *they* anyway? Why should anyone care what I am?' Damon rested his hands on Murat's broad, beefy shoulders and gave them an affectionate squeeze. 'Let them get on with it, that's what I say.'

And get on with it they did. Bigfun filled the front pages for the best part of a week. News, reviews, interviews and media debate, the likes of which had never been seen. But once the dust began to settle any number of things became clear.

Cassie was able to confirm that the overwhelming public response was both supportive and positive, the fan club having been inundated with messages of solidarity and support. The female fan base rang and wrote in their thousands to say they didn't care whilst the gay fan base wanted to assure the boys that they loved them all the more.

In fact, public response was so affirmative that the media were lost for an angle. Sure, people wanted to read and gossip about the band but they didn't want the same old homophobic nonsense. When the leading tabloid printed the headline 'With All My Arse' – a play on Cary's song title – outraged members of the public took them to the Press Complaints Commission. After which, they would reluctantly be forced to rethink their strategy. Enemies would suddenly become friends.

Rab had been attending to business in London for a full week when the call came through. It was something of a surprise to find himself being summoned to a band meeting and not the other way around. There had been no forewarning. Jayne passed the information on the band's behalf. Surprise turned into concern when he heard that the venue of the meeting was to be neutral territory. Not the London office, not the Manor, but a suite at the Dorchester. No explanation was forthcoming, simply a request to be there the following day at twelve noon.

At twelve o'clock precisely, Mitch opened the door and led Rab through to the drawing room. The room was light and the furniture was delicate, but a strange heaviness had settled over those seated. Just the five of them together, Rab and his boys.

'Take a seat, Rab.' Cary pointed to the high-backed easy chair.

Rab did as he was bid. 'What's this all about, lads? Why all the cloak and dagger?'

Damon spoke up. 'We've been talking and we've come to a decision.'

'And you couldn't tell me in the office?'

'That's your arena, Rab; that's where you're the boss, but we wanted to be on an equal footing,' Kenny replied, without taking his eyes off the floor.

Rab tried to laugh but failed dismally. 'So what's this all about? Come on, out with it.' The good-natured smile froze on his lips and the corner of his mouth began to twitch from the effort.

It was Mitch who finally broke the embarrassed silence. 'We've decided to part company.'

'With me?' Rab was stunned.

'With each other,' Cary replied.

Again, Rab tried to laugh but didn't convince anyone. 'You cannot be serious!'

Damon reached for the wine glass on the occasional table in front of him. 'Deadly serious.'

'So, on the crest of untold popularity, and after all we've been through together of late, you've decided to split?'

Kenny started to interject. 'Maybe not for ever but for an indefinite period, certainly for the foreseeable future. We want some serious time off –'

Damon finished the sentence: '– for good behaviour.'

Mitch began to argue the case, his eyes burning into Rab's. 'Look, we've achieved everything we set out to do and more. Now it's time to step out of the limelight and enjoy the fruits of all our hard work.'

Cary pressed on rapidly. 'We've talked it all through. We want our swan song to be three nights at Wembley Arena followed by a live double album and video. Then Jayne has told us that in doing so, all contractual obligations to the record company would be fulfilled and we could move forward into a new future.'

Rab's voice was subdued. 'Sounds like you've got it all figured out.'

Cary looked at his hands. 'Pretty much.'

'Don't suppose there's any point in me trying to talk you out of it?'

'Not a one,' said Mitch.

'Excuse me a minute.' Rab stood up and went into the bedroom, closing the door behind him.

'Now what?' Damon was perplexed.

'Maybe he just wants to go to the bog?' said Kenny.

'And I suppose he just couldn't wait?' Damon was dumbfounded. He looked at Cary. 'Is he actually being serious?'

Kenny was indignant. 'I always want to go when I'm nervous or upset.'

'That's you! Rab's a grown-up.'

Cary rolled his eyes to the ceiling as Mitch took charge of the situation. 'We'll leave him alone for a minute or two. He needs some time.' Mitch plucked a bottle of champagne from the ice bucket by the fireplace and promptly popped the cork.

Five minutes passed by. Rab stood in front of the bedroom window and stared down at the city streets below. His eyes were blind to the hustle and bustle, his ears deaf to the honking of horns, lost in thought. Mitch entered quietly, crossed the room to Rab's side and placed his hand lightly on Rab's shoulder. Long seconds passed before Rab turned to him. Mitch handed him a glass of champagne and, somewhat hesitantly, offered up a toast.

'To new beginnings?' The glasses clinked together.

Rab took a sip of champagne. 'So this is what you decided while I was away taking care of business?'

'Maybe you shouldn't have left us on our own?'

'No, Mitch. You're your own men. You have to be allowed to make your own decisions.' Rab turned back to the window. 'I don't think it's such a bad idea anyway. You deserve a break. And at least you never said "never again".'

'And I'm sorry about the other –' Mitch shrugged. 'You know.'

'What? For saying no to my other generous offer?'

'There's nothing wrong with wanting commitment, Rab. But I firmly believe there's also nothing wrong with not wanting it. There's nothing wrong with choosing to be a free agent – what you might call sleeping around. Can't we just agree to differ?'

'Do I have any choice?'

'If I learnt anything during my rehab it was to take responsibility for my own actions and decisions. How you react' – Mitch spread his palms wide – 'well, that's your own decision and, at the end of the day, your own responsibility. But believe me, Rab, I do love you.'

'I know, Mitch.'

'I'm just not . . .'

'*In love* with me?'

'Yeah. Guess that about sums it up.'

'Those are the breaks, my friend.' Rab smiled with his eyes, a smile of resignation. 'Don't feel bad. I don't.' He turned again and cast his eyes through the bedroom doorway to the main room. He caught sight of Kenny in animated discussion with Damon, and he smiled. Life was still full of possibilities.

Back at the mansion, Murat and Jack had been getting along famously. So famously, in fact, that Murat's cock was almost permanently docked in Jack's hole.

For the past few months, Jack had been hard at work converting the long-abandoned stable block into apartments. And it was here, amidst the hay and saddles, that Murat now rode him; drove him towards the finishing line as Jack, on all fours, whinnied and whined.

Murat didn't have to crack the whip; Jack wanted Murat to push him to the limits and beyond. Far from passive, Jack humped up to meet Murat's rhythmic thrusts. He had been well trained during the previous months. He wanted it all, jockeyed into position, as deep as Murat could go; to feel his powerful cock being driven home, time and time again.

When first he laid his eyes on his new neighbour, Jack could hardly believe his luck. Murat had been topless, soaping up the limousine; he had looked across the car roof and flashed his dazzling smile, before holding out a soapy hand. When their hands first gripped, it seemed to Jack as if a bolt of electricity had surged through his entire body. Now he felt the familiar surge once again, but this time specifically channelled through his arse. Murat had stuck his finger in Jack's socket, loosened him up for maximum overload.

Murat pummelled his prod ever deeper inside Jack's welcoming ring, and all the while marvelling at Jack's capacity to accommodate him. Here was a man who could more than match his passion, stroke for stroke; a man whose enthusiasm could spur him on to wild abandon – lost in the race for release. Murat's only aim now was to cross that line and, as it came into view, he found himself rushing forwards in a final spurt.

Neck and neck, Murat had bridged the final hurdle and with a decisive lunge he came, a cry of victory springing from his throat. He could almost hear a cheer go up from the imaginary crowd. Collapsing down on to Jack's back, he pinned him to the ground and remained inside him until they both had a chance to catch their breath.

It wasn't over. Now came the best part – the sugar lump: to rest in each other's arms, to wipe the sweat from each other's brow; to kiss and cuddle. Jack never ceased to be amazed by – and grateful for – Murat's capacity for tenderness. One moment a sex monster, and the next a honey bear.

'Good for you?' asked Murat.

'No, not good.' Jack paused, then winked as he snuggled against the crook of Murat's hairy armpit. 'Fuckin' brilliant!'

Having made the decision to call it quits the band had stipulated that they wanted everything wrapped as soon as possible. They really had no idea what they were letting themselves in for. The tidal wave of media interest that met the announcement of the farewell concerts threatened to overwhelm them. Then there were the practicalities. Whilst Rab and the team in the back office dealt with the practicalities of organising the event and the publicity, the band were put to work, not only rehearsing the set but also recording the 'farewell' single.

'Let's Go Round Again/It Ain't Over Till It's Over' was to be the final single, a double A-sided single – cover versions of two of the band's favourite songs. It surprised no one when it topped the charts in its first week of release. A week later saw the Wembley concerts take place.

The final night at Wembley was a charity event televised by satellite throughout the world. This was at Cary's instigation – his Lady Di complex coming to the forefront once again.

An upbeat, dance version of 'It Ain't Over . . .' opened the proceedings with a bang – literally. An explosion of fireworks lit the sky before the band even came on stage. A steady-cam followed the boys from the dressing room, through a labyrinth of corridors to the stage entrance while the band of musicians played on and on. By the time Cary and the lads entered stage left the audience were set to explode.

Cary raised a hand and waved, a gesture that was captured on two huge video screens suspended on either side of the stage.

'Hello, Wembley!'

The roar from the crowd was deafening. Yet another camera, positioned on a crane, swept over the heaving crowd and transmitted the pictures directly to the video screens. Mitch pointed to them.

'Smile. You're on television!'

Then they were into the first chorus, four voices blending effortlessly. It was a magic moment that brought with it a collective shiver. Four became one, facing an ecstatic sea of faces. No one else would ever understand the rush they felt in that moment. Only they had experienced it, and experienced it together.

The set consisted of musical highlights from the band's career in chronological order. Video clips and comic asides from the lads linked the whole thing together. The entire programme lasted just over two hours. It flew past at an unbelievable pace with barely a pause for breath. All too soon the show drew to a close.

Damon stepped forward. 'We're not one for long goodbyes. It would only make us cry – and then we couldn't sing –'

Kenny took over. 'We just want to say thank you for loving us –'

It was Cary's turn. 'We love you too!'

The crowd roared.

Mitch waited for the roar to die down. He had the final word. 'And who knows, if you still want us in a few years, maybe we'll come back.'

Another roar went up, even louder than before. Then came the final intro. The boys began to clap their hands and move to the beat.

Damon called out. 'You know this one. So come on, sing it with us! "Let's Go Round Again".'

This particular song had been a concert favourite and had ended each gig on the first and last world tour. Until the single release, their particular version had been unavailable. Now it was top of the charts and the boys were on top of the world. (Damon couldn't help but point out that the original version had only managed to reach Number 12!). Gayle had choreographed a spectacular dance routine to end the show but when the boys reached the chorus the crowd took over as if it were a football chant. The backing band quit playing save for the drummer beating out the time sequence. The lads sang along with the raucous crowd, repeating the chorus endlessly. At length, Mitch gave the signal for the musicians to start up again and the song continued to its inevitable conclusion.

More fireworks, more explosions, and the band made their exit in a cloud of smoke.

Damon spoke the final words. They echoed in every corner of the auditorium: '*We love you!*'

'It Ain't Over . . .' So goes the song. And the day to come would prove that things were far from over. Cassie and Damon's wedding was sure to be a blast. Place: a marquee in the grounds of Rab's mansion. Time: eleven-thirty in the morning. Groom: petrified!

Keeping the venue from the press had required a major miracle, but then they were aided by the trendy vicar who agreed to perform the service – and who also turned out to be yet another *number one* fan.

Formal dress was the order of the day and all the guys wore top hat and tails which, it has to be said, looked vaguely ridiculous on Mitch. Damon and Kenny stood side by side at the altar. Kenny was determined to get them through this without running off to the loo at the worst possible moment. Damon's eyes were fixed on his hands. Kenny's wandered around the elaborate interior of the marquee. Lavish one might have called it. Floral arrangements disguised the tent poles and, it seemed, decorated every inch of available space, including the one above their heads. Their combined perfume was overpowering, made him feel woozy, but he remained resolute.

A fleet of buses had been hired to transport the bulk of the guests from designated pick-up points both far and wide, and much to Rab and Mitch's chagrin they managed to arrive all at once. The marquee went from being virtually empty one moment to full the next. It was Mitch and Rab's job, as ushers, to show the guests to their seats. They certainly had their work cut out for them.

All the immediate family arrived in one fell swoop. Aunts and uncles entered, nodding and waving as they took their seats. Then came siblings and cousins with partners and kids in tow. Damon's dotty old gran was led to the front pew, flanked by Rab and Mitch. At last all were seated and all grew ominously silent save for the odd cough and the shrieking of Damon and Cassie's one-month-old baby, Celine.

Blast off, and the organ suddenly lurched into an ear-splitting rendition of the Wedding March, the familiar wail sending shivers of anticipation through the entire assembly. Damon continued to study his knuckles, which were white with fear. For the first time in his life he knew what it meant to be truly nervous. Kenny turned to watch the star turn make her big entrance. Against all odds, the bride did indeed wear white with all the trimmings, a Baywatch babe in form-fitting silk and lace, led by Murat and framed by her entourage of Cary, plus Damon's three sisters – bridesmaids all. A grey top hat and a fat blur of Kelly green chiffon barrelling down the aisle behind him. And the main event began.

Outside it was a cool but sunny day. Ideal for photographs, millions of photographs. Drinks were served on the front terrace of the main house where the guests retired to drink sherry and champagne and where they toasted the happy couple whilst the marquee was rearranged. The tables were all laid out. Top table (where the immediate family and the priest would sit) and a whole series of round tables. Ten to a table. So many tables that when everyone had taken their seats there was barely room for the prissy waiters to squeeze through and serve a traditional wedding breakfast.

Kenny made his speech, read out telegrams from far and wide, and lied about the bridesmaids looking pretty as a picture. All of which seemed to pass agreeably. No one got indigestion. Everyone relaxed back and waited for the evening event. Aunties loosened their corsets, uncles, the top button on their trousers. The beer flowed free and old acquaintances were renewed.

The evening disco with buffet began at 8 p.m. Damon's gran loved it; she loved weddings full-stop. She sat herself at a corner table and allowed everyone to come and talk to her, like a queen holding court. Cassie and Damon paid tribute. Early on in the proceedings, Damon waltzed her around an empty dance floor. Everyone clapped. She was in her element and having a whale of a time. And as the day progressed and more and more alcohol was consumed, so did everyone else.

Cassie's brothers commandeered one end of the packed bar, Perry, the eldest, taking up the most space. He was as dark and rugged as Cassie was blonde and petite. The only thing they seemed to have in common was an impressive chest – though for distinctly different reasons. He spent his time gesticulating wildly over some tall story, and threatened to spill his Guinness with the broad sweep of his hands. He towered over baby brother Lawrence who, aware of the threat, ducked and weaved. At nineteen, he was already bearded and brawny ... but agile.

He had to be! Henry was a little tub. Short and round with a permanent flush to his moon face. And alongside was Elliot's crooked smile. Elliot the big bruiser with his roman nose. They were a big hit with Murat and Jack who had volunteered to help staff the bar and then flirted with the four all night.

An arm slipped around Kenny's shoulder, it was Damon. A big, beery grin on his beautiful face; dewy eyes smiled directly into Kenny's.

'Thanks for everything, mate.'
'My pleasure, bro.'
Damon began to sway. 'Look, I know this has cost you a lot.'
'Why?' Kenny said in mock alarm. 'I thought Rab was paying!'
'You know –' Damon swallowed a hiccup. 'You know what I mean. And you didn't lose control of your bladder, not once.' And again that meaningful look.
'Leave it out, Damon. You'll make me cry. I've been on the beer too.'
'Just wanted you to know.' Damon looked down at his own feet. 'I love you, Kenny.' He squeezed Kenny's shoulder.
'Ah! Look what you've done now.' Tears came to Kenny's eyes. 'You soft sod. I told you what would happen.'

At ten o'clock it was time for the bride and groom to exit to their honeymoon destination. Kenny held the limousine door as Cassie stepped in with babe in arms. Next came Damon. Kenny paused as Damon held out his hand and instead threw his arms around Damon's neck and kissed his cheek. Just as suddenly they was gone. Most of the guests remained, though Kenny's duties for the day were fast drawing to an end.

Rab appeared and drew Kenny to one side. 'You did him proud, Kenny,' he said. 'You really charmed the whole family today.'
'I only did what was expected.'
'You shouldn't underestimate yourself, Kenny. 'You always have. You're a good boy.'

Kenny's throat tightened. 'I've told you before, Rab, I'm not a boy. I'm a man.'

'Bigger than most, if I my recollection is accurate.'

'I'm surprised you remember.'

'How could I forget?'

'You tell me. You say you want me one minute, then the next it's as if I don't exist.'

An embarrassed silence fell. Rab broke it. 'I need time to sort things through, Kenny.'

'Yeah? Well, how much time is enough time? When you've made up your mind what exactly it is you want perhaps you'd be so kind as to let me know. I'm sick of this: "Yes, tonight, Kenny. Not tonight, Kenny." Get it sorted! I'm not playing your game any more. I'm fed up.' And with that, Kenny turned and made his way back to the tent.

Jayne and Jo were sitting at on the sidelines when Cary crossed to join them.

'You seem a bit subdued,' he said, as he took a seat alongside them.

'You'd be subdued if you'd had the responsibility of looking after Celine all day.'

'Yeah!' Cary laughed. 'She's a bit of a handful.'

'Must take after her father,' said Jayne.

'But she is beautiful, isn't she?' Cary added.

'*That* she gets from her mother,' Jo replied.

Jayne rubbed his arm. 'Oh, don't mind us, Cary. We're just feeling a little bit . . . *broody*.'

Jo leant forward. 'Jayne wants us to have a baby.'

Jayne sighed. 'Unfortunately, we would need a little bit of help to make that particular dream a reality.'

Jo looked at Jayne then at Cary. 'What about you, Cary?'

'I've never thought about having kids. Not really. Can't see the point, it ain't going to happen.'

'No? What I actually meant was, what about helping us out?'

Cary was caught short. Stunned. 'Ask me when I'm sober. No, better still, ask me when we're all sober.'

Jayne gently ruffled his hair. 'Don't panic! It's an idea, Cary. Just something to think about.'

Gayle and Rab filled their glasses as they drained another bottle of champagne.

Gayle raised her glass. 'What shall we toast to this time?'

'My ex-wife, Linda. May she rest in peace.' Rab went to clink glasses but a stunned Gayle placed hers directly on the table.

'But, Rab, you never said. Is she really dead?'

'Unfortunately not.' Rab took a cigar from the inside pocket of his jacket, removed the film, and prepared to light it. 'However, she has been much quieter of late. Especially since I played her the tape you got from Des Foster.' A broad smile spread across his face. 'It was almost worth all the hassle just to see the look on her face.'

'Did you ever love her?'

He sat back in his chair and exhaled a puff of smoke. 'I can't honestly remember. She never loved me, I know that much. I met her on a business seminar, you know. The theme was 'finance'. That's all I ever was to her — an investment. Then again, I have to accept some responsibility. I was so scared of being gay, I let myself become her pet project.'

'I'm sorry, Rab. You didn't deserve it.'

'That's true. Nobody could possibly be so rotten as to deserve Linda.' He reached for his glass. 'Let me propose another toast. To you.'

'To us both. Cheers!'

'Cheers!' Rab took a sip from his glass. 'I owe you an apology, Gayle.'

'Not another one, Rab. You've apologised enough.'

'Then one more won't hurt.' He spread his palm on the white table cloth and examined his fingers as he spoke. 'If you hadn't tipped me off about Clive Foxx he would have trashed everything. You didn't need to warn me. Let's face it, after what I did, it's one thing I didn't deserve.'

'Rab, it's all in the past —'

'I let my dick rule my head, Gayle. I should never have sacked you and I'm sorry.'

Gayle covered his hand with hers. 'Well, that's all right then.'

Rab looked up into her eyes. They were smiling.

After suffering through countless rugby songs, watching them drop their trousers, throw up against the side of the marquee, and finally crash out in a drunken heap, Murat and Jack had managed to manoeuvre Cassie's four brothers on to the bus and waved them goodbye.

'Handsome but thick as pig-shit,' said Jack as they watched the tail lights disappear down the drive.

'Which one would you have?' Murat asked.

'Are you joking?' Jack replied. 'I'll stick with you, buddy. I like a man who knows what he is and what he wants.'

'Time for bed?'

'I thought you'd never ask!'

The stress of being Mr Social had taken its toll. Kenny felt it when he confronted Rab earlier, and felt it again now as Rab reappeared by his side. It was half past two in the morning and the two of them stood amidst the wreckage in the marquee.

'I've made up my mind.' Rab wore a determined expression.

'Let's hear it before I fall asleep. I'm knackered,' Kenny replied with a yawn.

Rab leant in so close his bushy moustache tickled Kenny's ear and whispered, 'Sleep with me tonight?'

'No chance. You want a quick fix? Find somebody else. I've had it with you messing me about!' He turned to walk away again.

Rab caught him by the arm. 'I don't want a quickie.'

'You want a longie? Sorry, that would definitely cost extra.'

Roughly, Rab pulled Kenny close. So close, they were eye to eye. 'I want you. I want you in my bed. Tonight and the next night and the next –"

Kenny frowned and tried to struggle free. 'I don't think you really know what you want.'

Rab held fast. 'Then you don't know me. And I want you to know me, really know me. I've been waiting, Kenny, waiting until the dust settled. I can't be accused of favouritism now. You've nothing to gain but my love.'

Kenny stopped struggling and held still. 'I want to know where I stand, Rab. And I won't settle for being second best.'

'You could never be second best. Not to me. Mitch and I are ancient history, almost prehistoric.'

'If you say so.'

Rab hugged Kenny to his chest. 'I do say so.'

Kenny spoke into Rab's shoulder. 'And you'll let me get a good night's kip?'

'If that's what you want.' Rab held Kenny at arm's length.

'Now I never said it's what I want but I fear it's all I can manage. But tomorrow' – a grin – 'I'll give you the full works.'

Rab slipped an arm around Kenny's shoulder. 'And I intend to keep you to that promise. C'mon. Let's go.'

Mitch and Cary were already curled up under the patchwork quilt. Mitch took the relatively small, stylishly gift-wrapped package from the drawer in the bedside table and placed it on the palm of Cary's hand. Cary's fingers fought to unwrap it. Finally he held up the token of Mitch's commitment. It was a big, silver cock-ring.

'Hope it fits,' Mitch said. 'The guy in the shop said they could enlarge it if it wasn't big enough.'

'Very funny,' said Cary.

'Check it out. I had it engraved.'

Cary spun the ring round until the light hit the inscription. '"With all my arse – Mitch." How sweet.'

'That's me all over,' said Mitch. 'Want to taste?'

idol

IDOL NEW BOOKS

BOOTY BOYS
Published in September — Jay Russell

Hard-bodied black British detective Alton Davies can't believe his eyes or his luck when he finds muscular African-American gangsta rapper Banji-B lounging in his office early one morning. Alton's disbelief – and his excitement – mount as Banji-B asks him to track down a stolen videotape of a post-gig orgy.
£7.99/$10.95   ISBN 0 352 33446 0

EASY MONEY
Published in October — Bob Condron

One day an ad appears in the popular music press. Its aim: to enlist members for a new boyband. Young, working-class Mitch starts out as a raw recruit, but soon he becomes embroiled in the sexual tension that threatens to engulf the entire group. As the band soars meteorically to pop success, the atmosphere is quickly reaching fever pitch.
£7.99/$10.95   ISBN 0 352 33442 8

SUREFORCE
Published in November — Phil Votel

Not knowing what to do with his life once he's been thrown out of the army, Matt takes a job with the security firm Sureforce. Little does he know that the job is the ultimate mix of business and pleasure, and it's not long before Matt's hanging with the beefiest, meanest, hardest lads in town.
£7.99/$10.95   ISBN 0 352 33444 4

Also published:

CHAINS OF DECEIT
Paul C. Alexander

Journalist Nathan Dexter's life is turned around when he meets a young student called Scott – someone who offers him the relationship for which he's been searching. Then Nathan's best friend goes missing, and Nathan uncovers evidence that he has become the victim of a slavery ring which is rumoured to be operating out of London's leather scene.
£6.99/$9.95   ISBN 0 352 33206 9

DARK RIDER
Jack Gordon

While the rulers of a remote Scottish island play bizarre games of sexual dominance with the Argentinian Angelo, his friend Robert – consumed with jealous longing for his coffee-skinned companion – assuages his desires with the willing locals.
£6.99/$9.95   ISBN 0 352 33243 3

CONQUISTADOR
Jeff Hunter

It is the dying days of the Aztec empire. Axaten and Quetzel are members of the Stable, servants of the Sun Prince chosen for their bravery and beauty. But it is not just an honour and a duty to join this society, it is also the ultimate sexual achievement. Until the arrival of Juan, a young Spanish conquistador, sets the men of the Stable on an adventure of bondage, lust and deception.

£6.99/$9.95   ISBN 0 352 33244 1

TO SERVE TWO MASTERS
Gordon Neale

In the isolated land of Ilyria men are bought and sold as slaves. Rock, brought up to expect to be treated as mere 'livestock', yearns to be sold to the beautiful youth Dorian. But Dorian's brother is as cruel as he is handsome, and if Rock is bought by one brother he will be owned by both.

£6.99/$9.95   ISBN 0 352 33245 X

CUSTOMS OF THE COUNTRY
Rupert Thomas

James Cardell has left school and is looking forward to going to Oxford. That summer of 1924, however, he will spend with his cousins in a tiny village in rural Kent. There he finds he can pursue his love of painting – and begin to explore his obsession with the male physique.

£6.99/$9.95   ISBN 0 352 33246 8

DOCTOR REYNARD'S EXPERIMENT
Robert Black

A dark world of secret brothels, dungeons and sexual cabarets exists behind the respectable facade of Victorian London. The degenerate Lord Spearman introduces Dr Richard Reynard, dashing bachelor, to this hidden world.

£6.99/$9.95   ISBN 0 352 33252 2

CODE OF SUBMISSION
Paul C. Alexander

Having uncovered and defeated a slave ring operating in London's leather scene, journalist Nathan Dexter had hoped to enjoy a peaceful life with his boyfriend Scott. But when it becomes clear that the perverted slave trade has started again, Nathan has no choice but to travel across Europe and America in his bid to stop it. Second in the trilogy.

£6.99/$9.95   ISBN 0 352 33272 7

SLAVES OF TARNE
Gordon Neale

Pascal willingly follows the mysterious and alluring Casper to Tarne, a community of men enslaved to men. Tarne is everything that Pascal has ever fantasised about, but he begins to sense a sinister aspect to Casper's magnetism. Pascal has to choose between the pleasures of submission and acting to save the people he loves.

£6.99/$9.95   ISBN 0 352 33273 5

ROUGH WITH THE SMOOTH
Dominic Arrow

Amid the crime, violence and unemployment of North London, the young men who attend Jonathan Carey's drop-in centre have few choices. One of the young men, Stewart, finds himself torn between the increasingly intimate horseplay of his fellows and the perverse allure of the criminal underworld. Can Jonathan save Stewart from the bullies on the streets and behind bars?

£6.99/$9.95 ISBN 0 352 33292 1

CONVICT CHAINS
Philip Markham

Peter Warren, printer's apprentice in the London of the 1830s, discovers his sexuality and taste for submission at the hands of Richard Barkworth. Thus begins a downward spiral of degradation, of which transportation to the Australian colonies is only the beginning.

£6.99/$9.95 ISBN 0 352 33300 6

SHAME
Raydon Pelham

On holiday in West Hollywood, Briton Martyn Townsend meets and falls in love with the daredevil Scott. When Scott is murdered, Martyn's hunt for the truth and for the mysterious Peter, Scott's ex-lover, leads him to the clubs of London and Ibiza.

£6.99/$9.95 ISBN 0 352 33302 2

HMS SUBMISSION
Jack Gordon

Under the command of Josiah Rock, a man of cruel passions, HMS *Impregnable* sails to the colonies. Christopher, Viscount Fitzgibbons, is a reluctant officer; Mick Savage part of the wretched cargo. They are on a voyage to a shared destiny.

£6.99/$9.95 ISBN 0 352 33301 4

THE FINAL RESTRAINT
Paul C. Alexander

The trilogy that began with *Chains of Deceit* and continued in *Code of Submission* concludes in this powerfully erotic novel. From the dungeons and saunas of London to the deepest jungles of South America, Nathan Dexter is forced to play the ultimate chess game with evil Adrian Delancey – with people as sexual pawns.

£6.99/$9.95 ISBN 0 352 33303 0

HARD TIME
Robert Black

HMP Cairncrow prison is a corrupt and cruel institution, but also a sexual minefield. Three new inmates must find their niche in this brutish environment – as sexual victims or lovers, predators or protectors. This is the story of how they find love, sex and redemption behind prison walls.

£6.99/$9.95 ISBN 0 352 33304 9

ROMAN GAMES
Tasker Dean

When Sam visits the island of Skate, he is taught how to submit to other men, acting out an elaborate fantasy in which young men become wrestling slaves – just as in ancient Rome. Indeed, if he is to have his beautiful prize – the wrestler, Robert – he must learn how the Romans played their games.

£6.99/$9.95 ISBN 0 352 33322 7

VENETIAN TRADE
Richard Davis

From the deck of the ship that carries him into Venice, Rob Weaver catches his first glimpse of a beautiful but corrupt city where the dark alleys and misty canals hide debauchery and decadence. Here, he must learn to survive among men who would make him a plaything and a slave.

£6.99/$9.95 ISBN 0 352 33323 5

THE LOVE OF OLD EGYPT
Philip Markham

It's 1925 and the deluxe cruiser carrying the young gigolo Jeremy Hessling has docked at Luxor. Jeremy dreams of being dominated by the pharaohs of old, but quickly becomes involved with someone more accessible – Khalid, a young man of exceptional beauty.

£6.99/$9.95 ISBN 0 352 33354 5

THE BLACK CHAMBER
Jack Gordon

Educated at the court of George II, Calum Monroe finds his native Scotland a dull, damp place. He relieves his boredom by donning a mask and holding up coaches in the guise of the Fox – a dashing highwayman. Chance throws him and neighbouring farmer Fergie McGregor together with Calum's sinister, perverse guardian, James Black.

£6.99/$9.95 ISBN 0 352 33373 1

THE GREEK WAY
Edward Ellis

Ancient Greece, the end of the fifth century BC – at the height of the Peloponnesian War. Young Orestes is a citizen of Athens, sent to Sparta as a spy. There he encounters a society of athletic, promiscuous soldiers – including the beautiful Spartan Hector.

£6.99/$9.95 ISBN 0 352 33427 4

MORE AND HARDER
Morgan

This is the erotic autobiography of Mark, a submissive English sadomasochist: an 'SM sub' or 'slave'. Rarely has a writer been so explicitly hot or so forthcoming in the arousingly strict details of military and disciplinary life.

£7.99/$10.95 ISBN 0 352 33437 1

------- ✂ -----------------------

Please send me the books I have ticked above.

Name ....

Address ....

....

....

.... Post Code ....

Send to: **Cash Sales, Idol Books, Thames Wharf Studios, Rainville Road, London W6 9HT.**

US customers: for prices and details of how to order books for delivery by mail, call 1-800-805-1083.

Please enclose a cheque or postal order, made payable to **Virgin Publishing Ltd**, to the value of the books you have ordered plus postage and packing costs as follows:

UK and BFPO – £1.00 for the first book, 50p for each subsequent book.

Overseas (including Republic of Ireland) – £2.00 for the first book, £1.00 for each subsequent book.

We accept all major credit cards, including VISA, ACCESS/MASTERCARD, DINERS CLUB, AMEX and SWITCH.

Please write your card number and expiry date here:

....

Please allow up to 28 days for delivery.

Signature ....

------- ✂ -----------------------

idol

WE NEED YOUR HELP . . .
to plan the future of Idol books –

Yours are the only opinions that matter. Idol is a new and exciting venture: the first British series of books devoted to homoerotic fiction for men.

We're going to do our best to provide the sexiest, best-written books you can buy. And we'd like you to help in these early stages. Tell us what you want to read. There's a freepost address for your filled-in questionnaires, so you won't even need to buy a stamp.

THE IDOL QUESTIONNAIRE

SECTION ONE: ABOUT YOU

1.1 Sex (*we presume you are male, but just in case*)
   Are you?
   Male ☐
   Female ☐

1.2 Age
   under 21 ☐   21–30 ☐
   31–40 ☐   41–50 ☐
   51–60 ☐   over 60 ☐

1.3 At what age did you leave full-time education?
   still in education ☐   16 or younger ☐
   17–19 ☐   20 or older ☐

1.4 Occupation _____

1.5 Annual household income _____

1.6 We are perfectly happy for you to remain anonymous; but if you would like us to send you a free booklist of Idol books, please insert your name and address

_____
_____
_____
_____

SECTION TWO: ABOUT BUYING IDOL BOOKS

2.1 Where did you get this copy of *Easy Money*?
- Bought at chain book shop ☐
- Bought at independent book shop ☐
- Bought at supermarket ☐
- Bought at book exchange or used book shop ☐
- I borrowed it/found it ☐
- My partner bought it ☐

2.2 How did you find out about Idol books?
- I saw them in a shop ☐
- I saw them advertised in a magazine ☐
- I read about them in _____
- Other _____

2.3 Please tick the following statements you agree with:
- I would be less embarrassed about buying Idol books if the cover pictures were less explicit ☐
- I think that in general the pictures on Idol books are about right ☐
- I think Idol cover pictures should be as explicit as possible ☐

2.4 Would you read an Idol book in a public place – on a train for instance?
    Yes ☐   No ☐

SECTION THREE: ABOUT THIS IDOL BOOK

3.1 Do you think the sex content in this book is:
    Too much ☐   About right ☐
    Not enough ☐

3.2 Do you think the writing style in this book is:
   Too unreal/escapist ☐   About right ☐
   Too down to earth ☐

3.3 Do you think the story in this book is:
   Too complicated ☐   About right ☐
   Too boring/simple ☐

3.4 Do you think the cover of this book is:
   Too explicit ☐   About right ☐
   Not explicit enough ☐

Here's a space for any other comments:

SECTION FOUR: ABOUT OTHER IDOL BOOKS

4.1 How many Idol books have you read?

4.2 If more than one, which one did you prefer?

4.3 Why?

SECTION FIVE: ABOUT YOUR IDEAL EROTIC NOVEL

We want to publish the books you want to read – so this is your chance to tell us exactly what your ideal erotic novel would be like.

5.1 Using a scale of 1 to 5 (1 = no interest at all, 5 = your ideal), please rate the following possible settings for an erotic novel:
   Roman / Ancient World ☐
   Medieval / barbarian / sword 'n' sorcery ☐
   Renaissance / Elizabethan / Restoration ☐
   Victorian / Edwardian ☐
   1920s & 1930s ☐
   Present day ☐
   Future / Science Fiction ☐

5.2 Using the same scale of 1 to 5, please rate the following themes you may find in an erotic novel:

- Bondage / fetishism ☐
- Romantic love ☐
- SM / corporal punishment ☐
- Bisexuality ☐
- Group sex ☐
- Watersports ☐
- Rent / sex for money ☐

5.3 Using the same scale of 1 to 5, please rate the following styles in which an erotic novel could be written:

- Gritty realism, down to earth ☐
- Set in real life but ignoring its more unpleasant aspects ☐
- Escapist fantasy, but just about believable ☐
- Complete escapism, totally unrealistic ☐

5.4 In a book that features power differentials or sexual initiation, would you prefer the writing to be from the viewpoint of the dominant / experienced or submissive / inexperienced characters:

- Dominant / Experienced ☐
- Submissive / Inexperienced ☐
- Both ☐

5.5 We'd like to include characters close to your ideal lover. What characteristics would your ideal lover have? Tick as many as you want:

Dominant	☐	Caring	☐
Slim	☐	Rugged	☐
Extroverted	☐	Romantic	☐
Bisexual	☐	Old	☐
Working Class	☐	Intellectual	☐
Introverted	☐	Professional	☐
Submissive	☐	Pervy	☐
Cruel	☐	Ordinary	☐
Young	☐	Muscular	☐
Naïve	☐		

Anything else? _____

5.6 Is there one particular setting or subject matter that your ideal erotic novel would contain:

_____

5.7 As you'll have seen, we include safe-sex guidelines in every book. However, while our policy is always to show safe sex in stories with contemporary settings, we don't insist on safe-sex practices in stories with historical settings because it would be anachronistic. What, if anything, would you change about this policy?

SECTION SIX: LAST WORDS

6.1 What do you like best about Idol books?

6.2 What do you most dislike about Idol books?

6.3 In what way, if any, would you like to change Idol covers?

6.4 Here's a space for any other comments:

Thanks for completing this questionnaire. Now either tear it out, or photocopy it, then put it in an envelope and send it to:

Idol
FREEPOST
London
W10 5BR

You don't need a stamp if you're in the UK, but you'll need one if you're posting from overseas.